TROUBLE AFOOT

at

The Three Hounds Bakery

JULIE TITTERINGTON

Contents

To my muses: Snuggles, Inga, Silky, Esper, and Mila. You were and are the goodest of girls.

The Dogs

Wilhelmina Lattner stood on the curb, looking uncertainly at the scrap of paper in her hand. She re-read the scribbled address and raised her eyes to the house before her, blinking as she tried to take it all in.

There was no mistake. This was 535 West Sequoia Lane, which meant that the sprawling, many-gabled monstrosity before her—replete with seven balconies, a widow's walk, and a massive turret—was now hers. Every last, ludicrous inch of it.

It was a masterpiece of Victorian architecture, she had to give it that. The whims (and unlimited pocketbook) of the original owner had produced an unusually elaborate mansion, even for the time. The most recent owner had imposed her own personality by repainting the structure a florid pink and touching up the decorative scrollwork with the brightest of whites. Deep blue hydrangeas lined the front porch and wrapped the sides of the house. The overall impression was a technicolor nightmare.

"Ugh," Willa muttered, to relieve her feelings.

She averted her eyes, looking instead at the pale yellow house next door, a less fanciful example of Victorian wealth. Demure and tasteful, it presented an almost reproachful contrast to its neighbor.

Willa turned back to number 535 and shuddered. The more she looked at it, the pinker it got.

The front door opened, and a thin, elderly man emerged, walking slowly with the assistance of a cane. He waved a hand in greeting and beckoned her up the neat walkway.

"Ms. Lattner, I presume," he said, in a curiously high-pitched voice. "Daniel Pilkington of Pilkington, Pilkington, and Gump, at your service. I am," he began, and then stopped. "Er, I *was* your great-aunt's attorney. We spoke on the phone last week."

"Of course."

He beamed at her.

"I'm glad you were able to come so soon. I know you are very busy with your writing, but there are complications to settling the estate that I was not expecting. But where are my manners? First things first! What do you think of your new property, Ms. Lattner? It's something, is it not?"

He looked admiringly up at the house. Cautiously, Willa agreed that *something* was the word for it.

"Come in, come in!" he entreated, leaning on his cane. "May I assist you with your luggage?"

She declined the offer as politely as she could. The wispy man before her did not look up to carrying a five-pound bag of flour, let alone her giant suitcase, and she had no wish to hurt his feelings by testing that hypothesis.

"I'll take care of all that later," she said, waving vaguely down the street where her car was parked in the shade of a broad shore pine. "I'm dying to see inside!"

Mr. Pilkington held the door open for her, and she walked in. Houses on the ocean were inclined to be damp, but this one was nice and dry, and there was a faint scent of lavender, which she traced to a bowl of potpourri on the entry table.

Willa peered about, allowing her eyes to adjust to the darkness. She was just admiring the crown molding in the hall when she turned with astonishment to the attorney.

"Is that barking?" she asked, incredulous.

"Yes," he said, embarrassed.

"There's a dog here?"

"Not *a* dog, per se. There are—ahem—three."

"Yours?" she said.

"Well, my dear, I'm afraid the answer to that question is complicated."

Color flooded into Mr. Pilkington's rather large ears but did not quite extend to the tip of his nose, which remained white. *Like Rudolph, but in reverse*, Willa thought, fascinated.

"Complicated how?" she demanded, but his answer was drowned out by increasingly frantic barking.

A door swung open down the hallway, and three long, low dogs rushed out, followed by an apologetic-looking man.

"Sorry!" he called out, in a pleasant, deep voice. "I tried to keep them in the kitchen, but the boys got too excited."

Willa looked down in some confusion to see three dachshunds frisking around her ankles.

"This is Mr. Harrison," explained Mr. Pilkington, hurriedly, as the other man scooped up two of the dogs and gently moved the other one away with his foot. "He has very kindly been watching your aunt's dogs for the last few weeks."

"I wasn't aware she had dogs," said Willa, bewildered.

Mr. Pilkington was still pink with embarrassment.

"I see explanations are in order," he said, faintly. "Ms. Lattner, Mr. Harrison—if you'll follow me down to the kitchen we can sort this all out. The, er, the doggies should come too."

"Sorry about this," said the stranger, restraining the barking dogs with difficulty. "They heard you talking and got the wrong idea, poor little buggers. You're Mina's great-niece—the mystery writer?"

"Wilhelmina Lattner," said Willa, shaking his hand.

"Same name, same hair, same voice," he murmured. "Do you go by Mina as well?"

"No," she said, with emphasis.

She put her hand up automatically to cover the Lattner nose, a dubious inheritance from her great-grandfather. All Lattner noses had a slight tendency toward crookedness. Her father's beak was legendary, but Aunt Mina's had approached near-witch status. Willa's was beginning to bend as she hurtled toward middle age, and she was very self-conscious about it.

"You may sound like her, but you don't look much like your aunt," he commented, and Willa withdrew her hand from her face, relieved. "Apart from the red hair, that is. It's nice to finally meet you. C'mon boys. There are nibbles in the kitchen!"

He strode down the hall carrying two yapping dogs under each arm, pursued eagerly by the third. Willa followed him toward a wide, swinging door, wondering if by any chance she had stumbled into the city pound instead of a private home.

Then she pushed open the door and gasped out loud.

The Victorians, restrained as they had been in other areas, had known how to cook, serve, and eat well. At least three times the size of an average modern kitchen, the space was expansive and sunny. At one end of the cheerful room was a large tiled fireplace, and an antique stove sat in the corner, next to a more practical gas-powered range.

Willa's eyes darted with pleasure from the large farm sink to the charming built-in window bench that served as seating for the kitchen table. Mr. Harrison dropped onto the bench and motioned the others toward a couple of pine chairs.

"Nice, isn't it?" he said, smiling at Willa.

"It's really something!" she responded for the second time that day, with much more sincerity.

"What do you think of your view?" he asked, looking out the window toward the bay, where the water sparkled in the late afternoon sun.

"That's something too," Willa said, drawing in a breath. "This is my first time in Humboldt Cove. Is that the harbor?"

"Yep. We have the smallest useable harbor on the California coastline, but in my opinion, it's the prettiest. I'm glad you like your view. How do you feel about the house in general?"

Willa hesitated, and the man grinned at her.

"Mina had her own aesthetic," he said, frankly. "And putting paint aside, there aren't many houses like it—even down in Eureka, where the old lumber and shipping magnates didn't exercise restraint when building their homes."

"It's certainly one of a kind," Willa agreed.

"The McKinley House is a masterpiece of Victorian architecture," said Mr. Pilkington, a trifle stiffly. "That's why it's on the register of historical homes."

"No arguments here," the other man said peaceably, reaching down to scratch the belly of the fattest dog, which had stopped barking to roll on its back at Willa's feet. "I think you and the dogs will be happy here, Ms. Lattner. I hope you plan to stay with us awhile."

"The dogs?" she repeated.

"Sure. They're your dogs now."

Perplexed, Willa stared at the fat dachshund lolling by her toes. Its tongue had flopped out the side of its mouth and was nearly touching the floor.

"I'm afraid Mr. Harrison is right," twittered old Mr. Pilkington, in some distress. "Ms. Lattner left written directions about the disposal of her pets, but I didn't find them until I opened her safe this morning. She did *not* inform me personally of her wishes in this matter, I assure you, or I would have tried to prepare you ahead of time. As you know, she changed her will in your favor only days before she died, and I've been scrambling to adapt to all the new arrangements."

"You'll love the boys," said the other man, lifting the chubby, black and tan dog off Willa's sandals. "This one's called Killer."

He fondled the dachshund's long black ears, and it barked in his face, wagging its tail ecstatically. Willa had never seen anything so inappropriately named.

"You're kidding me."

"Killer's a good boy, yes he is," he said, fatuously. He set Killer down and scooped up a smaller, red-brown dog. "And so is this guy. Meet Sir Reginald Waggington the Third. We usually just call him Wags."

"And who's that fellow?" asked Mr. Pilkington with interest, gesturing to the other black and tan keeping its distance in the far corner of the room.

It was curled in the little basket near the fireplace, watching the three humans with wary attention through half-lidded eyes.

"Him? That's Kyle. He's a little standoffish with strangers, but you'll love him once you get to know him."

"Hang on a sec," Willa said, trying to get ahead of the situation. "I don't want to get to know any of them. I can't care for one pet right now, let alone three."

Let alone a sausage dog named Kyle, she added, silently. This overgrown pink house was one thing. Three wriggly dachshunds were quite another.

"I'm afraid that maintenance of the dogs is a condition of the bequest," squeaked little Mr. Pilkington, miserably. "I regret that I was unable to inform you of this before you came. But really, considering the size of the estate and Ms. Lattner's significant fortune..." he trailed off into tactful silence.

"You'll be fine. The boys are easy as pie," said Mr. Harrison.

He clocked her stricken face, and added, "Truly! They're sweet dogs, and they don't require much. They're in mourning at the moment, so you're not seeing them at their best, but I've known them forever. And I live just down the road if you have any questions."

"Well," said Mr. Pilkington, rising from his seat. "You've had a long journey, Ms. Lattner, and I'm sure you want to get settled. I'm staying in Eureka for a few nights, but I fly back to Sausalito on Monday. I'll drive up here again first thing in the morning to walk you through the paperwork, if I may. There are a lot of documents to sign."

"I'll be off as well," said the other man, once Mr. Pilkington had handed over the keys to the house and bustled away. "I left the dog crates in the laundry room, and there's food in the cupboards there. Watch out for Killer, though. If left to his own devices, he'll eat Kyle's food as well as his own. Poor old Kyle. He hasn't had much appetite since Mina...well, since the accident."

He took a pencil and some paper off a butcherblock counter and wrote his name and number.

"Call me if you get overwhelmed," he said, "and I can come back to help. I live just down the hill, like I said."

"I'm sorry, but *who* are you again?"

Willa was overwhelmed and not disposed to be polite to this stranger who had just dumped three wiener dogs in her lap.

"Brian Harrison. I was a friend of Mina's. A good friend," he said.

"Your name is Brian?" she said, alertly.

He bent down to scratch Killer's ears one more time.

"Yeah. I'm a pastry chef—I managed the bakery for Mina. You knew Mina owned a bakery right? The Three Hounds? She and I were partners. And now you and I are partners," he said, more cheerfully.

"We're what?"

"Partners," he said, his grin fading as he saw the look of outright shock on Willa's face. "Or didn't Mr. Pilkington tell you? Mina left her half of the business to you."

"He failed to mention that point," said Willa, reflecting grimly that there were a lot of things the old man had forgotten to tell her.

"If you're anything like your aunt, we're going to get along just fine. So long, Ms. Lattner."

"Willa."

"So long, Willa. Holler if you need anything. And you should probably stop by the bakery sometime tomorrow so we can talk shop. You can't miss it. Just walk down the hill, turn left onto Main Street, and you'll see The Three Hounds under a pink-and-white striped awning."

Willa let Brian out the front door, shut and locked it, and returned to the kitchen, Killer and Wags at her heels. She exchanged looks with Kyle, who had not left his basket by the fireplace and seemed just as confused by being saddled with her as she was by being saddled with him. He curled himself into a tighter ball and she slumped down on the window seat and put her head into her hands.

The dogs were the least of her worries.

She reached into her pocket and drew out an envelope. With shaking hands, she removed the single sheet of paper within. She had read it already at least a dozen times, and almost had it memorized by this point.

My dearest Willa,

It's never been my way to skirt unpleasantness, so I'll get right to the point.

If you're reading this, then I've been murdered, and it's up to you to do something about it...

Mail

To Wendoline Lattner-Santini

Dear Wendy,

I tried returning your call but realized just in time that it was two AM in Rome and bailed. Call me as soon as you wake up. And don't pretend you haven't read this email, because I know you check your inbox the minute your alarm goes off.

I arrived in Humboldt Cove this afternoon and found Aunt Mina's house right away. It was impossible to miss. For one, it's at the tippy-top of an impossibly steep hill that juts out into the ocean. For two, it's four stories tall, with a turret and about a hundred windows. And for three, it's pinker than a flamingo.

I've attached a picture because I know you won't believe me. However pink it looks in the pic, it's pinker in real life. Pinker than your Barbie Dream House. It's PINK, Wendy.

Aunt Mina's lawyer was there waiting for me. He's a bit of a dear and looks exactly like Mr. Peanut (with the cane but without the monocle).

The inside of the house is amazing and almost makes up for the pinkness of it all. The kitchen is massive—bigger than the one in Downton Abbey. The original owner must have had a dozen servants. The attic is full of tiny, uncomfortable rooms where they sweltered in the summer and froze in the winter. I expect to see reproachful Victorian ghosts in caps and aprons whenever I walk down the hall.

There's an amazing view from the breakfast nook down to the harbor and you can see ships floating out there like pretty white dots. I think I'll be spending a lot of time in this kitchen. It almost makes me want to learn how to bake.

Almost.

Speaking of which, tell Guillermo I need one recipe for chocolate chip cookies and one for some kind of fudgy, rich cake. But not with buttercream—I used that in the chocolate cake from *Killed By Cocoa* and people will remember. I know he's busy with his new job, but where else am I going to get material for the books?

DON'T SAY ONLINE.

I need original recipes. People can tell when I've simply copied a baking blog. Don't ask me how they know but they do, and then poor Wallace gets nasty letters at his office and threatens to stop being my agent and only keeps me on because I send him baskets from Harry & David—and bless him, he can't resist a dried apricot.

It's no good telling me I should never have written a series set in a bakery because that ship has sailed. And you married a pastry chef knowing full well I'd take advantage of the fact, so this is partly your fault!

I'm stalling. But you know that already. Your twin senses are tingling.

There are DOGS, Wendy. Three of them. Dachshunds. All body and ears and no legs to speak of. And I can't take the house without taking them as well—or so says Mr. Peanut, and he would know.

There's Killer. He's black and shiny and looks like a sausage just about to burst.

Sir Reginald Waggington—the Third, no less—is brown and slender and I'll admit he has a lovely long coat and silky ears.

And then there's Kyle. YES, his name is Kyle, and YES that's an improbable name for a dog.

Aunt Mina was in rare form when she christened them, I'll tell you that for free.

Kyle does not like me yet, but that's okay because I can't actually keep any of them! I can't take care of three dogs. I can barely take care of myself!

Without G to cook and you to show me how to use the dryer, I am lost. I tried to make ramen the other day and burnt the bottom of the pan and then I laid on the floor and cried until the Uber Eats guy got there with my burrito.

If you guys would move back here, we could all live together again in this giant, rambling house, and you and G could play with the dogs to your heart's content.

I'm sorry. I'll stop asking. I know you're happy on your Italian adventure and it's time for me to start having adventures of my own, instead of sucking the life out of you both, as Mom so kindly put it when we last spoke.

There's one more thing I haven't told you yet.

Aunt Mina left me half her business, it seems. The other half is owned by a guy called Brian, who looks exactly like a Disney prince. Blond, blue-eyes, strong chin—the whole enchilada.

He seems okay, but you know I have trouble playing nice with other people. I'm not great at being an adult, and there's a lot of adulting to do here in Humboldt Cove. I have to go "talk shop" with him at the bakery tomorrow so I will keep you posted. (I know I just got out of a relationship, so you don't need to politely remind me of that fact when next we speak.)

I haven't been down to the town itself yet, but it looks pretty cute from up here. I did a little digging online and discovered that there are two diners, one Mexican restaurant, a teeny-weeny radio station, and a newspaper. An actual newspaper, that still prints the news!

The Humboldt Cove Gazette is online as well, so I bought a subscription and dug out Mina's obituary, written by an enthusiast journalist with a sticky keyboard and an indifferent approach to spelling. I've attached it below for your amusement and edification. Check out line three, which I'm pretty sure is supposed to be about CRIMINALS. I think I'm in love with this town.

I'm off to feed the three sausages their kibble, or whatever it is that dogs eat. Call me when you wake up. Call me before you wake up. Call me, Wendy.

Your loving sister,

Willa

Obituary of Wilhelmina Anne Lattner: January 5th, 1941 - May 7th, 2024

Wilhelmina Anne Lattner was born in 1941 in YAkima, Wshington, to Richard Neal Lattner and Henrietta Faye Lattner (nee Gershwin).

In 1965, Ms. Lattner moved to SAn Franciisco to attend law school, where she graduated with honors. She went on to become a prosecutor for the state of California and superintEnded the placement of many cannibals behind bars.

Between 1985 and 2005, Ms. Lattner successfully ran sevERAl political campaigns, includign twice for Govenor Blair McNelty, and once for Senator Bill Jones.

She moved to Humboldt Cove in 1999 and took up residence in the famed McKinley House. She is survived by her thrEe dogs, her brother Henry Lattner, her nephew CrAIg Lattner, her great-nephew Josh, and her great-nieces Wilhelmuna and Wondy.

In lieu of flowers, donations can be made to the California Canine Fund.

The Albatross

Willa woke up with a start and stared at the ceiling, trying to remember where on God's green earth she was.

What's that awful racket? she wondered furiously. Where was she, anyway? Who had misplaced her windows and put the door on the wrong side of the room? And how dare they wake her at the crack of dawn?

She sat up in bed and put on her glasses. The world went back into focus.

She was in her Aunt Mina's guest room, at her Aunt Mina's house. No. At her *own* house. And that racket was...?

Barking.

The dogs were barking. *Her* dogs were barking.

Willa sighed. It was a lot to take in at five-thirty in the morning. She hauled herself out of bed and put on her robe and slippers. The whimpering was getting louder and more insistent.

"Keep your tails on!" she muttered, rushing down the stairs toward the small modern laundry room in the very back of the house, where the dogs were waiting in their crates.

Killer burst out of confinement, wriggling happily on his back until she deigned to reach down and pet his tummy. Wags sniffed her hand and then looked pointedly at the empty food bowls in the corner. Kyle slunk out of his crate with his tail between his legs and gazed up at her with a mournful expression. She let them outside to do their business, then filled the bowls and put some water out. Once they were back inside and occupied with their kibble, she wandered into the kitchen to make herself some toast.

She saw her Aunt Mina's letter lying where she had left it the evening before and promptly lost her appetite. Outside the large kitchen window, the sun was rising over the harbor. A lump rose in her throat. In other circumstances, she might have really enjoyed living here.

Mina had hung a real albatross across her neck, and she had no idea what to do next.

She forced herself to open the letter again, skipping past the first paragraph to get to the crux of the matter.

If I'm not dead when you receive this letter, please disregard it. I will tell you all about it later. Otherwise, keep reading. Unless I have passed peacefully from an aneurysm or a heart attack—conditions verified by a thorough autopsy—you should assume I have been murdered.

I'm aware the claim is outrageous. Nevertheless, it is true, and you're enough of a Lattner (thank God) to face facts.

We have never been close. However, I have read all of your novels, which despite their silly premise are quite clever. I know you have a good head on your shoulders. Your grandmother always said you were her favorite, and that's good enough for me.

You will want to know what evidence I have to cry "murder." Sensible girl! I have already narrowly escaped from three separate and distinct accidents, all cleverly arranged by a third party.

The Ladder Incident: Last week the second-to-top rung on the ladder I was using to touch up the scrollwork was purposefully damaged. I would have fallen twenty feet onto the pavement if I had not clutched the drain pipe and found a foothold on the rung below. The ladder is in the shed. You will see faint saw marks where the rung gave way.

The Bicycle Incident: On Wednesday, the brakes on my bicycle were disabled. I set off to town as usual and realized a quarter of the way down Sequoia that the brakes were useless. I happened to be next to a strip of lawn so I tossed myself off and rolled onto the grass. I broke my elbow in the process and was considerably shaken, but otherwise fine. The bike is also in the shed. If you take it to an expert, they will tell you what they told me. Deliberate sabotage was employed.

The Hazelnut Incident: Today, I went to make my usual afternoon snack—a peanut butter and banana sandwich with a glass of buttermilk. I am allergic to tree nuts and have trained Kyle (a remarkable dog) to sniff out hazelnuts and macadamias. He sounded the alarm before I had time to bite into the sandwich, and closer inspection showed a small quantity of hazelnuts ground into the peanuts. An amateurish attempt, but even a broken clock is right twice a day and even an incompetent murderer may strike it lucky.

I wish I knew why I have been subject to these attacks. I have my suspicions—of one person in particular—but I don't want to influence your judgment. I'd prefer you approach the matter with an unstained mind.

This is a heavy burden to lay at your door, but I believe you can carry it. The Klamath County Sheriff is an oaf and a moron. He wouldn't believe me at any rate, and he won't believe you. Your father is a sweet man but he lacks imagination. Your grandmother—the only person I've ever trusted implicitly—is dead.

But you are a writer—and a writer of mysteries, which means you're clever, you're resourceful, and you've learned the art of believing six impossible things before breakfast! I know you'll do me proud.

A few words of final advice:

Don't speak of this to anyone but my dear friend and attorney, Daniel Pilkington. Choose your moment well. He's an old maiden at heart and may take some convincing, but Pilky WILL help you.

The two of you can bear this burden better together. And you may find an ally in my good friend Brian. I have always found him a man of good sense, and I trust you'll do the same.

Don't trust ANYONE in Humboldt Cove. Not a soul except the dogs, of course. They will serve you faithfully.

Best of luck, and happy hunting. I wish I were there to help you, but please believe I'm cheering you on from wherever I happen to be.

Yours affectionately,

Aunt Mina

Willa threw the letter down again. A heavy burden indeed! How was she—incompetent, impractical old Willa Lattner, who could not even boil water correctly—supposed to solve a real-life murder?

So far, she had respected her aunt's wishes in one respect at least. No one else knew about the letter. But she wasn't sure how long she could keep it a secret.

She looked down to see Killer and Wags jumping against her legs. She had a vague sense that dogs needed walking fairly often. Even these dogs, who lacked even the pretense of real legs, must need exercise. She spied a trio of leashes hanging by the back door and decided to get breakfast in town after she had bathed and worked a bit on her novel. She was on a tight deadline now, and couldn't afford to fall behind.

While she was down there, she could do a little sleuthing. Humboldt Cove was a small place. She'd find *someone* who had known her aunt. And she might as well drop by the bakery and talk to her new partner.

Mina's letter had said she might find an ally in Brian. Willa fervently hoped she was right.

The Author

Willa cleaned herself up in the master bathroom, taking a long soak in an ancient, claw foot tub. There was a stunning view out the bathroom window to what she called the "wild" ocean, to distinguish it from the relatively tidy and domestic harbor. The hill on which the house stood jutted far into the sea, creating the north end of the sheltered cove that gave the town its name. If you looked south, you could see the entire town hugging the edges of the bay and climbing into the hills. To the north, it was all open ocean, except for three enormous, weatherbeaten rocks—the Hags—that stood like broken giants, guarding the town.

There was a low, mournful sound from the south, and Willa closed her eyes, sinking further into the tub. The foghorn had startled her at first, but she was growing fond of it—and increasingly excited about her new house. She realized, with mixed emotions, that this would be the first home that was hers, and only hers.

She had always lived with someone else, before. Her parents. A long series of roommates. And most recently, she'd spent five happy years with her twin sister and her brother-in-law in *their* home. There had always been someone else to cook the food, make the grocery lists, or figure out the electric bill. Willa had stayed in her lane, writing bestsellers, and bringing in the big bucks—very happy to pay more than her fair share of the rent if she could pass the responsibility for plunging the toilets to someone else.

For the first time, she was truly on her own, and the feeling was two parts exhilaration and one part sheer terror. There was no safety net in Humboldt Cove. If the toilet overflowed, she'd have to plunge it herself.

After a nice, long, wallow, she toweled off, put on her old flannel robe, and unlocked the doors to let the dogs bound in.

She applied a thick layer of leave-in conditioner, already painfully aware that the moist, sea air wreaked havoc on her curls. She had come to town yesterday as an ordinary person and ended the day as Bozo the Clown.

Then she went downstairs, grabbing her laptop and power cord from the pile of luggage by the front door, most of which she had not bothered to unpack. Ironically, if the house had been smaller, she might have found places for everything already. But there were too many options. Such an embarrassment of riches could be paralyzing.

Wherever Willa went, the dogs went with her like three wiggly shadows. She'd already tripped on Killer twice, both times narrowly missing a tumble down the stairs. It was enough to make her wonder if Mina's accidents had been dachshund-related, after all!

Clearing a few dirty dishes off the table, Willa set up her computer in the breakfast nook. If she was going to live here, she would need to work here, and she had already decided that the kitchen was where she wanted to spend most of her time. It was bright and cheerful and had the added appeal of being close to the snacks and coffee.

She cracked her knuckles, opened a file, and prepared to get to work on revisions for the final chapters of *Fatal Fudge*, the latest Violet Valentine novel. She stared at the screen for a full five minutes before shutting her laptop again with a violent thud that made poor Kyle jump in his corner basket. Lately, she had developed a hearty aversion for her heroine. After solving twelve successful cases, Violet was becoming unlikable as a character—so self-assured and one-dimensional, and always a hundred steps ahead of the police. If Willa ever met someone like Violet in real life she'd slap her smug little face.

She had written herself and Violet into a nasty hole with *Fatal Fudge*, that was for sure, and her editor would be out for blood unless she could fix it. She opened the lid of her laptop again, but her eyes strayed over to the counter, where she had left Mina's letter. That was a much more interesting puzzle to solve.

Just write a thousand words, she told herself sternly. *Then you can detect a real-life murder.*

A thousand words. She could do that. Just fix the second-to-last chapter, miraculously close up about five plot holes, and call it a day. After she returned those calls to her agent, of course. And dealt with a nagging insurance issue.

Five hundred words, she amended, telling herself she'd make up for lost time tomorrow.

She looked down to see Killer wagging his tail and Wags looking meaningfully up at the hanging leashes.

Two hundred words it is, she thought.

Mail

To Safe & Sound Insurance, LTD

To whom it may concern,

This is the fifth time I've reached out, and I
hope to God it's the last. Last night I spoke
to someone called Gail (ID number 55588453) and
she put me through to someone called Karen (ID
number 66675483) who gave me this address and a
claim reference number: 932-G-VI-777.

I'll tell you what I told them, and what I
have been telling your agents for the past
three weeks. I cannot get verbal permission from
Wilhelmina Anne Lattner to speak to you on her
behalf because *as previously stated*, my aunt

is quite dead. I've sent the death certificate three times now. She died in an accident on the very boat in question. It's safe to assume she's still dead—unless you have proof of resurrection in the form of, say, the second return of Christ or a zombie virus.

I've read the policy in detail and the boat was covered by acts of God, including the storm that destroyed it and drowned her. If you don't want to pay for God's mistakes, I suggest you rethink the wording of your policies. I've attached a copy of the incident report filed by the Sheriff's Department of Klamath County, California. I know you already have a copy. Here's another one for the collection. Good luck trying to 'misplace' this one.

I've CC'd my attorney on this email, and my next move will be to talk to some of my aunt's old cronies in Sacramento. She still has plenty of friends who'd enjoy a chat with your CEO. There is also such a thing as the California Department of Insurance. Ever heard of it? They're always very happy to oblige.

I work for myself, and my time is my own. I have twenty-four hours each day to make your lives a misery and I will gladly spend each second gumming up the phone lines of every Gail and Karen you've got.

You owe my aunt's estate $50K, as per the policy, and I expect written confirmation of your intention to pay up by Friday, or I release the hounds.

Sincerely,

Wilhelmina Wendonline Lattner

Incident Report Filed By Deputy B. J. Anderson of The Klamath County Sheriff's Department

We received a call at 10:07 AM on the morning of May 7th from the harbormaster of the port of Humboldt Cove, informing us that a fishing boat had gone out at 6 PM the previous evening and failed to return to dock after a storm warning was issued.

Upon arriving at the port offices, located at 645 F ST in Humboldt Cove, I spoke personally with Captain Douglas Burch, the harbormaster. He informed me that Ms. Wilhelmina Lattner had taken out her boat 'The Old Girl' for a salmon fishing expedition on the 6th. A storm was forecasted for the following morning. At 8 PM, Burch radioed Lattner, who agreed to come back to port if conditions became unsafe. He successfully contacted her again at 12 AM and she verbally confirmed her intention to return immediately. At 2:15, he radioed again to tell her the storm was approaching faster than predicted and was unable to make contact.

The storm, which hit the coast around 3:30 AM, was brief but severe, with wind gusts of up to 80 MPH. The Coast Guard found the remains of the craft, a Defiance Admiral 220, equipped with a Yamaha F200XC outboard motor, at around 1 PM on the 7th. It had dashed against the rocks on the south end of the Cove and taken on water. Ms. Lattner was not on board. She was declared dead after a search lasting forty-eight hours.

Several fishing boats were blown out to open sea during the same period, and the wreck

was deemed accidental by the Coast Guard. Ms.
Lattner's body has not yet been recovered.

The Plaques

Willa managed to wriggle all three dogs into their harnesses and leashes and got out the door around ten AM, feeling like she was being drawn and quartered. One arm was nearly wrenched out of its socket by Killer's eagerness to bound out into the yard, and the other was working at full capacity to drag the depressed and unwilling Kyle along. He sat back on his heels inside the kitchen and they had a massive battle of wills. Willa only prevailed by filling her pocket with lunchmeat and seeding it along the kitchen tile and out onto the gravel path that led up to the sidewalk. Mollified by ham, Kyle finally consented to go with them.

Consented was the only word for it. Willa was beginning to realize that dachshunds had definite, fully formed opinions of their own.

It was a beautiful morning, and the omnipresent layer of coastal fog had already begun to burn off on the hill. In the town below, a few rays of sunlight peeped through the haze, making the bay waters sparkle.

Willa had already noted the prominent bronze plaque in front of Mina's house. It was large and ugly, spouting a detailed history of the McKinley House and its builder, James McKinley—the first mayor of Humboldt Cove. As she made her way out to the sidewalk, dogs in tow, she spotted a similar plaque in front of the yellow mansion next door. She had been too distracted by the pinkness of Mina's house to see it the day before.

Interested, she walked over to read the sign.

Garber House, it said. *Erected in 1879 by Hezekiah Garber.*

She was peering down to see if there was any other information about Hezekiah Garber or why his house might merit its own plaque when Killer, Wags, and Kyle began barking all at once.

"Hush, boys," she said, trying to determine what had set them off.

Willa heard the gentle clearing of a voice behind her. She turned to see a brisk, elderly lady with silvery blond hair, cut short. She was only five feet tall, but she had a decided chin and looked like she could handle anything thrown her way. Her black Nike tracksuit was fashionable, and she sported an agreeable dimple on her left cheek.

"Good morning," said the woman, flashing the dimple in Willa's direction.

Wags and Killer continued barking, and Kyle was baring his teeth and snarling.

"I'm so sorry," Willa said, trying to quiet the dogs.

"Oh, don't worry about it. I know them well. Quiet, boys! It's just me. Mina never could get them under control," she said confidentially, bending down to pat Killer. "All they need is a little training, but as it is they'll bark at anything! Cats, squirrels, and people, indiscriminately! They absolutely terrorize my Blue Persian, Fluffy. I keep telling her dachshunds are nothing to be afraid of. They're good boys, at heart."

She stood and stuck her hand in Willa's direction.

"Lucy Garber! I live here," she said, jerking her head toward the door of the stately yellow house.

"That makes us neighbors then," Willa said.

Embarrassed by the barking and desperate to make it stop, she dropped a pile of ham by her feet. The dogs commenced a tiny feeding frenzy.

"You must be Mina's grand-niece," said Lucy, cheerfully. "I've waited *ages* to meet you! I couldn't put *Berry Dangerous* down! I left a whole load of laundry to rot while I read away—but I had to know who the murderer turned out to be. You had me completely fooled! I have the whole set, from *Delicious Death* to *Pineapple Upside Down Peril*, and I want you to autograph each one."

"Sure," said Willa, smiling at her. "I'm always glad to meet a fan."

"Is it true that you own the place now? Will you be living here, in Humboldt Cove? Or do you plan to sell?"

"Well..."

"Sorry to pry," Lucy apologized. "I haven't got a tactful bone in my body. I'm just curious, that's all. Mina was a dear friend, and I'm heartbroken she's gone. Such a sad accident—the kind that makes you take stock. After all, if it could happen to Mina, it could happen to me. And she was a much better sailor. So fearless! She's been a great loss to the community. I hope you plan to stay awhile, because it would be sad to have a strange family move in next door, and I would miss the dogs so much."

She cast a delighted eye over the three dachshunds, who had finished their ham and were gearing up to bark at her once more.

"I'd better get going," said Willa, hastily. "It was very nice to meet you."

"Stop by anytime!" said Lucy. "In fact, come by this afternoon for tea."

Willa hesitated, unsure whether it was a real invitation or a polite nothing.

"I insist. Three o'clock. We'll get the china out, and I'll make some of my famous apricot bread."

It would have been rude to refuse so pointed an offer, so Willa accepted. It was early days to start offending the neighbors. She waved goodbye to Lucy and made her way south. She had only gone a few steps beyond the yellow house when she ran into an elderly man wearing slippers and a robe, who had clearly come out to fetch the morning newspaper. She stooped to pick it up for him.

"Thank you!" said the man. "I don't know you, but I recognize these fellas."

He bent down to pat Wags and allowed Killer and Kyle to sniff his hands.

"You related to Mina?"

"Great-niece. Willa Lattner's my name."

"Jonah McNaught. Own the house now?"

"Yes."

"Gonna keep it pink like that?"

"I hadn't thought about it yet," said Willa, honestly.

"Get started thinking then," he said, grinning at her. "Nice to meet you."

Willa allowed the dogs to pull her down the hill and toward the town. There wasn't far to go. She passed only ten cross streets before descending onto the main street of Humboldt Cove.

It didn't take her long to spot The Three Hounds under a wide pink and white awning. *More pink,* she thought, with resignation. She noted, bemused, that there was another bakery directly across the street. The Humboldt Cove Patisserie had a somewhat threadbare exterior, and she wondered how a town this small could support two bakeries. As she walked by, a woman came out of the shop to sweep the pavement. She stopped short when she saw the dogs and retreated inside, giving Willa a look of pure hatred.

Stunned, Willa tripped over Killer's lead, became entangled between Kyle and Wags, and fell backward onto her rear end, skinning up her hands in the process. Brian Harrison came running out of the front entrance to The Three Hounds. He helped her up, disentangling her with some difficulty from the dogs, who barked the whole time. He took control of the leashes while she limped into the shop, embarrassed and covered with dust from the street and smudges of blood.

"What happened?" he asked, his lips quivering as he tried not to smile. "Quiet, Killer, for Pete's sake!"

He was just as good-looking as Willa remembered; maybe more so. Strong jaw—dazzlingly blue eyes.

"I don't know," Willa said, crossly. "A woman out there gave me an absolutely poisonous look and I got flustered. It's not easy walking three dogs, especially ones this stubby. They get under your feet."

Brian led her into a small lavatory in the back of the shop and left her there to clean up her skinned hands as best she could. She tried, unsuccessfully, to smooth down her mop of crazy auburn curls and pinch a little color into her cheeks. Despite the lavish amount of conditioner she had applied, she was still cultivating the Bozo look.

He was waiting for her with a cup of coffee and a pain au chocolate when she emerged.

"I thought you might need a pick-me-up," he said. "I took the liberty of guessing what you'd like best, but I'm happy to exchange this for chai tea and a kruller."

Gratefully, she took the coffee and gulped it down.

"I've never needed a caffeine fix more," she said, honestly. "Between my long drive yesterday, sleeping in a strange bed, and these dogs, I'm worn to a nub. And apparently, I'm already making enemies around town!"

She pointed out the large shop window to the bakery across the street.

"A lady came out that door, took one look at me, and rushed back inside. Did I grow an extra head? Or is she offended by dachshunds?"

Brian grimaced.

"Small woman, sandy hair?"

"That's the one."

"That's just Harriet Snelling. She owns the Humboldt Cove Patisserie. When Mina set up shop here she took it hard. Her 'patisserie'—I am using the term lightly—was the only game in town for about twenty years, but there isn't a real oven in the place. She orders pastries from the Safeway in Arcata and heats them in the microwave. Obviously, people prefer the real deal, and she's going under. She blames Mina."

"Bad luck for her, having another bakery move in across the street," Willa said, sympathetically.

Brian laughed.

"Luck had nothing to do with it. Your aunt paid the people who owned this building to move their shop down the road. She set up here on purpose. Harriet hates her guts."

Willa looked down at her sore hands, plaintively.

"Why does she hate *me* though?"

"Guilt by association. Everyone in town knows the boys. But I'm not sure you can blame the fall on her. I saw the whole thing. You must be as accident-prone as your aunt was!"

Willa looked up, sharply.

"How so?"

"She was pretty clumsy. Always burning herself on the ovens here or stumbling over the dog leashes. She actually broke her elbow right before she...well, before she died."

"How'd she do that?"

"A tumble down the stairs, I think."

Willa frowned. Mina hadn't trusted Brian enough to tell him what really happened to her. She had said he might be a good ally, though. It was hard to know what to do. Should she unload the whole story on him? Should she hint around and see what happened? Or should she keep her mouth shut?

"Speaking of which," he went on, blithely unaware of this internal struggle, "do you have time to go over a few items of business? Or were you on your way somewhere else when you ate it outside my shop?"

"I was out in search of breakfast. But you've provided that," she said, taking a giant bite from the pain au chocolate and nearly swooning.

Crisp, buttery pastry. Melting dark chocolate. The flaky interior was ever so slightly warm and smelled like the gates of heaven. It was enough to make her want to confess everything to him at once.

"Oh my gosh. Oh my *gosh*," she raved, her mouth full. "This is the best thing I've eaten in, well, *ever*. You have to give me the recipe."

Brian beamed.

"It's a trade secret, but since you own half the business now, I'll share it gladly. I didn't know you were a baker!"

"I'm not," said Willa, taking another bite.

"Why do you want the recipe then?" Brian asked, leading her into a small office in the back of the kitchen, where Killer, Wags, and Kyle were happily curled up in three respective baskets, chewing on rawhide.

They looked up at Brian as he came in and barked as a formality, but soon returned to their bones.

Willa gave him a sheepish look.

"I write cozy mysteries, set in a bakery. In every chapter, the heroine makes some kind of delicious cake or pie and there are recipes in the back."

"Seems like an odd choice, if you don't like to bake."

"I like to eat," she said, proving her point by devouring the last, buttery morsel of the pastry. "I enjoy describing the food. I just have no idea how to make it."

"Where do you usually get your recipes, then? Old cookbooks?"

"My brother-in-law is a pastry chef. He used to be my recipe lifeline, but he and my sister recently moved," she gulped. "Overseas. It's been harder to pick his brain."

"Well, you can pick mine any time," Brian said, and he looked as though he meant it.

The Employees

Talking business was not as complicated as Willa had feared. Brian showed her the books, walked her through that month's profit and loss statement, and gave her a brief tour of the ordering system.

"I order regular supplies on Mondays and Thursdays," he said, "and bring in specialty stuff once a month. If there's a cadence you'd prefer I'm open to hearing it. Mina always gave me carte blanche, but I'm open to changing the software as well…"

He trailed off, watching her anxiously.

"Whatever rope Mina gave you, you can take double from me. I only own half the bakery."

"Fifty-one percent, actually," he said, embarrassed.

"Close enough. You don't need to ask my permission to do stuff. If anything, I need to ask yours."

"But I want this to be a true partnership," he said, leaning in and taking her hand.

He saw her look of surprise and released her immediately.

"Sorry," he went on, miserably. "I tend to come on a little too strong."

Willa laughed, to put him at ease.

"Hey, I get it! 'Comes on too strong' was the caption on my high school yearbook photo."

He grinned at her, relieved.

"Well, I meant every word of it. I do want this to be a true partnership."

"Great! As long as you don't expect me to contribute much," Willa said, apologetically. "I don't know a thing about running a food service business. I've never even worked as a waitress. I assume you've got years of experience, or Mina wouldn't have partnered with you. How long had you worked together?"

"I've known her forever, though she didn't set up the bakery until about a year ago. It was perfect timing. I had just burned out on business school and started over as a pastry chef. I was looking for work in Eureka when Mina started talking about opening a shop in town. She was debating between a boutique and a cafe, but I persuaded her to go the donut, cake, and pie route and take me along for the ride. It's only been eighteen months, but we've made a real success of it!"

"You certainly have," said Willa, admiringly.

Everything in the bakery looked tasteful and expensive, and the pastries themselves were excellent.

"We started simple—just donuts at first. Bear claws, jellies, krullers. But we've expanded into croissants, bread, wedding cakes, you name it! Donuts are our specialty, but wedding cakes are the real bread and butter, if you'll forgive the expression. They pay for everything else. We get orders from as far south as San Fransisco and as far north as Ashland."

"I'm impressed," she reassured him. "I completely trust your expertise. But I would like copies of some of the reports and financial statements, if you don't mind."

He grinned at her.

"Go ahead and audit me, Willa Lattner! I'm not scared of you."

"As an author, my tax situation is complicated," said Willa, hastening to explain herself. "I want my guy to make sure I'm filing correctly."

"I'm just teasing you," he said, taking her hand again self-consciously. "It's going to take some getting used to, this partner thing. But I'm looking forward to it."

"So am I," she said, embarrassed but pleased all the same.

As if on cue, Wags, Kyle, and Killer looked up from their bones and woofed in her direction.

"So are they, it seems!"

Brian finished showing Willa the company bank statements and then introduced her to his assistant, a quiet woman in her early twenties hiding behind long bangs and the industrial mixer.

"Willa Lattner, meet Heidi Forrester."

"Oh! I didn't realize there was another employee," said Willa, pleasantly.

"Not just an employee! She's my right-hand man here in the kitchen," he said. "She's in charge of all the decorating. You should see her wedding cakes! Impeccable!"

Heidi blushed all over, gave Brian a look of pure adoration, and muttered hello to Willa. She immediately excused herself to fetch something from the walk-in freezer, as though Willa might have the plague and she was afraid of close contact. Brian saw Willa flinch.

"She doesn't take to strangers," he whispered.

Willa nodded politely, but the resentment in Heidi's eyes had looked personal—not general. The girl was clearly in love with her boss. *Who wouldn't be, though?* Willa wondered, taking in Brian's handsome profile.

"She'll get used to you soon enough," he said. "What do you think of the bakery? Mina and I decorated it together, so it's a little of her and a little of me. A very good combination, I think."

Willa looked around to see if she could tell who had contributed what to the decor. Most of the wall art was dog-related—hardly surprising since the name of the shop was The Three Hounds. Stylized paintings of dachshunds covered the walls, and black and white photos of Killer, Kyle, and Wags featured heavily as well. But every now and then, there was a painting, sketch, or stencil of a magnificent butterfly. It was a strange combination of artistic sensibilities, but the overall effect was pleasing.

"Who chose the name?" she asked. "Why 'The Three Hounds'?"

He snorted.

"Look around. The boys are everywhere. Mina had studio portraits made of all of them."

"But they're *sausage* dogs. Not like, bloodhounds or hunting dogs."

"Dachshund means 'badger hound' in German. They were bred to tunnel in holes and fight badgers."

"You can't be serious. They're so small and stubby!"

"They don't seem to know that," he laughed. "Heaven help you if a dachshund takes a dislike to you, that's all."

"What's with all the butterflies?" she asked, pointing to a large case of pinned and mounted butterflies, prominently displayed on the wall. "Are those real?"

"Every one of them," he said, enthusiastically. "Have you met Lucy Garber yet? Your neighbor up there on the hill?"

"Just this morning!"

"To know her is to love her. She was my favorite teacher in high school—biology. Anyway, her great-grandfather was a famous lepidopterist."

"A what now?"

"A butterfly collecter. That case was his. It's a valuable antique now. Lucy gave it to Mina once she knew about the whole dogs-and-butterflies theme. I'm a bit of an amateur lepidopterist as well. Butterflies are my spirit animal. My mascot. Look here!"

He peeled back his sleeve to show the monarch butterfly tattooed on his muscular shoulder.

"What is it you're drawn to about butterflies?" she asked, resisting the urge to touch his arm.

"They're so free," he said, dreamily. "Such a symbol for life and change."

"That's lovely. And I don't know why, but wiener dogs and butterflies make a good combination. Stout and brave meets delicate and free."

He smiled at her and her heart flip-flopped.

"So what are your plans?" he asked.

Her heart flop-flipped this time, but she tried to play it cool.

"Well, I've had my breakfast and we've talked shop, as arranged. Now I've got to hoof it back up the hill in time to meet with Mina's lawyer again. It was nice to see you."

"I was wondering more about your long-term plans," Brian said, delicately. "I'd be thrilled if you stay, but I'll understand if you need to get back to your normal life in Seattle. I can always send the monthly reports via email."

"Oh, I'll be around a while," Willa said, hoping she sounded vague enough. "I've got no plans to leave Humboldt Cove just yet."

At least not until I figure out who killed my aunt, she added silently.

Mail

To Craig Lattner

Hey Dad,

Sorry I missed your call. It's been nuts here, and the cell reception isn't that great. I blame the lead paint that's almost certainly lurking beneath every layer of floral wallpaper. This place is a DIY'er's paradise. The previous owners laid a horrible carpet over the original oak floor. (I refuse to believe Mina was guilty of such an atrocity.) The house won't be happy until the evil has been exorcized, so if you come down, you can yank out carpet to your heart's content.

The drive was easy. I took your advice and went up the coast, and you were right: the 101 is much prettier than the 5. Unfortunately, there are fewer bathroom stops—I was floating up to my eyeballs by the time I reached Crescent City. I found a Taco Tower there and scared the daylights out of the one person working that shift by sprinting in and demanding the keys to the restroom. I got a decent burrito out of the deal, so I'm calling it a win.

I'm guessing Mom or Wendy already told you about the dogs. Those crazy little sausages are growing on me. When Wags is asleep, the very corner of his tongue slips out of his mouth. I've texted you a picture of it.

Before you ask, YES, I am still fighting with the insurance company about the boat, and YES, I am using a firm tone. I channeled Grandma and threatened them with everything from the insurance oversight committee to Aunt Mina's old buddies in the Senate. Once the money comes in, I promise I will talk to your "guy" about investing it in IRAs or whatever.

On second thought, I may need every penny to remodel the house. The books pay well, but they don't bring in Victorian mansion-restoration money. I'll use up all the cash and die alone here with twenty cats. Or maybe I'll start collecting dachshunds in earnest.

By the way, Mom let something slip, so if Steve does call you, please don't pick up. It will start innocently—a Mariner's game, for old time's sake, and a beer afterward—but then he'll try to worm his back into my life and I'd rather not give either of you false hopes. We're never getting back together. Transfer your man crush fully onto Guillermo, or if you must attach it to one of my male belongings, Kyle, Killer, and Wags are all handsome fellows.

I'm speaking with the lawyer again in a minute or two, and I'll ask him what's to become of Mina's china and Great-Grandma Lattner's lace tablecloths. I know you want them, and I certainly don't.

I'll try to call you guys tomorrow. Meanwhile, can you have Mom take a picture of Grandma's

recipe for seven-minute icing and text it to
me? It's in the back of the recipe box, under
miscellaneous.

Love and hugs,

Willa

P.S. I am deadly serious about Steve. Don't let
him take you in. It will start with baseball
and lager and end with you trying to Parent Trap
us.

The Lawyer

By the time Willa walked back up the hill, the sun was burning fairly hot. She only had a minute to return a few emails and run a pick through her mop of curls before Mr. Pilkington rang the doorbell at precisely eleven-thirty-five.

"Good morning, my dear," he said, eyeing Willa with unflattering attention as he walked into the foyer and down toward the kitchen. "You, er—you seem to have something on your cheek."

Embarrassed, Willa reached up and felt a smear of chocolate, leftover from her breakfast. This is what she got for combing her hair without looking in the mirror. She realized, horrified, that the smudge had come from the croissant, which meant that Brian had seen it while they were talking business, and kept silent to spare her feelings. She felt almost prickly with humiliation.

Mr. Pilkington looked away, tactfully, while she scrubbed out the chocolate with her index finger and a little spit.

Wags and Killer ran up to sniff his shoes, and Willa—hoping her face was now chocolate-free—offered him a cup of tea or coffee.

"No, thank you," he said, with evident regret. "I'm afraid I can't stay long. We have a lot to do in a short space of time. There are several documents to sign, and I've arranged the transfer of Mina's banking accounts to your name. My clerk showed me your message to the insurance firm, by the way."

His voice held mingled approval and reproach.

"The apple does not fall far from the tree. Mina would have relished that email, though I question the wisdom of making threats you cannot keep."

"I meant every word I said," Willa replied, raising her eyebrow at him. "I went easy on them, if anything. I still have a card to play. Mina was friends with the governor. He owed her a favor from three elections back."

"How do you know?"

Willa laughed.

"We were in the same line for cheese cubes and punch at her memorial, and he thought it was a clever anecdote. I doubt he would have admitted she helped him win if she was alive to collect on the IOU, but if Safe & Sound keeps stonewalling me, I am not above calling his office and reminding him he owed Mina big time."

"I cannot imagine why they are being so tiresome."

"They're trying to make the case that Mina was reckless," Willa said. "Well, she wasn't. I'm going to get a signed affidavit from the harbormaster and the deputy who was on call that day. Safe & Sound can put the whole file into their pipe and smoke it, and I hope they choke to death."

"Such a tragic accident," sighed Mr. Pilkington, sadly.

"Strange too, don't you think? I sometimes wonder if it *was* an accident," Willa said, putting out a gentle feeler to see how he would react.

She wondered, uneasily, if showing Mr. Pilkington the letter at the wrong time might provoke a heart attack or a stroke. Mina *had* said to choose her moment wisely.

"What do you mean?" he squeaked, increasing her uneasiness.

"Oh, I don't know. Aunt Mina was the kind of person who got herself into trouble. Someone may have ill-wished her," she said, lightly. "Called up a storm to wreck the boat."

"My dear," said Mr. Pilkington, sternly. "There is a difference between wishing someone ill and *deliberately* trying to kill them. The most skillful sailor can be caught off guard by the ocean. It is dangerous to underestimate Mother Nature, and your aunt was inclined to er, risk-taking."

Willa considered dropping the subject, but she saw Kyle's dejected little form curled up in his basket and decided to plunge deeper.

"I don't know much about her life. I only saw her once a year or so, at Christmas. I know she played a mean game of Hearts and liked fruitcake—the boozier the better. I know she had strong opinions about football and politics. But I'm curious how she behaved around strangers. My father says she wasn't particularly popular down here."

Mr. Pilkington smiled to himself.

"You really are your aunt's niece. You sound just like her. If she were here, she'd say *Pilky*—she called me Pilky, you know—*Pilky, stop being such a fussy old lady and spill the tea!* Lord, I loved that woman," he said, sentimentally. "She and I—well, it never came to anything, but I did love her."

"What was Mina like?"

Attracted by the mention of Mina's name, Kyle slunk out of his basket in the corner and crept over to Willa. She picked him up and set him on her lap, stroking his ears. His little body shuddered for a moment, and then he relaxed into her legs and shut his eyes.

"Amazing," said Mr. Pilkington, his eyes watery with suppressed emotion. "Kind. Funny. Smart as a whip. But she didn't brook fools easily. She had a habit of telling people where they got off. That's what made her an effective prosecutor and a successful politician."

"How long did you know her?"

"Oh, years and years. I met her in law school. She was the only woman in our class and she whipped us all soundly. Pretty as a picture then, with hair as red as yours is now, but she wouldn't give anyone the time of day. Never married, though I asked her, more than once."

"Did she have enemies?"

The old man became cautious.

"Enemies is stretching the point. But, as I said before, she didn't mince words. What's more," he said, with a little nervous cough, "she, er—she didn't mind taking what she wanted, as long as no laws were broken."

Willa ran her hand down Kyle's spine and smiled.

"Like when she rented the space directly across from another bakery, you mean?"

"Exactly so," he replied, dryly. "The owner, a Ms. Snelling, threatened legal action, but she didn't have a leg to stand on. The woman is unbalanced, in my opinion."

"Who else did Mina offend around here? Lately, I mean."

Mr. Pilkington's expression became even more cautious—almost wary.

"She had just decided to run for County Sheriff," he said, uncomfortably. "Klamath has had the same one for dog's years now, and he didn't relish the competition. He's never had any real challengers. Klamath is the smallest county in California—just a sliver running west to east between Humboldt County to the south and Del Notre County to the north."

"She wanted to be a sheriff?" Willa said, skeptically. "But she didn't have any law enforcement experience!"

"It's an elected position, my dear. A political role. And she was a criminal prosecutor, don't forget."

"What's this guy's name—the one she would have run against?"

"Gary Poole. He is a bit of a—ahem—well, some people would call him a blowhard. Mina had a stronger term but I hesitate to use profanity."

"Gary Poole, Gary Poole," muttered Willa, trying to commit the name to memory. "Anyone else have a bone to pick with her?"

Killer trotted into the kitchen in search of a snack and rolled himself amiably at Mr. Pilkington's feet.

"Hmm," he said, thoughtfully. "I don't know if you're aware of this, Ms. Lattner, but your aunt was writing a book."

Willa sat up. This was definitely new information.

"A *book*? What kind of book?"

"A history of Klamath County, I believe. Logging barons, and the Gold Rush, and so on. I don't know much about it, but she mentioned to me in passing that one or two families here were in for a rude awakening when the book was published. I didn't press for details."

"Where's the manuscript?" Willa demanded, more strongly than she had intended.

"Oh dear," he said, taken aback. "I don't know. It wasn't in her safe. Perhaps it's about the house? Or with her publisher? Would you like me to help you look?"

"I'll dig it up somewhere. She didn't mention any definite names?"

"I think she said something about the mayor, but I could be mistaken."

"I see. Did my aunt have any other enemies, that you know of?"

Mr. Pilkington fidgeted in his seat.

"There's that word again: *enemies*. She had no enemies! Adversaries, perhaps, but...really, you are behaving as though your aunt's accident was deliberate," he said, distressed. "It was wind and waves that did the job. Not human hands."

Willa watched him for a minute and decided to risk the heart attack. She needed help, and she was tired of carrying the secret alone. Quietly, she stood up, walked to the counter, and grabbed the letter. She handed it to him.

"Why, this is Mina's writing," he said, astonished. "When did you receive it?"

"Just open it. Then we'll talk."

The old man drew the letter out and began to read. Willa saw his countenance change from curiosity to disbelief. His eyes returned to the top of the page several times, as though he hoped re-reading the message would change its contents.

"Remarkable," he murmured, finally folding the letter and handing it back to Willa. "Remarkable! I don't know what to say. I am really at a loss for words. Dear me. Dear, dear me. What was she thinking?"

"She was thinking she didn't have long to live. And she was right, as it happened."

"Goodness, gracious me," he twittered, upset.

She poured him a cup of coffee and added two sugars.

"Here," she said, forcing it into his hand. "Drink this, and then we'll come up with a plan."

He slurped the coffee down in one draught and asked her for another cup. When he had drunk that as well, they sat in silence, staring at each other.

"Well," she said at last, "what now?"

"How could she have been killed? It was an accident! The boat went into the rocks," he mumbled. "Drowned, they said, right in the police report. Police don't lie."

"Why didn't she return to port after receiving the initial warning? It should only have taken twenty or thirty minutes to get back. I think she might have met with another boat."

"What other boat?"

"There may have been other people out fishing that night. Isn't it possible that she encountered someone and—" Willa stopped herself abruptly, taking a cue from the horror and distaste on her companion's face. "Nevermind. We can talk it out later. You need some time to adjust to the idea, I see."

"Hmm," said Mr. Pilkington unhappily. "I can hardly bring myself to believe a word of it—and yet Mina was a very truthful woman. Dear, dear, dear. Well, there's no help for it. We must take this letter to the police and let them deal with it."

"Mina expressly told us *not* to do that!"

"What other choice do we have?"

"She wanted us to work together to figure it out. She didn't trust local law enforcement—it's right there in the letter."

"We *must* go to the police! It is their job to investigate suspicious death. And who are we, after all? Just a tired old man and very young woman, if you'll excuse me saying so, without much experience in the world."

"Mina believed we could do it."

There was a long silence.

"You loved her," said Willa, gently. "You told me that yourself. We owe it to her to at least *try*. It's Monday today. Give me until Friday, Mr. Pilkington. Stay here with me until Friday. If we haven't made progress by then, you can take this letter to the police and I'll go with you."

"Well..."

Willa stuck out her hand.

"C'mon, Pilky. Partners? For Mina?"

He shook his head, doubtfully, but he took her hand.

"For Mina."

Unwilling to shirk his primary duties, Mr. Pilkington refused to talk murder until he had walked Willa through every exhaustive clause of Mina's will.

Poor old Mr. Peanut, Willa thought, after she signed the last paper. *He doesn't like this one bit.*

He was a bit of a fussy old maiden, as Mina had called him. He didn't like mess and he had a very pure mind. That was all well and good, and very appropriate in a respectable law firm, but she didn't know how effective he'd be as a partner in a murder investigation.

"That's the last of it," Mr. Pilkington said, sighing as he leaned back against his chair. The paperwork ordeal had been hard on him, and he looked absolutely exhausted. "She had a vast estate, as you can see. You're a very rich woman now."

"I'd rather have my aunt back."

"So would I," he said. "But I believe you're right. We owe it to Mina to respect her final wishes, at least until it becomes impractical or dangerous to do otherwise. I accept your invitation to stay here. I shall return to Eureka to gather my things and check out of my hotel, and meet you back here later this afternoon."

Willa accompanied him to the door and watched as he drove safely away. Then she returned to the kitchen to think. Mr. Pilkington had already given her several helpful leads.

She wasn't previously aware of her aunt's prospective run for Sheriff of Klamath County. She'd need to look more into this Gary Poole. Men like that could be dangerous when crossed.

Then there was the book…

Willa chewed on the end of her pencil, absentmindedly petting Kyle with her other hand. She was becoming more and more fond of him, and he seemed to be resigning himself to her.

The book held definite possibilities, especially if Mina planned to expose old scandals or uncover ancient skeletons. Willa decided to have a good, hard look for the manuscript that afternoon. *But first, I've got to have tea next door*, she reminded herself.

She was looking forward to it, actually. As an old friend of Mina's, Lucy might shed more light on what had happened. Plus, the apricot bread sounded pretty darn tasty. If she was lucky, she'd come away with a lot of useful town gossip *and* a brand-new recipe for her latest novel.

Win-win.

Mail

To Wendoline Lattner-Santini

Wendy,

Got your message, but I am furious that I missed your call. I swear, this house exists outside of time and space in some kind of weird third dimension. I can't get bars here to save my life, except inside the linen closet on the fourth floor. Every time I have to call someone, I stuff myself in there and all three dogs insist on coming along. One of these days, I will punch through the back and find myself in Narnia, and the dogs and I will sit on the four thrones at Cair Paravel until I get lonely for you and find my way home.

When are you coming for a visit, by the way? Did I mention this house has seven guest rooms?

I did see cute-bakery-owner-guy again, thank you for asking. Not only is he the nicest guy I've met in months, he can *bake*. His pain au chocolate is better even than Guillermo's. Those are not fighting words, but the literal truth. If you come and visit, you'll find out for yourself.

I DON'T think he's interested in me, so you can put that to bed right now. He did offer to be my recipe guru, which seemed promising at first. But the bulk of our conversation was about business, and he called me accident-prone, which does not bode well. Also, there was a large smear of chocolate on my face the whole time I was there. He was too much of a gentleman to say anything about it.

When I am eighty, I will still wake up at night and think about that smear.

Steve hasn't called, thank goodness. He has been making sneaky overtures to Dad, though. If I

ever do talk to him again it will be to rip him
a new one.

Oh! Before I forget! I met with the lawyer (Mr.
Peanut) this morning and he told me that Aunt
Mina was writing a book! And I thought I was
the only writer in the family! That was four
exclamation points in a row! I am aware of them
but I'm going to leave them in! I'm going to
look for the manuscript this afternoon and see
if I can touch it up and find a publisher for
her. I hate to think of her doing all that work
for nothing.

Mr. Peanut also tells me Aunt Mina was planning
to run for local office. Between that and the
book and the color of this house, Mina had more
layers than I knew.

Remember that Christmas when she and Grandma
played bridge against Dad and Grandpa and almost
started a fistfight? I always thought that was
an anomaly brought on by fruitcake and brandy,
but now I think it was Mina being Mina (and
Grandma being Grandma). Sounds like she went
through this town making enemies and taking

names, and I may have to watch my back. I've already attracted the negative attention of one of her victims, so if I go missing, tell the police to look for a Ms. Snelling. She has the face of a ferret and according to cute-bakery-owner-guy, she can often be found buying stale donuts at Safeway.

Thankfully, I have three stout protectors in Killer, Kyle, and Wags, and as you can tell, they have wriggled themselves under my defenses already. I may actually keep them. That's how nuts things are, Wendy. I'm considering it. Please come visit, so you can talk me out of it (or into it, as the case may be).

Thanks to Guillermo for the recipe. I have questions about it but I will save our relationship by directing them to him and not to you.

Love, love, love, and lots of kisses,

Willa

The Neighbor

Willa let herself out the front door and walked up the neatly kept path toward the Garber House, marveling as she went at the scrollwork. Mina's house was far more decorative, but this one had a truly impressive elegance and simplicity. Lucy opened the door before she could knock.

"I saw you leave your house," she said. "At my time of life, one begins to embrace one's nosy tendencies. In another ten years, I'll sit at my window with binoculars, I'm sure. But come in, come in! Let me take your jacket!"

The interior of the house was even more stunning than the exterior. The whole space had been meticulously restored, and even the furniture looked original—and expensive. A downy, blue-gray cat walked casually up and rubbed itself on Willa's leg, leaving quite a bit of dander on her black denim jeans. It looked up at her smugly, as if it knew what it had done.

"This is Fluffy," said Lucy, proudly. "She's my baby. And she likes you! I was fairly sure you and I would get along, but now I'm certain. Anyone who gets Fluffy's seal of approval gets mine. Go on! Pet her! She'll allow it now that she's marked you, so to speak."

"I'm allergic to cats," Willa said, looking regretfully down at her jeans.

She'd be itching for days if she didn't get the hair off soon.

"Ah, what a shame. Well, nobody's perfect."

Lucy had laid out a tea table in the front parlor. There were several different kinds of cake, and a bowl of lump sugar, and a pitcher of cream, and it all looked unspeakably delicious and charming. Willa couldn't remember the last time she had felt quite so enchanted by a meal.

"Try this," Lucy said, and without waiting for Willa's consent, she piled her plate high with moist slices of apricot bread. "Eat! Eat!"

Obediently, Willa took a bite. And then another. And another.

"It's like eating sunshine," she raved. "So tangy! And yet it's still sweet. You must give me the recipe. I could base a whole book around this cake. *Arsenic and Apricots*. Or, let me see...*The Case of the Appalling Apricot*. Not *that*, of course, but something like that."

Lucy seemed delighted at the prospect of one of her recipes appearing in print.

"Your aunt was particularly fond of this cake! And you wouldn't believe it, but it's low-fat, too."

"How well did you know Mina?" Willa asked, sliding another piece of the apricot bread onto her plate.

It was low-fat, after all...

"Oh, we've been thick as thieves ever since she bought the house next door. That must have been...hmm...twenty-five years ago, now. It was very exciting to have a famous neighbor—and such a breath of fresh air to the town! Mina brought her own flavor with her."

Willa snorted into her teacup, and Lucy laughed. She had a delightful, low chuckle that made you want to join in.

"I'll admit the pink is very startling at first. I used to tell her she had the taste of a colorblind toddler."

"How did she take that?"

"She'd call me Grandma Moses and ask me when my dentures were arriving. She always gave as good as she got. But the truth is, we needed revitalization. Believe me, I would know! I've lived in Humboldt Cove all my life. Grew up in this very house. This is where I took my first steps—rode my first bike. I had my first kiss, right out there on the steps, me and Dougie Burch," she said, dimpling mischievously. "My mother caught us and grounded me for a month! That was back in the early fifties, you know, when women were expected to be demure and chaste and goodness knows what else. My parents were absolutely scandalized that I was 'necking' with a boy like Doug. The Burchs lived on the other side of the tracks, you see, and we were the fabulous and exclusive Garbers. A lot of nonsense, really, but my great-grandfather Hezekiah Garber did found the town and my parents were very proud of that fact."

"Oh really?"

"Yes! I won't say they were wrong to be proud, either. He was a great person—way, way ahead of his time. Most of the men back then were bigoted, sexist old dinosaurs, but he was an abolitionist, a conservationist, and a great believer in women's rights. He used his wealth to buy a tract of old-growth redwoods and then donated it to the government before he died in the early twenties. I suppose you've heard of Garber National Forest," she said, modestly. "It's twenty square miles of the most beautiful redwoods around. I hike there most weekends—you should come with me sometime! And I don't mean to brag, but Hezekiah was one of the only people to find gold in this part of California. There were plenty of claims here, but one by one people gave up and headed further south or east. He stuck it out and struck it rich."

"How interesting. I hear my aunt was writing a book about the Gold Rush and the history of Klamath County," Willa said, watching Lucy carefully.

Mina had said the book would take one or two people off their high horses, and Lucy Garber came from an old, established family—and seemed proud of the fact.

But Lucy nodded at her, enthusiastically.

"Yes, she was! We were collaborating on it. I have scads of old family documents, and we did a lot of the research together. Every Friday night, we'd order pizza and beer and Mina would sneak an entire cake out of The Three Hounds. We'd stay up all night stuffing our faces and working on the manuscript. The whole process has been tremendously exciting. Or it was," she said, her face falling. "I don't know what's to become of the book now."

"Mina's lawyer mentioned that she may have stumbled across one or two illuminating secrets about the town."

Lucy nodded again, more soberly.

"Yes, I'm afraid we did find some, er, unsavory things about certain founding members of Humboldt Cove."

"Like what?"

Lucy flushed.

"I shouldn't say. Especially since the book won't be published after all."

"Do you happen to know where the manuscript is?" asked Willa, hopefully. "I looked on Mina's computer but there was no sign of it."

"Mina didn't use a word processor," said Lucy, smiling a little. "She hated computers. And she called me the old lady!"

"How did she survive as a working attorney in the twenty-first century?"

"She kept assistants and aides to handle anything even remotely digital. And at home, whenever there was a problem she'd call me. I set up her TiVo for her. I'm a bit of a whiz with new tech," said Lucy, modestly. "I have a scientific bent. I taught high school biology, and have spent most of my adult life at the Garber Wildlife Foundation, researching local insects. Anyhow, Mina was a true luddite. She used a typewriter whenever she had to write anything of length, and handwrote everything else. I know she typed out the book because I sat with her many a night while she clacked away on that old thing, picking up the bits of pepperoni she dropped onto the keys. You say you can't find the manuscript?"

"No. There's nothing in her desk. Just some bills and blank paper."

"It's in her wall safe, then. Or maybe she entrusted it with her attorney."

"No dice there," Willa replied, grumpily. "Mr. Peanut doesn't have it, and it isn't in the safe either. He told me so himself."

"Mr. Peanut?"

"Oh, that's just what I call Mr. Pilkington, Mina's lawyer. He knew about the book but he doesn't know where it is."

"Why are you so interested in finding it?"

"I thought I might be able to finish it up for her—as a sort of tribute."

Lucy blinked a few tears out of her eyes, slightly smearing her mascara.

"No wonder Mina was proud of you. She always said that apart from your hair, you were the spitting image of your grandmother Wendoline, who as you know, she loved more than anyone in the world."

"They named my twin sister and I wrong. *I* should have been Wendoline and she should have been Wilhelmina. It's a big family joke. Grandma and Mina were best friends," Willa explained. "Aunt Mina introduced my grandma to my grandpa, in fact. Even though they were only sisters-in-law, they were closer than most sisters. I saw a lot of her when I was growing up. She came to every Christmas, every Easter, every family vacation. But after my grandma died, Mina sort of faded away. I was surprised when her will was read and she'd left everything to me."

"Mina felt you were a kindred spirit," said Lucy, pouring herself another cup of tea. "With similar ambitions and on a similar course. As I understand it, you—er—are not married. And you've got a very promising career. Mina was always a career woman, through and through."

So that's why she left me the house, Willa thought, a little displeased.

"Mina didn't let many people in, as I'm sure you're aware. But I loved her very much. Her death has been one of the most devastating experiences of my life," said Lucy.

Fluffy jumped up on her mistress's lap, sensing her distress.

"It must have been very unexpected," agreed Willa sympathetically—and rather mechanically.

She was surprised by the look on Lucy's face.

"It was unexpected, wasn't it?" she probed.

There was a slight pause.

"Very," said Lucy, stroking Fluffy firmly. "More tea?"

Willa attempted to lead the conversation back to Mina's death, and Lucy squelched her at every turn. Eventually, she admitted defeat.

But there had been something in the older woman's eyes—an awareness that Willa found both disconcerting and encouraging. She wondered if Lucy knew more than she let on about the circumstances of Mina's accident, or whether Mina had confided any fears or suspicions before she died.

"Have you met your new partner yet?" Lucy asked, when tea time was almost over and they were beginning to clear up the dishes.

"Brian? Yes."

"Do you like him?"

"So far! We've only talked a couple of times, but he seems like a solid guy."

"The best. And cute as a dang button," said Lucy. "I've known him since he was about three years old. Watch out, though," she warned Willa, winking. "He has a definite weakness for redheads."

Mail

To Wallace Schmidt

Wallace,

Thanks for checking in. *Fatal Fudge* will be completed on schedule, and I'm working with my editor now on final revisions for the last two chapters, which—if you'll recall—you called 'stinky' and 'full of holes.' As much as I relish my work being compared to Swiss cheese left to sweat at room temperature, I agree that the bit with Violet and the horse is silly and I'll cut it out. The whole passage will be rewritten to tone down the stink and I'll add one more red herring (a fish known for its odor, so the irony is not lost on me). I will humbly submit it for your approbation in a week or two.

Don't bother pestering me for it sooner. I just
moved into my aunt's old Victorian mansion, and
I'm up to my ears in busywork and dachshunds.

Not to worry, though—I'm gathering lots of local
color for a new series set in San Fran around
the turn of the century. I predict you'll have
another best-seller on your hands.

I don't know when I'm coming back to Seattle, so
if you want to take me out for one of your famous
poached-eggs-with-guilt-sauce brunches, you'll
have to come down here. There's an airport in
Arcata, and the fog occasionally lifts enough
to allow a plane or two to descend. I hear they
trained American pilots here during WWII so they
could navigate the fogs of London—how's that for
local color?

Speaking of which, it turns out that my aunt—a
celebrated prosecutor here in California—was
writing a book about the Gold Rush. I'm going
to finish it for her, and YOU'RE going to find
me a publisher. Yes, Wallace, you are. It will

be your penance for introducing me to Steve all those years ago.

That man, if you can believe it, has been asking around for my current email address and phone number. If you tell him where I am or how to reach me I will find a new agent and take my books with me and that IS a threat. I know you, Wallace. You're a sucker for a sob story.

If you still want to talk through the premise for *Grisly Ganache*, we'll have to schedule a time. I don't get very good reception in the house. Don't ask me why. Asbestos, maybe. Or ghosts.

Talk soon,

Willa

P.S. I'm serious about Steve. Tell him how to reach me and we're through.

The Mayor

Willa returned from tea with Lucy, stuffed to the gills and uncertain what to do next. She opened up her laptop to do some work, shut it again, and wandered upstairs, where she hurled herself facedown on her bed, spreading out her arms and legs like a starfish. The dogs jumped up with her and they all settled in for a nice, long nap.

Willa was exhausted, physically and mentally. There was still no proof that Mina's death had been anything but accidental. She had a nice collection of potential motives now, but the *whys*—while nice to have—were useless if one did not know the *how*.

She lay dozing for a while, spinning on the various ways someone could wreck a boat, and awoke with a snort, none the wiser. *Oh well*, she thought, philosophically. The book was a good starting place. She decided to have a good, long look for that manuscript before Mr. Pilkington returned. She had just peeled herself off the bedspread to get started when the doorbell rang.

Wags, Killer, and Kyle, all of whom had been asleep in various poses next to her, struggled onto their feet like upturned pill bugs, flew off the bed, and began barking as though their little lives depended on it.

What now? thought Willa, rising wearily to answer the door.

Mr. Pilkington wasn't due for another hour. It was probably someone selling solar panels or collecting canned food for the Boy Scouts. She hurried down three flights of stairs, irritated by the persistent ringing of the doorbell, which sounded every ten seconds. Every time it rang, the dogs burst into another frenzy of barking.

By the time she reached the front door, it took every ounce of self-control not to throw it open and scream *"What is it?"* at the bell-ringer. She stopped herself just in time and overcorrected, opening the door with slow ceremony like a butler from a drawing-room comedy.

The dogs planted themselves reassuringly behind her, ready to pounce. They had accepted her as one of their own, and she found their willingness to rip out the throats of her enemies touching, given their size.

A man and a woman stood on the doorstep, and even now, the woman's finger was on the doorbell.

"Oh!" she said, mercifully withdrawing her hand. "Who on earth are *you*?"

The question was blunt beyond the bounds of normal convention, and the man with her sensed Willa's surprise and chagrin.

"Er, hello," he said, quickly. "My name is Ian McKinley and this is my wife Patricia."

"Yes?" said Willa, nudging Killer back with the heel of her right foot.

"We weren't aware that the house had a new owner yet," he said, by way of explanation. "We—we understood that Brian Harrison was staying here."

"He's not. Nobody's living here at the moment but me."

"This is outrageous. Mina assured us we'd have first refusal if she ever sold," Patricia broke in, angrily.

Deciding that it was most politic to pour oil on these troubled waters—at least until she knew who the couple was and what they wanted—Willa conjured up a pleasant, social smile and held out her hand to the man called Ian. Of the two, he looked the least likely to bite.

"My name is Willa Lattner," she said. "Mina Lattner was my aunt. I'm not in the market for a buyer, but if I ever decide to sell, I'll let you know."

Patricia McKinley's right eye twitched expressively, and her husband's body grew very still.

"I see. We weren't aware she had an heir," he said, waiting expectantly for Willa to reply.

There was an awkward silence, which Willa did not choose to fill this time. Neither of them had given her any reason why they should be privy to her personal business, and she had no intention of satisfying idle curiosity.

"I'm sorry," said the man, eventually. "You must think we're very rude! May we come in?"

Willa shrugged and opened the door a little wider. If they turned out to be dangerous, the dogs were small but they had sharp teeth.

The couple walked in and Willa gestured to a rather hard velvet couch in the front sitting room.

"Have a seat," she said, taking the comfortable armchair for herself.

Wags and Killer sat on her feet, occasionally uttering a low woof just to remind the visitors who was in charge. Kyle jumped onto Willa's lap and sat there, ears back, body tense, ready to attack if needed. Willa's heart melted. She was getting attached to these little bratwursts.

"Remind me of your names again," she told the couple. "I've got a terrible memory."

"Patricia and Ian McKinley," said Patricia, who had reined in her temper and was using a reasonably polite tone.

She was an attractive woman, with stylish, blond hair and expensive clothing. Her skin was tight and youthful but the effect was unconvincing. You could always tell the real thing, no matter how skillfully the Botox was applied, and there was a telltale paralysis of movement around the eyes. Willa guessed she was nearer sixty than forty.

"McKinley," she repeated, thoughtfully. "I see. As in the McKinley House?"

"Exactly. My husband's family founded this town."

"I thought the Garbers founded the town," said Willa, immediately regretting it.

Both her guests turned a queer shade of purple.

"Hezekiah Garber owned the land on which the town was built," explained Ian, smiling at her in a terrifying way, "but my great-great grandfather, James McKinley, was the town's first mayor. And this was his home."

He looked around the sitting room.

"I grew up here," he said, still smiling, though he gazed at her with dead eyes. "We were forced to sell back in '86, but for many years I have been attempting to acquire the property again."

"I'm sorry to hear that," Willa said, lamely.

She did feel somewhat sorry for the man, but she wasn't going to apologize for inheriting the house.

"I'm the mayor of Humboldt Cove, by the way," said Ian, and again he paused as if waiting for Willa to deliver the correct response.

"How nice."

"This is a large house for one person," said his wife.

"One person and three dogs."

"It costs a lot to heat in the winter. The insulation is quite poor," added Ian.

"I don't mind the cold."

"The property taxes are extremely high."

"Is that so?"

"The insurance costs the earth, this close to a tsunami zone."

"We're well above the evacuation route. I checked."

"The neighborhood is falling to bits," said Patricia, desperately.

"Suits me just fine. I like a little character."

"Are you actually planning to live here?" asked Ian, outright.

He seemed frustrated by Willa's unwillingness to engage with their hints.

"As a matter of fact, I am."

"I see. May I use the restroom?" asked Ian, after a brief pause.

"Uh, I suppose so," said Willa. "It's just up those stairs to your—"

"I know where it is," he interrupted her, coldly.

Ian disappeared up the stairs, followed by Killer and Wags, who accompanied him as two bouncers might accompany a troublemaker in a club.

Patricia stared, unsmiling, at Willa.

"So what do you do for work?" she asked, after a silence of some twenty seconds.

"I'm a mystery writer."

"Have I heard of you?"

"It seems not," said Willa, briefly. "What do *you* do for work?"

Patricia flinched as if the question was inherently rude.

"How well did you know Mina Lattner?" she asked, abruptly changing the subject.

Willa blinked.

"Pretty well. She was my dad's aunt."

"So you knew what she was like?"

Willa blinked again, baffled by the question and growing tired of the visit in general.

"I spent a lot of time with her growing up," she said.

Above them, the creaking of human footsteps along the floorboards was followed by the pitter-patter of dog feet and the jingling of collars.

"Where are you from?" asked Patricia, glancing briefly upwards.

"The Seattle area," said Willa, listening distractedly for sounds on the second floor. What was Ian doing up there?

"Tacoma? Olympia? Bellevue? We have friends in Bellevue. Do you know them? The Wrights."

"I don't know anyone called Wright."

More footsteps, and the creaking of boards overhead.

"I'd better see if he got lost up there," said Willa. "He seems to be having trouble finding the bathroom."

Before Patricia could protest, Ian McKinley returned, flanked by Wags and Kyle.

"I hope you found what you were looking for," Willa said, exasperated. Ian smiled at her, nastily, and the hair on her arms stood on end. "Now if you'll excuse me, there's somewhere I have to be. It was very nice to meet you."

"Wait just a minute, now. Do you know what Mina Lattner was like?" Patricia pressed, rudely. "Do you know the kind of things she got up to? The kind of company she kept? Do you know where she went on all those boat excursions of hers?"

"Dear," said Ian, a warning in his voice.

"I know everything about my aunt," said Willa, wishing it was true. "Good night. Thank you for coming."

She stood, with Kyle in her arms. After a moment, the couple stood as well.

"It was nice to meet you, Ms. Lattner. Welcome to Humboldt Cove," said Ian, but it sounded more like a threat than a welcome.

"Thank you," said Willa politely, and shut the door behind them.

She quickly locked and leaned against the door, her heart racing.

Woof, said Kyle, contemptuously.

"You're telling me, buddy," she replied.

The encounter with the McKinleys shook Willa up more than she cared to admit. She locked and bolted every entrance and retreated to the kitchen to make herself a cup of tea and try to calm her nerves. Ian McKinley gave her the creeps. If he or his wife had been responsible for Mina's death, what was to stop them from going after her as well? It was an extremely unpleasant thought.

The kettle was just beginning to boil when there was a firm knock on the kitchen door. The dogs went crazy and Willa nearly jumped out of her skin.

"Who is it?" she called with a wavery voice, unwilling to open the door.

"It's Brian—Brian Harrison? From the bakery? What's wrong with you?" he asked, once she let him in. "You look like you've seen a ghost."

"It's nothing," she said, trying to laugh it off. "To what do I owe the pleasure?"

"Sorry for barging in. I tried to call, but your phone kept going to voicemail."

"I can't seem to get a signal here."

"Are you sure you're okay?" Brian persisted. "You sounded almost scared."

Willa sighed and poured herself a cup of tea.

"I had an odd visit this afternoon. A couple called the McKinleys—do you know them?"

Brian began laughing.

"I'm sorry," he said. "I should have warned you. Those two had quite a grudge against Mina."

"They seemed to resent me for occupying the house," she said, her mood lightening.

"That's an understatement," he said, shaking his head. "Any room in that kettle for me?"

She handed him Mina's tea caddy and a spare cup.

"Ian McKinley's been trying to buy back this house for years. The family lost all their money in the sixties and seventies—had to sell sometime in the eighties, and the house was bought by a young couple with kids from San Francisco. They used it as a vacation place, if you can believe it. Big tech money. But they put it on the market sometime in the early part of the century, and Ian thought he'd finally get his mitts on it again. I think there was even a preliminary sale in the works when Mina swooped up here from Sacramento and offered cash. Ian and Patricia own the big cannery next town over, and they do alright, but they didn't have enough cash lying around to make a purchase that big. Mina poached the house, and they've never forgiven her. I bet they hoped they could buy it off the estate."

"They thought you were staying here, for some reason," she said.

"Oh," he replied, embarrassed. "After Mina died the dogs were inconsolable. I did bunk here for a few nights until I could get them comfortable enough with me to take them home."

"Ah. Well, the McKinleys were surprised and displeased to find me here instead of you. They hinted around a lot until I told them flat-out I was planning to stay."

"Are you?" he cried, warmly. "That's the best news I've had all day. This town could use a little fresh blood. It's not often we get a new citizen, and when we do it's usually a retiree. Now we've landed a famous author and a pretty, young one to boot!"

Willa blushed.

"What did you want me for?"

"I need your signature on something for the bakery. And I have that recipe you asked for. But my real motive was to see if you would have dinner with me tomorrow. There's a good Mexican place in town, but if you wanted, we could drive down to Eureka for some seafood, or..."

"I'll eat anything," said Willa, truthfully. "But I love me a burrito."

Brian grinned, delighted.

"Then it's a date."

The Case

Mr. Pilkington returned just in time for dinner. Willa ran up to the fourth-floor linen closet to call Seastar Pizza, the only restaurant in town that offered delivery.

"Pepperoni okay?" she yelled down the staircase.

"Add black olives, please," shouted the old man from the landing on the second floor, where she had made up a guest room for him.

They waited until the pizza arrived to begin strategizing their next moves in earnest. Small talk about the weather, the town, and the dogs occupied them until the food was on the table. It was easier to face grim realities when you were downing carbs and cheese.

"Enough chit-chat. It's time to make a plan," Willa said, surreptitiously feeding Killer a slice of pepperoni under the table.

"I wish I knew where to begin," Mr. Pilkington replied, making a helpless gesture. "I have never actively participated in a murder investigation. I've prosecuted many murder cases, of course, but it's hardly the same thing. I feel very underqualified."

"The two of us may bring more to the table than we think. For various reasons, we've been knee-deep in violent death for years."

"Ugh," he said, distastefully.

"It's sad but true! You've tackled murder in court; I've studied famous murderers for my books. We both make a living from murder. Death happens no matter what. Your work helps bring bad guys to justice and provides closure to the victim's families. And my books may be a little silly, but they paint the world as it *ought* to be—mysteries are solved, evil is punished, the innocent go free. We're on the side of the angels. We can do this, Pilky. Let's treat it like any other job. When I'm writing a book, I always start with the list of characters—their relationships and motivations."

"Do you indeed? Fascinating. Murder cases are much more sterile, I'm afraid. Hard evidence is what we work with," said Mr. Pilkington, handing Killer a stray olive. "Weapons, witness statements, autopsy reports, and so forth. The personal element is often lacking."

"Two different approaches, then. We should use them both."

"Very well. If this was a book, who would the main characters be?"

"That's the problem! I didn't write the plot of Mina's murder story, so I'm struggling to identify the characters."

"I'm not sure I follow."

"It might help to think of it as a play or a movie. Right now, we don't know who has speaking parts, and who walks on and off in the background. Let's take the Sheriff, for example. He may be one of the primary actors in Mina's story. He may play a bit part, with one or two lines. Or he might appear in the background, a mere piece of set dressing. Do you follow?"

"I think so."

"Based on what I know so far, I've put the County Sheriff, the local bakery owner, and the town mayor in the suspect's column."

She told him briefly about her encounter with the McKinleys.

"I wish I had been here," he said, wrinkling his nose. "That couple sounds like trouble."

"Definitely. But there may be others with equally compelling motives. That's what we need to work on tomorrow. Who knew Mina? Who liked or disliked her, and for what reason? Who and why—those are my specialties."

"Fascinating. My work is very different. If you can prove that John Doe shot the gun that killed his wife, it doesn't matter why he did it. Maybe the wife was having an affair, or maybe his dinner was cold one too many times. Maybe he was possessed by a devil! I've seen the gamut of excuses in my time. The end result is the same no matter what: she is dead and he is sent to prison."

"The books I write focus on character and motive, which as little of the *how* as my readers will allow. But you're right—in real life, once you know how, you usually know who, and the why doesn't matter. Right now, we're very short on answers for who, why, and how," she said, gloomily. "All we really have is the what and where! It's like the end of a game of Clue!"

Mr. Pilkington chuckled.

"Mrs. Peacock, in the boat, with the Pacific Ocean."

Willa groaned.

"I feel hamstringed, Pilky. I don't know anything about boats—the tides—the ocean in general! I've got no reasonable theories for how someone caused Mina's boat to capsize. What we need is real data."

"I have been considering our assets in that respect," said Mr. Pilkington, fastidiously wiping pizza grease from his fingers with a paper napkin. "We have the report made by the deputy. That is hard evidence. We can speak with the harbormaster personally to garner more details about the night.

For now, we will operate on the assumption that Mina drowned, until it is proven otherwise. We can also attempt to trace her movements on the day of her disappearance. It may help to know with whom she spoke or dined that day."

"And then there's the book," said Willa, taking another slice of pizza.

Wags and Kyle had figured out that the pickings were good, and all three were collected under the table now, begging. Willa reckoned that they had already snuck nearly a quarter of the pizza to the dogs. She wondered, guiltily, whether it was okay for dogs to eat cheese and tomato sauce. They *liked* it, but maybe dachshunds would eat anything...

"Mina's neighbor Lucy Garber was helping with research for the book. She confirmed that there's some pretty hot stuff in the manuscript—details and stories that may have angered more than one family in town."

"But she doesn't know where it is?"

"No. She handled research, notes, and historical documents, but Mina did all the actual writing. If Lucy doesn't have it, and you don't have it, then where is it? We'll need to spend some time tomorrow looking for it."

"Agreed. One step at a time."

"What if we can't find the book?"

"I'm not allowing myself to contemplate that scenario."

"What if we find the book, and it gets us nowhere? What if we fail?"

"We shall not fail."

"I'm afraid of letting my aunt down," Willa admitted, after a short pause. "She trusted me with her dogs and her house. She trusted me with her *death*, Pilky. She's counting on me for justice."

"Take heart, my dear. We will crack this case, yet. Together, we make an excellent team. To the hunt, and to Mina!" said Mr. Pilkington. "May she rest in peace."

He looked vaguely around him for a glass and was forced to hold up his pizza crust instead.

"To Mina," echoed Willa, tapping the end of her slice against his.

Mail

To Joshua Lattner

Hey Josh,

Got your email last week but have been too busy
sorting out Aunt Mina's estate to reply. It's
almost midnight here and I'm about to turn into
a pumpkin.

I'm glad to hear that Jen and the girls are doing
well. I wish I could have made it to Charlotte's
recital. Thanks for sending the recording.

Tell her and Isabel that if they visit Aunt
Willa, they'll get unlimited access to a trio of
wiener dogs. I've attached several pictures and

a video of the one Aunt Mina christened "Kyle" (for obscure reasons of her own) chasing a ball. Most dachshunds lack a retrieving instinct, preferring to burrow for imaginary badgers, but he loves a good fetch.

My love life is rotten, thank you for asking. I'm sure Mom told you about the breakup, and I know you heartily hated Steve. I will allow you exactly one I-told-you-so. You were right, as big brothers always are.

There IS a guy here I'm slightly interested in, and before you ask, he has a steady job, no criminal record, and a deft hand with donuts, which I know you will find endearing. Nothing has come of it yet, but we'll be working together pretty closely AND we are having dinner tomorrow night at the best restaurant in town, which is genuinely called Fat Oscar's Taco Shack.

With my luck, he will turn out to be a serial killer OR have two wives stashed in the basement OR be into country music.

How's work? I heard you recently got an assignment on union busting (or possibly onion growing) in Walla Walla. Mom was unclear on the distinction but she assured me it was definitely unions or onions. I'd love to read the articles. Send me the links when you have time.

I doubt there are any breaking news stories *here* for you to investigate, but we do have a newspaper—The Humboldt Cove Gazette.

I dug through the archive for a few stories I thought you'd enjoy, including an unhinged op-ed that is definitely about Aunt Mina. For flamboyant read *pink*. I'm pretty sure I know who wrote it and he doesn't like me either, so in a few months I may be able to send you another one.

Love you,

Willa

Op-Ed From the Humboldt Cove Gazette, 14th April, 2015

We've all been warned about invasive species, haven't we? Bark beetles. Coral root. Scourges of the Redwoods that plant themselves in our backyard, turning what once was paradise into a wasteland.

There are such things as human parasites, dear reader. They come to Humboldt Cove, not to blend in harmony with the existing community, but to uproot what we hold sacred, to spit on our traditions, blaspheme our history, and destroy our heritage. We all know what I'm talking about.

'Tourist' is not the right word, for they do not stay to gawp at the Redwoods or fish for recreation in our waters. They come to this town, buying property here as if they had the right to it, shutting down good businesses with their boutiques, "gentrifying" old neighborhoods, and spreading their liberal stink over us all.

It's time for our Bay Area visitors to take their money, their flamboyant style, and their big, long noses right back to where they came from. Let's reclaim Humboldt Cove.

The Deputy

The dogs did not allow Willa to lie abed much longer than dawn. She rose, poured the kibble, and took the boys for a brief walk through the morning mist. When she returned around eight o'clock, Mr. Pilkington was only beginning to stir above.

She was just sharing the remains of her buttered toast with Killer when the doorbell rang. Willa's heart skipped a beat or two, and then she got a firm grip on herself. It was unlikely the McKinleys had come back. But if they had, so what? It was broad daylight. She had the dogs and Mr. Peanut with her, and if worse came to worst, she could scream and get the attention of Lucy Garber next door.

Killer and Wags accompanied her to the front door, and she opened it to see a man with dark brown hair and the beginnings of a stubbly beard. He wore a green uniform and carried a wide-brimmed hat under his right arm, along with—oddly—a plastic container that looked to contain cookies.

"Can I help you?" she asked, looking up and down the street for signs of a police vehicle.

Except for the Tupperware, the man looked nothing if not official.

"I hope so," he said, blandly. "Hey, boys."

Wags and Killer had gone out onto the porch, tails wagging, to say hello, and Kyle trotted out now too, his ears perkier than Willa had ever seen them. The man knelt to pet them and Kyle jumped up to lick his bearded face.

He let the dogs swarm him but straightened up, eventually, and stuck out a thin, tanned hand to Willa.

"Sheriff's Deputy Anderson, ma'am. You're related to Mina Lattner, I take it?"

"Yes!" she said. "I'm her great-niece. Come on in."

He entered the house, wiping his feet carefully on the doormat.

"Come on back to the kitchen," she invited him. "I'm just finishing breakfast but I was about to make myself some coffee."

The Deputy followed her back and accepted a mug of coffee. He sat down at the window seat and all three dogs jumped into his lap, jockeying for position.

"Did you know my aunt personally or is this a professional call?" asked Willa, looking curiously at the container in his left hand.

"Both," he said, giving her a crooked smile.

"Do you live in Humboldt Cove?"

"Nope. I live in Arcata."

"How did you know Mina?"

That he had known her, and known her well, seemed evident by the relaxed manner of the dogs.

"Used to work for her at the courthouse in Sacramento," he said, opening the Tupperware and extending it toward her. "Law clerk. Chocolate chip cookie?"

Never one to turn down chocolate, even at eight-thirty in the morning, Willa accepted the treat and took a bite. Chewy. Crispy. A hit of vanilla and then a massive dose of bittersweet chocolate.

"Mmmph," she said, sticking the rest of the cookie into her mouth, whole.

"Good, huh? My mom's recipe. Mina sent me home with a casserole before she died," he explained, and there was a very slight tremble in his hand. "I wanted to return it, full. To whoever happened to be in possession."

"That's me," said Willa, wondering if she dared to take another cookie so soon.

As if reading her mind, he held one out to her.

"Have another. Hey now, down boys! Sorry Wags, sorry Kyle—no chocolate for dogs. But I brought you guys something," he said, removing a couple of dried pig's ears from the inside pocket of his uniform and tossing them onto the floor.

Willa raised her eyebrows at him.

"You come prepared."

He shrugged.

"Is that all you wanted? To return Mina's Tupperware?"

He gave her another one of his crooked smiles.

"I have some official questions to ask, actually. On behalf of the Klamath County Sheriff's Department."

"Oh! How convenient. Because I have some questions to ask the Klamath County Sheriff's Department," said Willa, archly, "on my own behalf. Or on Mina's, if you prefer. Are you the B.J. Anderson who wrote the incident report?"

He looked at her, surprised.

"I go by Jake. Only my mom calls me B.J. You read that?"

"I had to get a copy for the insurance company. They're refusing to pay the claim."

His face grew grave, and he took a bite of cookie, chewing in silence for a time.

"They say the accident was due to negligence and improper usage of the boat," she went on. "I'm contesting it, but I may have to get the governor involved at this point."

"The governor?" Jake said, incredulously. "Are you serious?"

"Yep."

"The policy is that big, huh?"

Willa flushed at his tone.

"She paid her premiums faithfully. They should hold up their end of the bargain."

"Insurance companies never pay if they don't have to."

"That's not the point. Mina wasn't careless, and she wasn't negligent. They can't just say her death was her problem! You know—you wrote the report! Mina told the harbormaster she was coming back to port and she always kept her word. So whatever happened to her that night, it wasn't her fault."

"No," he agreed, quietly. "What happened wasn't her fault. But I'm curious why you have such strong opinions about it. You barely knew her."

"Excuse me?"

"Why are you so interested in the circumstances of your aunt's death?" he pressed. "You never came to visit her. You didn't show much interest in her life when she was alive. You weren't even the main beneficiary of her will until a few weeks ago."

"How do you know that?"

"I was investigating her death. I know a lot of things. So why all the curiosity about Mina now? Is it the money? How large was the policy on that boat, anyway?"

"*Excuse* me?" Willa repeated, angrily. "That is none of your business."

Again, he gave her that odd, crooked smile.

"I'm an investigating officer, like I said. Anything related to Mina Lattner or her death is my business."

"Oh yeah?" she said, watching him through narrowed eyes. "Because I heard her case is closed."

Jake reddened immediately.

"Technically, you're right," he said, with formality. "My boss was convinced by the Coast Guard's findings. They combed the wreckage for traces of explosives or engine interference. There were none. By all appearances, the craft was driven into the rocks by the wind."

"So what is there to investigate?" she challenged him. "Sounds like everyone agrees it was an accident."

"You don't appear satisfied with that explanation," he shot back. "Do you suspect foul play, Ms. Lattner?"

She blinked, startled both by the question and the intense expression in his eyes. An unpleasant thought struck her.

"Hang on—you don't actually *suspect* me of something, do you?"

His face grew a shade redder.

"Seriously?" she said, unsure whether to be angry or amused. "You said yourself the investigation is closed. What's to suspect?"

"I've continued looking into it. Informally."

"Fine. That's what I'm doing too. Looking into it. Informally."

"How much did you say the policy was on Mina's boat? The Old Girl was in great condition—almost brand new, and an expensive model, too. Mina took out $50,000 on it?"

"It seems so," said Willa, coldly.

"And she left you the house, too?"

"Yes."

"How much cash was in her accounts? Did you get the whole pot?"

"Excuse me? My lawyer is upstairs. Do I need to get him down here for this conversation?"

He saw the disgusted look on her face and let up.

"This is off the record. You don't need to sic your lawyer on me. Look, cards on the table, Mina was special to me. We were actually supposed to go out for dinner the night after she died, to celebrate me passing the bar. I'm protective of her memory. And her stuff."

"Well, so am I. I'll take good care of everything she left me."

"Even these guys?" said Jake, looking at the dogs.

"Even these guys."

"They're a handful," he said, scratching Kyle's ears.

"I'll make sure they're okay."

"I believe you," he said, after a pause.

There was an uncomfortable lull, punctuated only by the sound of Killer's tail thumping against the window bench as it wagged. Willa gathered her courage.

"Let me ask you something," she said, impulsively. "You claim to have known Mina well."

"I did know her well. What's the question?"

"Was she a good person?"

"What do you mean?"

"As far as I can tell, my aunt went through life offending people left and right. The owner of the bakery across the street from The Three Hounds definitely hated her. The town mayor and his wife hated her—she poached this house right out from under them. And she was writing a book about Klamath County that was going to put quite a few noses out of joint."

"Do you have it? Where is it?" he said, quickly.

A little too quickly, Willa thought. He seemed awfully eager to get his hands on the manuscript. Her hackles rose again, and she gripped the bottom of her coffee mug a little tighter.

"You're not going to answer the original question, huh?" she said, trying to keep things light. "Maybe that says it all."

"Mina was a good person," he said, firmly.

"It sounds to me like she was ruthless."

"She was. The two things are not mutually exclusive. I will add, though, that sometimes good people do bad things."

"What is that supposed to mean?"

"Do you know anything about Mina's life here? About her work or—extracurricular activities?"

"Nothing," said Willa, narrowing her eyes at him. "Do you want to explain what you're hinting at?"

"Not really," Jake replied, popping the last bite of cookie into his mouth. "But if you do know anything, it would be better to tell me now."

"I have no idea what you're talking about."

Without warning, he rose, displacing the dogs into a heap on the floor. He handed her the Tupperware with the remaining cookies.

"Suit yourself. I'd better be going now. It was nice to meet you, Ms. Lattner."

"Willa," she corrected, automatically taking another bite of cookie.

"Willa. See you later. I've got to get to the office before nine-thirty or Sheriff Poole will have my hide. If you find out anything more about Mina's accident—you know, to 'sort things out with the insurance company'," he said, using air quotes, "here's my number."

He handed her a card, which she pocketed, sure she'd never use it.

"I'd be careful, though."

"What do you mean?"

"Curiosity killed the cat."

"Is that a threat?" asked Willa, whose pulse began to race.

"Nope. Call it a passing remark. You just got chocolate on your face, by the way."

He dabbed a finger in the corner of his own mouth to show her where it was, gave the dogs one last pat, and let himself out the back door.

Mail

To Walter P. Blumenthal, CPA

Hi Walt,

Thanks for the message.

Fatal Fudge is set to release just after the Christmas holidays. My publisher expects roughly the same number of sales we saw for *Pineapple Upside Down Death* last January, plus the usual uptick in sales for the rest of the series. I've attached the projections, but it's safe to say we should withhold a little more for Q1 than usual.

The value of my aunt's estate all told is between three and four million dollars—not including the business, of course. That's split between the house, her car, her boat, checking, savings, and the value of various stocks and bonds, which I'm still sorting through with her attorney. Her boat was destroyed, but I'm expecting roughly $50K in cash from the insurance company.

The house itself is valued at $1.3 million and the property taxes will make you weep—a cool ten grand, if not more. Looks like California doesn't have an inheritance tax, thank goodness, and from what you said I'm well within the threshold where federal estate taxes kick in. You'll be getting a packet of documents from Pilkington, Pilkington, and Gump soon with more details. Sorry for the extra mess.

I appreciate you looking over that stuff from The Three Hounds. I knew there wouldn't be any funny business with the taxes—Mina wasn't like that. I suspected it was running on thinner margins, though. I'm happy and relieved to hear how much we're netting per month!

Sounds like their tax guy knows his business so I'm going to leave all that to him and won't bother you with the books again. He'll forward the earnings statements and so on to you whenever needed.

I may end up selling the condo as Wendy and Guillermo have permanently moved overseas, but for now, we can assume I'll own property in Washington and California and work out of both states. Again, sorry for the mess.

Let me know if you need anything else from Pilkington, Pilkington, and Gump.

Thanks again,

Willa

Mail

To Guillermo Santini

G,

Received the ganache recipe and your
instructions.

Can I have the ganache be dark chocolate? Dark
chocolate is all the rage right now, and you know
how willing I am to swing myself onto whatever
bandwagon is rolling by. I think it tastes like
old coffee grounds but I am a woman of the
people. If I switch it to dark, do I have to
change the amount of cream in the recipe?

Also, does it have to be cream? Sometimes people write Wallace and ask stupid questions about substitutions and I never know what to say. What about the people who drink 1% and don't have whipping cream lying around? Or the oat milk crowd? Are they supposed to go cakeless? Have a heart, G.

Things are going well thanks for asking. Give Wendy a hug and a kiss from me, and tell her I miss her. She doesn't believe me. She thinks I am too in love with my nice big house and my new dogs to feel homesick. Well, I'm not. I miss you both horribly and I don't like living alone.

Tell your mother "ciao" for me. I hope she's starting to feel better.

I am off to walk the dogs to town and try to meet some new neighbors. Meeting people is not my strong suit so please click your rosary for me once or twice and ask the saint of lost causes to give me a holler. I am going on a first date tonight for the first time in seven years so if there's a saint for that, have them look me up as well.

I have some papers I'd like you to look over—ordering forms and reports from the bakery. Mina's partner has things well in control but I always like to get a second opinion. I'm out of my depth, G. I had no idea how many pounds of flour you pastry chefs could get through in a week. And gelatin. Why all the gelatin? What needs gelling so desperately? And don't even get me started on marzipan. Tubs and tubs of it. Whole forests worth of almond trees, mowed down in the sacred name of patisserie.

Love you guys,

Willa

P.S. I don't like marzipan, so I can afford to be snarky and environmental about it.

The Rival

Willa let the dogs out to run around a bit and tried to get some work done. She hadn't been on her laptop long before she heard the telltale creak of the stairs above her. Soon, Mr. Pilkington wandered into the kitchen, wearing his robe and slippers and rubbing his eyes.

"Sleep poorly?" she asked, sympathetically.

"I confess I spent the bulk of the evening thinking about Mina."

"Me too," Willa admitted.

Before they could speak further, there was a casual knock on the back door. Willa peered cautiously through the window and saw Lucy Garber, holding a loaf of apricot bread. People were practically lining up to bring her baked goods this morning.

"It's my next-door neighbor," she informed Mr. Pilkington, opening the door.

"Good morning, sweetheart," said Lucy, giving her a quick, informal peck on the cheek.

The gesture surprised Willa a bit, but Lucy smelled like lilac and vanilla and had a comforting maternal presence that was much appreciated. The world had become a scary place, and Humboldt Cove seemed populated with bogeymen and potential murderers. Lucy was a safe harbor in the storm. Plus, she came bearing apricot bread, and Willa would have admitted a grizzly bear with a chainsaw if it offered her a slice of that bread.

"I'm sorry to drop in unannounced," Lucy said, sitting on the window seat. "I just returned from my morning run and thought I'd pay a friendly call."

Her legs were so short that they dangled off the polished pine floor. She looked questioningly at Mr. Pilkington, who was peering down at his slippers, horrified to have been caught in such a state of undress by a stranger.

"Don't worry about it!" Willa assured her. "Have you met Mina's lawyer? This is Daniel Pilkington—Mr. Pilkington, I'd like you to meet Mina's dear friend, Lucy Garber."

"Charmed," said Mr. Pilkington, cultivating the Rudolph look again.

Every bit of his visible skin was a bright scarlet, except the tip of his rather pointed nose. He looked like a beet with features.

"Excuse me, ladies, won't you?" he murmured, rising before either woman could reply.

"Do you run every day?" Willa asked Lucy, to distract her from Mr. Pilkington's slippered feet as they scurried out of the kitchen.

"Four miles! Up and down the hills. It's fantastic exercise. Did I see an officer from the Sheriff's department here a little while ago?"

"At the window again with your binoculars?" Willa teased, but she noted that the other woman did not smile. "As a matter of fact, I was just visited by the Klamath County Sheriff's Deputy—a guy named Jake. Do you know him?"

"I do," said Lucy, gravely. "He is a former student of mine. Did he say what he wanted?"

"He was returning a Tupperware," Willa replied, puzzled by Lucy's tone. "Why the long face? Is there something wrong with that? Or with him?"

Lucy looked at the floor.

"Not exactly. But I would be careful, that's all. Are you aware that Mina had strong feelings about the Sheriff's Department?"

"I know she was in a minor feud with the Sheriff himself. She was planning to run for office."

"Yes, and she would have won! But she was wary of everyone there, not just Gary Poole. She suspected the entire organization was rotten, including Deputy Anderson, who she knew personally."

"Somehow, that doesn't surprise me," Willa said, frowning.

Her visit with Jake Anderson had been disconcerting, to say the least. The dogs were barking from the laundry room, making it hard for her to think, and the things Lucy was saying were deeply troubling.

"She always said it was a shame when a good apple got tossed into a rotten barrel. I believe she had written him off entirely as a lost cause. Too hand-in-hand with Sheriff Poole. Speaking of which, have you found the book yet?" Lucy asked, hopefully.

"Why 'speaking of which'?" Willa replied, beginning to feel like she was missing something important. "What's in this book, anyway? Everyone seems very eager for me to find it."

"What do you mean? Who else is looking for it?"

The old woman sounded genuinely frightened now, and the scared, tight feeling was returning to Willa's chest.

"The Deputy asked me to let him know when I located it."

"Why?" cried Lucy. "Did he say?"

"I have no idea," said Willa, noncommittally.

Inwardly, she cursed Mina's injunction to silence. Secret-keeping was not her strong suit, and she felt a strong desire to unburden herself to Lucy. The woman knew something, that was clear. And it would be so nice to have someone else to talk to.

Forcing herself to speak as normally as possible, Willa said, "Mr. Pilkington and I are going to look for the book today. Would you like to help? I can provide lunch, and we could make an afternoon of it."

The worry lines around Lucy's eyes receded instantly.

"Great idea," she said. "I'm very eager to find the manuscript. We worked so hard on it, and I would hate for—well, least said, soon mended."

"You would hate for what?"

"Nevermind. It's only that if the book were to—no, no, that's just silly. Don't mind me, sweetie."

Willa waited politely, hoping Lucy would stop dropping dark hints and say what was on her mind, but the other woman remained silent. Willa saw her eyes darting to the kitchen counter, where Mina's letter still lay innocently in its envelope.

"Excellent," said Willa, stepping slightly in front of the letter. She decided it was best to just ignore Lucy's non-sequiturs for now. "I'm planning to head down to town for a few hours this morning, but I'll be back around noon. You can pop over for some sandwiches and then we'll have a nice little search party."

"What fun! A search party! I don't know when I've been so excited," said Lucy, swinging her feet and looking more and more like a girl of six instead of a woman of eighty-five.

"See you around noon?"

"I can't wait!"

Willa locked the door after Lucy left. She cut herself a large slice of apricot bread and ate it standing over the sink. Moist crumb; deep vanilla flavor; lots and lots of plump apricots. This bread was to die for. Reflecting that she should share the wealth, she let the dogs in and split a second slice with them.

As she was going in for a third round, Willa caught sight of the letter again and decided to tuck it safely in her purse. The fewer people who saw it, the better. Mr. Pilkington crept down the stairs and peeked his head into the kitchen.

"It's all clear," Willa laughed. "She's gone."

"I'm terribly embarrassed to have been caught in my slippers by such an attractive woman!"

Willa, who had never considered Lucy's physical attractions one way or another, blinked. Lucy was very pretty, in her way.

"She was Mina's best friend here."

"Ah. She may prove a valuable resource, then."

"I invited her over to lunch to help us search for the book."

"Excellent. I look forward to cultivating her acquaintance."

He eyed the apricot bread, hungrily.

"Would you like to cultivate a closer acquaintance with this cake?" Willa asked with a laugh, handing him the end of the loaf.

Once Mr. Pilkington had devoured the last of the apricot bread and the dishes were virtuously washed and replaced, Willa harnessed Kyle, Wags, and Killer and led them outside, ready to explore the town.

Behind them, a tall grove of redwood trees receded into a bank of fog, and before them, a fine mist was rising from the water around the Hags.

"Lovely!" breathed Mr. Pilkington, enthusiastically. "Smell that fine, sea air! What is up that direction, my dear?"

"I think it's a dead end, but let's find out!"

They walked toward the barrier that signaled the road's ending. Willa peered down through a thicket of scotch broom and blackberries toward the open sea below. Waves crashed around the boulders at the bottom of the cliff, and she stepped back, suddenly giddy. It was on rocks like these that Mina's boat had been destroyed...

She snatched a few of the last remaining blackberries off the nearest bush and handed some to Mr. Pilkington, munching appreciatively as they moved south toward the town. A few of the neighbors were out watering their hydrangeas or checking the mail, and she waved at them. Most of them waved back and called out a "hello," but one or two stared at them without replying.

The town of Humboldt Cove was laid out on a neat square grid, and most of the streets were conveniently named after letters going north-south, and numbers going east-west. They reached the bakery and Willa looked in the window briefly to see if Brian was working. Heidi was stacking a variety of tempting cake donuts in the front pastry case. They made brief eye contact, but Heidi pretended not to see her.

"Care for a donut, Pilky?"

"I'm full, thank you. But I am eager to see inside Mina's business. More pink, I see," he said, peering up at the awning. "Do they do chai tea?"

"I think they do everything!"

Willa pushed open the door to let the old man in.

"Good morning! Those donuts look amazing," she said brightly, giving a verbal greeting this time so that Heidi couldn't in decency ignore her.

Heidi shrugged.

"What flavor are those? The ones with the slivered almonds on top."

"Almond," was Heidi's withering reply, and Willa felt extremely foolish.

"Hey boys," Heidi said, her tone softening as the dogs approached her, tails wagging. "Hang on a sec, I'll get your treats."

She walked behind the counter and emerged holding three milk bones.

"We keep them here for pets," she told Willa, distantly.

"Great idea. Is Brian around, do you know?"

"He's busy with a batch of sourdough," Heidi replied, turning her back on Willa to fiddle with some bread on a warming tray behind the counter. "I'll tell him you stopped by."

Snubbed again, thought Willa, refusing to let herself be hurt. The girl was probably just shy. She ordered a chai tea latte, a to-go cup of coffee, and a cream-filled donut. Heidi gave her a martyred look, as though Willa had marched in and demanded she spin some straw into gold. Stomping over to the steamer, she heated the milk for Mr. Pilkington's chai latte and smacked the finished drink on the counter without a word. Then she returned to her work.

"What are you doing now?" Willa asked, trying to keep things light and friendly.

"Decorating," spat Heidi. "We've got a cake going out in two days."

"You start two days ahead?" said Willa, flummoxed at the idea.

"We started yesterday."

"How interesting! I had no idea it took that long to make a cake. What happens after they're baked?"

Heidi gave her a very dirty look, but Willa maintained a neutral—and she hoped pleasant—expression. Internally, she was fuming at the younger woman's attitude. She owned the bakery, didn't she? She could ask as many questions as she darn well pleased, and Heidi could lump it.

"They chill and rest overnight."

"Then what?"

Heidi sighed again.

"Then I add the crumb coat and filling. *Then* I add the fondant. *Then* I do the flowers or whatever other decorations are needed. And *then* we have to box it up carefully and drive it wherever it's going and set it up again, which takes hours and hours too."

"Sounds like a lot of work!"

Heidi did not respond, and Willa gave up. She'd get to know Heidi more as the weeks went on, and hopefully, they'd come to an understanding. She took the latte and her coffee and said goodbye, but Heidi did not turn around.

"A strange young woman," said Mr. Pilkington, once they were outside. "Unfriendly. She dislikes you, Willa. Why?"

"I have no idea."

"Perhaps we should add her to our list of suspects," he said, sipping his chai latte and wincing at the heat. "Her hostility is suggestive. And she did not like your questions about the wedding cakes. Odd subject to be touchy about."

"I don't think it's the cakes. I think it's me, in general. Why would she hurt Mina, though? How could she possibly benefit from her employer's death?"

Willa remembered Heidi's look of abject adoration yesterday at the oblivious Brian Harrison. *Maybe she killed Mina for Brian's sake*, she mused. *To give him more control over the bakery.*

It wouldn't be the first time a crime had been committed on behalf of an innocent party. Willa considered it for a moment longer and then shook her head. This was pointless speculation.

"Speaking of hostility," she said, "there's the rival bakery."

She pointed to the Humboldt Cove Patisserie, and Mr. Pilkington looked across the street.

"Aha. The provider of sub-par baked goods. Shall we go in and see what it's like?" he suggested, with a touch of mischief.

Willa hesitated, but gathering up her courage (and the dogs), she crossed the street with Mr. Pilkington and entered the bakery. The interior was dim and smelled vaguely of baked goods, but the odor was more reminiscent of the bread aisle in the supermarket than the heady, yeasty aroma of The Three Hounds.

Two or three questionable cakes were on display, and an indifferent assortment of baguettes lay limply in their packages, beginning to collect condensation. Harriet Snelling came out of the back room, flinching when she saw the dogs, who began cheerfully barking at her in unison.

"No pets allowed," she said shrilly, pointing to the door.

"I'm so sorry!" said Willa, embarrassed she hadn't thought about it. It was a reasonable request. Food service businesses had to be careful about hygiene. "I'll tie them up out front," she began, but the woman cut her off.

"Don't bother. I assume you're related to Mina Lattner. She wasn't welcome in my shop and neither are you."

Willa and Mr. Pilkington stared at her, astonished. Harriet pointed to a sign that hung below the cash register.

"I reserve the right to refuse service to anyone," she said. "The old fart can stay, but *you* have to leave. Get these dogs out of my store or I'll call the police."

"The police?" Willa repeated, incredulous.

"Old *fart*?" said Mr. Pilkington, with equal incredulity.

Harriet stalked back behind the counter and picked up the phone.

"You have five seconds to get out."

"My dear lady," fluttered Mr. Pilkington.

"I don't understand what's happening!" Willa protested. "Let me put the dogs out and then we can start over."

"One!" shrieked Harriet, beginning to dial. "Two!"

Willa yanked the dogs and the indignant Mr. Pilkington out of the store before the other woman could count any higher. She was shaking with anxiety, the more so when she spied Heidi watching them through the window.

"I am flabbergasted. Flabbergasted!" repeated Mr. Pilkington, taking Willa's arm to steady himself. "I would never have expected such treatment. It is a public shop, and we had every right to enter. Our money is as good as everyone else's!"

"It's okay, Pilky," said Willa, soothingly. "If she doesn't want us, we don't want her, right?"

They were striking out at all the Humboldt Cove bakeries this morning, and Willa, for one, chose to take the hint. If you didn't pay attention to the closed doors and the open windows in life, you were liable to get hurt. Mina Lattner had pushed on one too many locked doors during her lifetime, and look where it had gotten her! A lonely death at sea.

Willa shivered and drew Mr. Pilkington away. It was a bad policy to pick fights with fate.

The Town

Turning left, Willa, Mr. Pilkington, and the dogs made their way onto F street, a lovely little avenue that led down to the harbor. It was a beautiful morning, and the bay was calm and glassy.

Several people said hello or stopped to pet the dogs, and Willa felt her spirits lifting. They window-shopped their way through the small downtown area, and could not resist popping into The Sea Hag, a charming shop that sold shells, driftwood sculptures, and other trinkets. While Mr. Pilkington admired a carved wooden mermaid in the back corner, the lady behind the counter gave the dogs a biscuit each and handed Willa a polished shell for luck.

"You'll need it," she said, rather ominously.

She was a fat, beautiful young woman with purple hair and dark makeup—rather like an attractive hippopotamus.

"You Mina Lattner's granddaughter?"

"Great-niece. My name is Willa."

"Justine Galway. You don't look much like your aunt. Same hair, though. Yours dyed?"

"No."

"Mina claimed hers wasn't either but I would have sworn in court that hers was straight outta the bottle. Halloween orange. Mind you, *I* liked Mina just fine. She was bossy as heck but she was smart and polite. You can be from the Bay Area without being *from* the Bay Area, you know? Mina wasn't stuck up. Well, on behalf of me and my man, welcome to Humboldt Cove," she said, and there was a strange pity in her eyes. "I don't believe everything I hear, if you know what I mean. I swim my own direction. And I, for one, am glad to have you."

"Uh, thanks."

"Don't mention it. You like fish?"

"Sure."

"My man Dale runs the fish and chips shop down on B Street. You want the best fried cod you ever had? Go there and tell him I sent you over. He always keeps back some of the guts for the dogs."

Puzzled (and a little revolted), Willa collected Mr. Pilkington and exited the shop. Absently rubbing the smooth interior of the shell, Willa wondered what Justine had meant by *I don't believe everything I hear.*

"There!" said Mr. Pilkington, interrupting her train of thought. "The harbor office, if I'm not mistaken."

He gestured toward a small, red building just off the pier. They walked eagerly in that direction, but when they reached the door of the red building, it was locked.

"Fiddlesticks," said Mr. Pilkington, peering through the window. "There doesn't seem to be anyone within."

"We'll have to come back later. Maybe after lunch."

Lunch.

With a slight twinge, Willa remembered that she had promised to provide lunch for the search party. Mina's cupboards were bare. There was nothing in the fridge except for some mustard and a jar of horseradish, and she wasn't quite ready to take on Justine's 'man', his fried cod, or his fish guts. She spied a corner market at the intersection of F and 6th and hoped it had a dog-friendly policy.

Doyle's was a charming, traditional small-town grocer, complete with a green and white striped awning and large wooden barrels of fruits and veggies outside. A thin, middle-aged woman with grey hair tossed into a messy bun was outside, unpacking nectarines from a crate. She looked up as Willa and Mr. Pilkington approached, and called out a cheery greeting.

"Kyle! Wags! Killer! You sweet boys," she crooned. She stooped as the dogs ran up so they could lick her face. "Hullo, hon. You belong to these dogs now?"

"Looks that way," Willa laughed.

"You must be Mina's niece," said the woman.

"Willa Lattner. This is my friend Mr. Pilkington—he's staying with me for a few days."

"Welcome! We heard you were coming. I'm real sorry for your loss, but I'm glad the boys have a nice person to go to. I'm Irene Doyle—my husband Sam and I own this place."

"Is it okay if we leave the dogs tied up out here?" Willa asked tentatively, having learned her lesson at the patisserie.

"Oh heavens, take them in! Everyone in town knows the boys. They wouldn't hurt a fly, any of them, and they're well-trained. Go on in, and get what you need. If we don't have what you're looking for, let Sam know when he checks you out and he'll order it for next time."

The woman resumed unpacking nectarines, and Willa grabbed a small green shopping cart and followed Mr. Pilkington in.

Doyle's was well-stocked for a small-town market, and there was something very pleasing about the neatly arranged aisles. There looked to be a real deli counter and a proper butcher, and the array of packaged and canned foods was attractively displayed. Willa took a lap around the store just to see her options. Then she selected a loaf of rye bread.

"Ham or turkey?" she asked Mr. Pilkington.

"Pastrami," he said, firmly, and asked the man behind the deli counter for a pound, sliced thin.

Hitting the center aisles, they picked up some lettuce, a few tomatoes, and a jar of pickles. Hopefully, Lucy liked sandwiches, because Willa didn't know how to make anything else.

They took their bounty to the counter, where a lanky man was fiddling with an espresso machine. Willa looked up, surprised, and saw a drink menu written in chalk above the counter. Apparently, this delicious little store doubled as a cafe. The man turned around and smiled at them.

"Mornin'," he said, congenially. Without waiting to be asked, he sprayed whipped cream from a can into three individual cups and handed them to the dogs. "Puppiccinos," he explained. "Mina always got the dogs somethin' when she came in for her lattes."

"Thank you," said Willa, hoping it was okay for dogs to eat whipped cream. They certainly seemed to like it, whether it was good for them or not. "You knew my aunt, it seems?"

"Everyone knew Mina," he said, still smiling. "Not everyone loved her, but everyone knew her."

Mr. Pilkington gave a dry, little chuckle.

"As for me and my wife, we were proud to call her a friend. She came in every day, regular as clockwork, getting her morning caffeine and a treat for the boys. She liked to support other businesses in town. No one had a stronger sense of civic duty than Mina had. Ask anyone! You're her niece, are you?"

"Yes. Willa's my name. This is my friend, Daniel Pilkington."

"Sam Doyle."

"Well, Mr. Doyle, I love your market. I suspect I'll be haunting it every day. At least as long as I'm here."

"I hope you stay a good long while," he said, firmly. "No matter what anyone else says."

Willa blinked, wondering what he meant by that, but he had already moved on to another topic and she felt rude interrupting.

"Are you two coming to the town meeting tonight?"

"Oh," she hesitated. "We don't know anything about it."

He finished ringing her up, printed off the receipt, and thrust it and a bright yellow flyer in her hand.

"Six o'clock, down at the community center. Stop by! It'll be a good chance to meet the neighbors. Might change a few minds, even."

"Change minds about what?" she began, but the person behind her had already begun unloading and was looking pointedly at the receipt in Willa's hand.

They went out, carrying their groceries. Irene Doyle, now unpacking another crate of produce, said goodbye to them as they left.

"Y'all goin' to the town hall meeting?" she asked, examining a Honeycrisp apple with a critical eye.

"I'm not sure."

"Come," Irene said, transferring her gaze from the apple to Willa's face. "You should be there."

"Why?"

"Might stop some of the talk. One or two people had strong feelings about Mina Lattner, and they've transferred those feelings onto you."

"I've only been here two days," Willa protested, trying to balance the groceries in her right arm as Killer, Kyle, and Wags pulled on their leashes.

They were eager to get home, and Willa didn't blame them. The streets of Humboldt Cove, which had seemed so cheery half an hour ago, were beginning to look sinister to her.

"Doesn't take two minutes for some folks to make up their minds, hon. But don't worry about it. Sam and I have got your back and Lucy Garber does too. You come tonight with your head held high, and all the tongues will stop their wagging."

"Wait, what are people saying about me?" Willa asked, but Irene only smiled at her and went to help an elderly woman fill a plastic bag with fresh corn.

Willa glanced over toward the small office on the pier, but it looked just as dark and empty as before. After a quick conference, she and Mr. Pilkington decided to get home and try the harbormaster again later. They began trudging up the hill, but the dogs were jumpy and unsettled and pulled at Willa's arm the whole way back.

Maybe that whipped cream is moving too quickly through their systems, Willa thought wryly, though she suspected they were picking up on her own uneasiness.

When they finally reached the top of the hill, Willa saw why the dogs had been so frantic. The side door of the pink house was wide open, and the bay window that looked out onto the town had been shattered.

"Merciful heavens," said Mr. Pilkington, dropping the bag of groceries he was holding.

Apples began rolling down the street, and Kyle jumped against Willa's legs, whining. She set her bag of groceries down and picked him up, noticing that they were both trembling.

Someone had broken into the McKinley House.

After they called the police from Lucy Garber's house and received comfort in the form of hot tea and several more slices of apricot bread, Willa finally began to calm down. The dogs would not stop barking, and Mr. Pilkington eventually helped her shut them up in Lucy's mud room so they could have a few moments to think.

"I don't know who has the *nerve* to break the window in broad daylight," Lucy huffed. "So stupid! And reckless."

"Dangerous, too," Willa mused.

"Ruffians, do you think?" asked Mr. Pilkington, without conviction.

"Have another slice of cake," Lucy told him. "And you both need more sugar in your tea. It's good for shock. Was anything taken?"

"I left my phone on the counter, and it's gone," Willa said, obediently adding three more sugar cubes to her cup. "Nothing else is missing."

She caught Lucy's eye and gave a sidelong glance at Mr. Pilkington. They were all thinking the same thing.

Her phone was gone, but her laptop was still where she had left it on the kitchen counter. Mr. Pilkington's belongings were intact. The only thing the housebreaker had done was turn out the contents of Mina's office. Strewn papers covered the entire third floor of the house. Whoever they were, they had been looking for something specific.

"Still fancy that book search party?" said Willa, trying to instill a little bravado into her voice.

"Good girl," said Lucy, approvingly. "Smart, too. You've got a little of your aunt's spunk in you. We all know the thief wasn't after your cash or your TV."

"Are you suggesting the thief came to steal Mina Lattner's manuscript?" said Mr. Pilkington, wide-eyed.

"Yes. But I doubt he had time to do more than pocket the cell phone and make a mess. How long were you gone?"

"Forty-five minutes," Willa said. "Maybe less."

"Why would someone steal the book?" asked Mr. Pilkington, looking very hard at Lucy.

"That thing was a ticking time bomb, Daniel."

"Indeed?"

"Indeed. Believe me, I would know. And I don't want it to fall into the wrong hands," said Lucy, suddenly hitting the tea table with her tiny fist. "By gosh, we won't let them beat us! We must find it before whoever it was comes back!"

Willa used Lucy's phone to call Brian at the bakery. He hurried up the hill, stopping to fetch his tools and a sheet of plywood to board up the broken window.

"You sure know how to make an entrance to a town," he said, once he was done nailing up the board. He stood back to admire his handiwork. "And talk about a welcome committee! I apologize on behalf of all the citizens of Humboldt Cove. We're not like this."

"One of you is," said Willa, bitterly.

He shot her a compassionate look, tinged with anxiety.

"Don't worry. I won't let anything happen to you," he said, but he sounded worried. "This should keep the rain and wind out but it won't deter any other burglars. And you aren't much of a deterrent either, are you boys?"

He reached down to pet Killer and Wags, who had been happily running in circles, barking at them all for the last fifteen minutes. Kyle was in his basket in the corner, woofing occasionally under his breath.

"Willa and Mr. Pilkington will be staying with me tonight," Lucy informed him.

"With the dogs, if we can ever get them to shut up. I hate to leave them here, all alone."

"They smell the cat hair on Lucy's clothes. She's the town's resident cat lady," Brian explained to Willa, in a whisper. "Fluffy's the only one left, but they say she used to have about a hundred."

"I hate to bring this racket into your house, Lucy."

"Nonsense. We'll put the boys in the guest room on the second floor. Fluffy never goes in there. If necessary, I'll shove her in the basement while you're there."

"You don't have to do that!"

"She loves it," said Lucy. "She would like to believe there are mice down there. Hours of fun, truly."

"That's settled then," said Brian, cheerfully. "I'll leave you folks to it. Heidi will never forgive me if we don't get ahead of the dough for tomorrow, and I've got to ice about a thousand donuts for the town meeting tonight."

"Oh!" said Willa. "Are you going to that?"

"Yeah, I have to. Catering. But don't worry, they always end on time. I won't be late for our date at seven-thirty."

"I was thinking about attending the meeting. We could go to dinner from there."

Lucy and Brian gave her identical looks of approval.

"You should," he said, "if you can stomach it. It might shut some mouths around here."

"That's the third or fourth hint I've gotten today. What are people saying about me, guys?"

"You met the McKinleys," Brian replied, uncomfortably. "Ian's spreading it all over town that you plan to knock his house down and build some kind of McMansion in its place."

"That's an outright lie!"

"Of course it is, but Ian and Patricia have sway here, and there are people who'd believe anything bad about Mina or her extended family. If you show up tonight, you can rub it in their noses and make Ian look like an idiot."

"Gladly," said Willa, cheering up.

There were few things she liked more than a good fight.

The Book

Willa, Lucy, and Mr. Pilkington spent the entire afternoon searching Mina's house for the manuscript. After four hours opening old hat boxes, sifting through file folders, lifting up bed skirts, and opening books to shake them out, Lucy was fading, Willa wanted to die, and poor Mr. Pilkington looked half-dead already.

Leaving Lucy to paw through the chaos on the fourth floor, Willa took Mr. Pilkington outside with her to search the shed. She wanted to spare Lucy the dirt and cobwebs of the disused shed, but she had another motive as well. Mina's letter had described one incident with a bike and another with a ladder. She wanted a chance to examine both objects with Mr. Pilkington and away from prying eyes, even eyes as kind and understanding as Lucy Garber's. She'd avoided the job thus far—Lucy was often at her window, peeking out, and she didn't want the older woman to get too interested in what she was doing. Jake Anderson was right. Curiosity killed the cat, and Lucy was becoming precious to Willa. She couldn't bear the thought of something happening to her.

The shed was dimly lit by one small window and smelt of grass clipping, gasoline, and fertilizer. Willa spotted the ladder right away, leaning against the filmy window. She took hold of one end, tripping over an old watering can as she dragged it out.

I'm as clumsy as Mina was, she thought. *Maybe all these accidents were just...accidents.*

After all, Mina could easily have put her foot through a rotten piece of wood and simply lost her balance. Wasn't that the most likely explanation?

One look at the second-highest rung in the brighter light and she abandoned that idea completely. Her aunt hadn't been exaggerating. The rung was split alright, but it hadn't splintered, and the wood was sound, without a trace of rot or decay.

"There are definite saw marks here," said Mr. Pilkington, grimly.

Willa rolled Mina's bike out, and the two of them crouched down to examine it together.

"Sabotage," said the old man. "I never quite believed it until now, but someone was definitely trying to kill her."

For the sake of thoroughness, they searched the shed from top to bottom for the manuscript before dragging the ladder back inside. There was nothing else to find.

"Does this shed have a lock?" asked Mr. Pilkington.

"Not that I know of. Why?"

"This ladder and the bike are evidence, now. We want to preserve them. This is good news, my dear," said Mr. Pilkington gently, sensing Willa's discouragement. "We have more facts—more data. These are things that can be used in court."

She nodded. She knew she should be happy about their progress, but all she felt was a deep sense of pity for her aunt. Poor Mina. She had lived a dangerous life and paid dearly for it. She had taken what she wanted and done as she pleased, refusing to bow to convention or basic good taste or the powers that be.

The world was not kind to uppity women in pink houses.

At five o'clock, the trio of searchers gave up, dirty, discouraged, and on the brink of tears.

No book, no research, no nothing.

"It's not here," Willa said, flopping down onto an antique fainting couch on the second-floor sitting room, and wishing she could pass out in earnest and be done with it. "It's either never been here, or the thief found it right away."

"I don't think he found anything," said Lucy, stoutly.

Less inclined than Willa to splay herself in an unseemly way, she perched delicately on the edge of a loveseat next to Mr. Pilkington.

"Mina was very careful with the manuscript—it was her pride and joy. And the historical letters and documents that we studied were valuable. I think she's hidden them all somewhere very clever."

"It's time you told us what's in this manuscript, Lucy. What on earth did you ladies dig up? It must be extremely damning, whatever it is."

Lucy sighed and twisted her hands together in her lap.

"Damning is putting it mildly. If we had published the book, two or three of the oldest families here would have thrown fits—maybe even sued us for defamation."

"Defamation?" repeated Mr. Pilkington, skeptically.

"What did all these founding families do that was so awful?" asked Willa. "Were they part of a cult? Did they eat people? Did they dress up like chickens in the light of the moon?"

"No, no," Lucy scolded. "Nothing like that. There are no corporate scandals—it's something different for each of them. I wouldn't want it to leave this room, but we found the most awful thing about James McKinley. He and my great-grandfather started the town together, you know. It was Garber money and Garber land, but James McKinley was a good friend. The Garbers and McKinleys and Doyles stick together. We always have. That's why it was so difficult for me when I found out that...well..."

"Just spit it out, Lucy," said Willa, wearily.

"Slave ships," whispered Lucy, looking around as though the walls might have ears.

"Dear me," said Mr. Pilkington, shocked.

"Dozens of them. James McKinley was a shipping baron. He came out here in 1867, set up a shipyard, and began importing things from India and the Far East. But before that, he was trading on human life out of ports in South Carolina. We found proof of ownership of several known slave vessels, and letters in his own handwriting discussing business with some of the captains. He shut down that part of his business in the early 1860s, of course, and was quite decorous and correct in his support for the Union, but before that, he spent at least twenty years profiting from suffering. Mina was going to print it all, and she wanted to add a paragraph or two to the plaque outside your house, mentioning the original source of James McKinley's money."

"Ian seemed almost fanatical about his heritage when we spoke."

"Hmm. Yes. And Mina did not mince words in the text," said Lucy, sadly. "I told her it might be more tactful to take a softer approach, but she wouldn't listen. And my great-grandfather Hezekiah Garber was a staunch abolitionist, after all, so I felt I'd be letting him down if we covered up the scandal."

"Good for you! What other muck did you two uncover?"

Lucy sighed.

"We did find something rather icky about the Doyles."

"As in Irene and Sam Doyle, down at the grocery store? Darn. I like them."

"They're wonderful people—so generous. Several years ago, they donated the old Doyle house to the city, and now it serves as the town museum. You may have seen it—the green Victorian mansion, down on H Street? I volunteer there several mornings a week. They live at the other end of town, now, in a nice big modern home. Well, anyway, Mina and I discovered that old Mr. Doyle, Sam's grandfather, ran liquor during the prohibition."

"Him and everyone else," said Mr. Pilkington, with a little smile.

"Well, maybe so. But Sam and Irene are very devout Baptists. They'd be ashamed if the truth came out. And George Doyle also dabbled in a few other vices. Prostitution," she said, wrinkling her nose. "There was actually a speakeasy in town, from what we understand, and people came from as far away as Eureka and Crescent City to get drunk and er..."

"Canoodle?" suggested the old man, delicately.

"Get off with loose women?" said Willa, who did not often trouble with delicacy.

Lucy made a face.

"It was icky, as I said. George was a pillar of the church at the time, with a wife and seven children. I didn't want to put it in the book, but Mina insisted that everyone loves a speakeasy."

Willa knew several people who would wear a liquor-running ancestor as a badge of honor, especially if said ancestor also ran a speakeasy. The whole thing conjured up interesting images of flappers in sequined dresses and cocktails and jazz bands. But the whole thing had probably been very sordid and unpleasant, flappers or no flappers.

"Okay, so we know the McKinleys and the Doyles might have resented the book. Anyone else?"

Lucy's hand-wringing became more obvious.

"Several families settled the town originally. The Garbers, of course. And the McKinleys and the Doyles you know about. But a man called Henry Anderson held the original claim on the land. How much do you know about the Gold Rush?"

"Almost nothing," said Willa, whose ears had perked at the name *Anderson*.

"Forgive the expression, because it's hackneyed—but it was the *Wild West* out here. Land was up for grabs, and the whole thing was handled in a pretty informal way. You laid claim to the land you wanted by staking out boundaries—rudimentary fences or stones that marked your territory. And then you filed an official claim for the land in Sacramento. But people were forever moving the boundary stones, or 'claim jumping,' as they called it. It was all legal—if someone abandoned their claim or was too busy prospecting on other land you could just come settle there yourself."

"Squatting, you mean?" said Willa.

"I suppose you could call it squatting," laughed Lucy, tickled by the word. "If you squatted long enough, the property became your own. Now, this man Henry Anderson staked the first claim on the land around here. He was a baddie—constantly jumping the claims of his neighbors and using violence and intimidation to drive people away. My great-grandfather Hezekiah was the only man around who wasn't scared of him. Anderson went off on drinking binges every so often and abandoned the land. In 1855, Hezekiah moved in on this territory—it was the dead of winter, and the coldest one for a hundred years before and after. He braved the rain and the ice and he stuck it out and officially took over the claim. When Anderson returned, he was furious, but Hezekiah would not be moved. The story goes that they had a nasty fight, and Anderson turned tail and disappeared out East. His wife and children lived nearby and settled in the town once it was established. They were good, quiet people, but there was always a little resentment between Henry Anderson's wife and my great-grandmother Matilda."

"I bet."

"Mina and I found several unpleasant accounts of Anderson's behavior from the local newspaper archives, and rumors that he died in prison out in Redding—on a murder charge, no less."

"Goodness!" said Mr. Pilkington.

"There are still Anderson family members in the area, you know..."

Lucy paused and gave Willa a meaningful look.

"I met one of them this morning. Is that what you're trying to tell me? To watch out for the Deputy?"

"Yes. I don't personally know anything bad about him, but as I said, Mina mentioned him once or twice and she had her opinions. I happen to know his parents—we attend the same church. They're proud people. They wouldn't have liked what we were going to print."

"You ladies really were knee-deep in muck and scandal, weren't you?" Willa laughed.

"It's amazing what you turn up with a little dedicated research."

"My editor will eat this up with a spoon. Don't worry, Lucy. We'll keep searching. If I have to tear up every floorboard in this house, we'll find that book."

"Oh my goodness!" squeaked Lucy, looking down at her watch. "It's getting on for five-thirty now! I need to run a comb through my hair and get down to the community center. I promised Irene Doyle I'd help her set out the chairs."

"Sounds good. I'll see you there in a bit. I'm looking forward to the meeting. Mr. Pilkington wants to go, too."

"It's been a long time since I lived in a small town," he said. "It should be quite interesting."

"Interesting," warned Lucy, "is not the word."

Mail

To Wendoline Lattner-Santini

Wendy,

Guess what?

You never will, so I'll tell you. I just finished
filing my first official police report!

Don't get too excited, though. It's not for
something cool, like diamond theft or attempted
assassination. Some idiot just broke into Mina's
house this morning.

DO NOT TELL MOM AND DAD.

Mom will cry and Dad will race down here with a baseball bat and I'm not prepared for that.

Don't worry, the dogs and I weren't home, and nothing but my phone was taken. They were content to shatter a window and throw some old tax forms around—annoying but not really dangerous. If it wasn't for the broken glass, I'd put the whole thing down to a poltergeist.

The local police blamed teenagers for the incident. I wish I could be that confident. There isn't a soul on this street that's younger than eighty. I suppose even the very old need some kind of thrill, but what would be the point of it? Oh well. If they wanted to make things inconvenient for me, they have succeeded, and that is its own kind of thrill.

The officer I dealt with—a very dull young man in his late teens—asked me fifteen times how much cash Mina kept in her desk, and each time I told him I didn't know, he raised an eyebrow at me and scribbled something on a little pad of paper. He had an annoying habit of sniffing

while he talked, and it made me want to blow my
nose badly on his behalf.

*Ms. Lattner, he sniffed, I regret to inform you
(sniff) that we don't usually find perpetrators
of minor crimes (sniff) or vandalism (sniff
sniff). I suggest you change the locks, ma'am
(sniff sniff sniff).*

I thought about asking him how changing the
locks would prevent the guy from BREAKING MY
WINDOW again, but I restrained myself. You would
have been very proud of me. I showed my contempt
by handing him a box of Kleenex in a way I hoped
was devastating. He thought I was being nice,
so that's what I get for taking the high road.

Fortunately, I had my purse with me and I didn't
leave any personal papers or things at the
house. The guy got my phone, but it was a new
one without much personality and no photos to
speak of.

Someone in Humboldt Cove doesn't like me, Wendy.
That's not just me being paranoid. It's the
truth.

The old girl next door has offered to put me, Mr. Peanut, and the boys up for the night and I think I'll take her up on it. At least until I can arrange for a better security system. She is a doll and I love her to bits.

Oh, I almost forgot! Cute-bakery-owner-guy asked me out! I can't believe I didn't lead with that. It is far more exciting than the break-in. Mexican restaurant—my choice. If a man does not like a taco, he is no man at all.

Before we gorge ourselves on carne asada and margaritas, we are attending a town meeting, and don't ask me what that entails, because I don't know. I suspect there will be about thirty people milling around a moldy grange building, drinking punch made from cylinders of frozen juice, a two-liter of Seven-Up, and a cardboard carton of vanilla ice cream. I can't wait.

Note: What is a grange? Didn't Grandpa Weaver belong to one? I'm picturing men driving around in tiny cars but I think that's something else…

I will tell you all about the meeting and the date tomorrow. I've ordered another phone, but we'll have to stick to email until I can get you my new number.

I miss you.

Stupid time difference. Stupid Rome. Stupid burglar, who steals phones. You will add "Stupid Willa, who won't face her fear of planes to spend a month eating homemade pasta in the most beautiful city in the world."

I'm glad to hear you're settling nicely and getting along well with G's family. I always knew they'd love you. (TBH I wasn't sure WHAT they'd make of you, but it sounds like they are good people with sensible taste.)

Send me a picture of your flat as soon as you can. I want to see the terrace with all the flowers.

Did I mention I miss you? A lot?

It goes without saying that you and G have a standing invitation to visit. You can set up camp on the entire fourth floor if you want to, and I'm sure cute-bakery-owner-guy wouldn't mind sharing the kitchen down at The Three Hounds with G for a week or two. Think about it. I'll pay for the tickets, Wendy. That's how lonely I am.

Okay, I'm off to get ready for my date. Wish me luck.

Love,

Willa

The Meeting

Before they left for the meeting, Willa and Mr. Pilkington took advantage of a little peace and quiet to gather their thoughts.

"We need to get organized," he told her. "There is too much information and not enough, at the same time. It is most irritating."

"Motives are littering every corner," Willa sighed. "At least the evidence is also starting to pile up nicely! The break-in was a giant, flashing red sign that we're on the right track."

"An unpleasant, but welcome confirmation."

"What a day. So much has happened, and I haven't even debriefed you on the deputy's visit yet."

Willa told the old man about her conversation with Jake Anderson.

"You say he asked about Mina's extracurricular activities? Those words, exactly?"

"Yes. And listen to this, Pilky. He claimed he knew Mina well and followed up immediately by saying that sometimes, good people do bad things."

"I don't like the sound of that."

"Neither did I! I'm not sure what he was implying, and I'm not sure I want to know. The whole visit was scary."

"Threatened you, did he?" asked Mr. Pilkington, concerned.

"Sort of. But he seemed more worried than aggressive."

She frowned down at Kyle, who had trotted over to her as soon as Lucy left and would not let her put him down. Jake Anderson was an enigma. His cookies were good, but that wasn't a guarantee of good character—more's the pity. And as an Anderson, he had a decent motive for suppressing the book.

Would he go so far as to kill Mina to prevent its publication?

"You know what happened to her, don't you?" she said, stroking Kyle's ears. "So do you guys," she told Killer and Wags, who looked up from their bones for a moment and wagged their tails. "It's a crying shame you can't tell us. We're on our own, here, fellas. And very short on clues."

Kyle licked her hand, encouragingly.

"What do we actually know?" she mused, depressed. "Not much."

"You're wrong, my dear," said Mr. Pilkington, with energy. "We know Mina believed her life was in danger. That belief has been justified. We know that more than one person had it out for her over—hmm, let's call it *personal spite.* That includes the owner of the Humboldt Cove Patisserie and the Klamath County Sheriff."

"That also includes Ian and Patricia McKinley, if their primary beef is losing the McKinley House to Mina."

"So childish. Then there is the matter of the manuscript. Grievances in *that* direction are not personal—the book is about what Mina knew, not who she was or what she did. Any member of the McKinley, Doyle, or Anderson families might have strong feelings about that book. Slave ships and prostitutes!"

Willa shook her head, frustrated. If this was a Violet Valentine novel, the murderer would be Ian McKinley. Easy! He was sneaky, and mean, and vaguely threatening. But she could not believe that anyone in real life would care enough about the events of decades past to kill a harmless old woman over them.

"You think that's not a believable motive," said Mr. Pilkington, reading her mind. "You haven't lived long enough to know how far people will go to defend mistaken beliefs. Miss Garber knows this town well. I already have a high respect for her intelligence—and her charm."

"Pilky, do you have a crush on her?" Willa laughed, delighted.

"No, no," he said, blushing. "I'm merely saying that if she believes the book is dangerous, we may take it that the book is dangerous."

Willa's stomach growled, reminding her that it was time to get a move on. It took at least ten minutes to walk into Humboldt Cove, and she didn't want to be late for her first town meeting. Especially since everyone here already seemed prepossessed to hate her. She looked at herself in the mirror, grimaced, tried to straighten her unruly mop of hair, and eventually just threw on some lip gloss and called it good.

After her last experience with dating, which had ended badly with dashed expectations on both sides, she was determined to enter into every new romantic encounter as authentically as possible. If cute-bakery-owner-guy didn't like messy hair, he could move along to someone else.

Or, she thought, gently shoving a very reluctant Kyle back into his crate, *I'll give up dating altogether and die alone with my dachshunds.*

The prospect was not unappealing, at this point. She blew the dogs kisses, shutting their crates and closing the laundry room door.

They really were very good boys indeed.

Double-checking the address on the flyer they got from Sam Doyle, Willa and Mr. Pilkington arrived at the Humboldt Cove Community Center with five or six minutes to spare. At least a hundred people were there, noisily talking, snacking on Brian's donuts, politely fighting over the best seats, and getting ready to do their civic duty. Brian saw them coming in and waved from across the room.

Willa waved back, but before they could move in that direction, they were accosted by a woman in a polka-dot blouse.

"Welcome!" she said, handing Willa the meeting agenda. "You're just in time. We'll be starting in a minute or two. I'm Doreen Belcher, by the way. I work down at Belcher's Hardware. You must be new to town!"

"Daniel Pilkington," said Mr. Pilkington, shaking her hand.

"Willa Lattner," said Willa, and was startled by the immediate change in the woman's face.

"Shame on you!" said Doreen, turning an unbecoming shade of purple. "Haven't the McKinleys been through enough?"

She whirled around and stalked away before Willa could even open her mouth to reply. Embarrassed and confused, she looked at Mr. Pilkington, whose mouth had dropped open in disbelief. Twenty feet away, Doreen whispered angrily with a group of older women, one of which was Patricia McKinley. They all turned to look at Willa, and then Patricia said something and laughed.

"What is happening?" Willa murmured to her companion.

"I'm quite at a loss, my dear. Shocking behavior. Absolutely shocking!"

A large, purple-haired woman materialized next to Willa with a skinny man on her arm, at least twenty years her senior.

"What's the matter with you?" she asked, amiably. "Tummy ache?"

It was the lady from the curios shop—the one who had given Willa the shell. Jennifer? Jessica? No, *Justine*. Justine somebody.

"This is my other half, by the way."

"Dale Snood, of Dale's Fish 'N More," Justine's partner said earnestly, removing his 49'ers ball cap to reveal a greasy ponytail.

"Daniel Pilkington, of Pilkington, Pilkington, and Gump," said Mr. Pilkington.

"Nice to meetcha, Danny. You like cod?"

"Certainly," he replied, blinking a little at Dale's informality.

"You're in luck, because we got cod. You like salmon?"

"Er..."

"We *got* salmon, Danny. You like abalone? Get on down the coast a ways!" he cackled. "That's too rich for our blood."

Mr. Pilkington smiled, as a courtesy, and Dale leaned in.

"Jokes aside, if you've got a taste for abalone, I could arrange that for ya. I know a guy. Hi there, gal," he said, moving on to Willa. "Dale Snood, Dale's Fish 'N More."

Willa shook Dale's hand, which was bony and a little moist—rather like an eel. He smiled at her through a mouth full of missing teeth.

"You want some Immodium?" said Justine, looking Willa up and down with concern. "No offense, but you look like you might need to make a run for it."

Mr. Pilkington made a little strangled sound in his throat.

"Uh, no," said Willa, hastily. "I'm fine, thanks."

Justine followed Willa's gaze over to the group of women, still sneering in their direction.

"Oh, I see. Don't worry about Doreen or—who's that one, Dale, with the orange lipstick?"

"Jenny Hershe."

"Right. Don't pay any attention to her or Doreen or Trish."

"Trish?"

"Mayor's wife. Miss High and Mighty Patricia McKinley. Ha! She does *not* like it when I call her Trish."

"She don't like it when Justine calls her Trish," Dale said, solemnly.

"She's got a stick up her you-know-what about it. But give me a break, 'Patricia' is too bougie for Humboldt Cove. Who does she think she is, Jackie freaking *Kennedy*? Her husband may be the mayor, but that don't make him the president of the United States of America!"

Somewhat confused, Willa agreed that it did not.

"Yeah, you get it. That's why I call her Trish—to take her down a notch. She's just a redneck from the hills above town, like me. She's my Momma's age, though. Older than Dale, even, and he's older than *God*. How old do you think I am?"

She twirled around, showing off her massive and shapely behind. Her large, beautiful eyes were lined in bright blue and she had not one, but three piercings in each ear. The overall effect was gorgeous but rather overwhelming, like Justine herself.

"Twenty-five?" Willa guessed.

"Thirty-five," said Justine, triumphantly. "I've got more to love than most women, and that irons out the wrinkles. Nature's botox. How much do you think I weigh?"

Willa prayed desperately for an intervention, and just then a man walked by and bumped her elbow, hard. She apologized—an automatic reaction—and he glared at her.

"Go back to where you came from," he said, swearing at her.

"You kiss your baby momma with that mouth?" snapped Justine, leaping to their defense. "Oh, that's right—you *can't*, cuz she's got a restraining order."

"Shut up, Jussie," said the man, uncertainly.

"You shut up. Now get out of here, or I'll tell Tiff you hit on me and Dale'll back me up."

"Get!" echoed Dale.

"There he goes. Sorry about that."

"That's okay," said Willa, feeling anything but okay.

"Brad's a hot mess."

"A mess," repeated Dale, earnestly.

"Deals crack up on Hag Hill."

"No, he don't."

"Yes, he does—Tiff told me so. Don't listen to him or anyone else. You're real sweet, both of you. What'd you say your name was? Winnie?"

"Willa."

"You actually planning to tear down that pink house, Willa?"

"Of course not."

"See, Dale? I told you she wasn't like that. It's all lies. Well, most of it. Your nose *is* kinda big, but if you change your makeup a bit you can...Oh, look, Dale," said Justine, her eyes wandering away from Willa. "Donuts! I told you there'd be donuts. And that stud is handing them out this time, instead of his emo-girl assistant."

She whistled, appreciatively.

"You gonna try to hit that?" she asked, elbowing Willa significantly.

Mr. Pilkington's eyes grew wide.

"Simmer down now, Justine," warned Dale, "or I'll start to get jealous."

"You get yourself one of them butts and then we'll talk. You're flat as a pancake back there."

The couple melted away into the crowd, arguing happily with one another.

"Merciful heavens," said Mr. Pilkington, faintly. "This is all very shocking."

Her heart racing, Willa scanned the room for signs of friendly life forms. She spotted Lucy sitting at the end of one of the front rows. Linking arms with the stunned Mr. Pilkington, she made her way toward Lucy, relieved. Left to herself, she'd never sit so close to the action, but she would rather be too close with someone guarding her back than on her own at a more comfortable distance.

"Hello, Daniel. Hey, sweetie," whispered Lucy, patting the seats next to her. "They're just about to get started, I think."

"What exactly happens at a town meeting?" Willa whispered back. "Is this the kind of thing where people say 'yea' and 'nay' and they read the minutes? What are minutes, exactly?"

"No, no," laughed Lucy. "You're thinking of a town *council* meeting. That's where elected officials meet to discuss official business and vote on important matters. This is just a gathering. We have one, every so often—especially ahead of the tourist season. The main topic of conversation will be our yearly crab festival but other topics might come up."

"Topics like me? Or Mina?"

"I don't think so. It's one thing to whisper behind closed doors but so embarrassing if the person you're talking about is right there, watching you."

"I should hope so," said Mr. Pilkington, flushed. "The treatment Miss Lattner has received already this evening is shocking. Shocking!"

There seemed no end to Mr. Pilkington's ability to be shocked.

"I'm not very popular here. That polka-dotted woman over there was openly rude once she heard my name, and the little creep in the hoodie behind her practically roughed me up! What do they think I've done?"

"Oh, don't pay attention to any of them. Mina was...well, she had opinions, you know."

"And money," added Mr. Pilkington, dryly.

"And money," agreed Lucy. "It's hard to know which people resented more. Small towns are always a little unfriendly to newcomers. Just hang in there. There won't be any more open unpleasantness. Hopefully, we'll discuss the crab festival and not much else. Oh, and someone will probably bring up the problem of the cracked sidewalk on G Street. They always do, and nothing ever gets done about it."

Turning around discreetly, Willa surveyed the crowd of people now beginning to take their seats. She saw Sam and Irene Doyle in the back and was pleased when Irene waggled her fingers at her in a friendly manner. She also saw Jake Anderson, sitting about three rows behind her with an older man and woman. There was enough of a family resemblance for her to guess they were his parents. Lucy had said something about his family living in town.

He saw her looking at him and nodded, a trifle cooly. She looked away, embarrassed to have been caught staring.

She didn't recognize anyone else in the room, except a small, sandy-haired woman in the very back corner. Harriet Snelling was sitting alone, speaking to no one, looking at no one, and doing a crossword. She was the only person in the room, so far as Willa could tell, not eating one of Brian's donuts.

"Check, check, check," said a voice from the front of the room, and Willa turned around to see who was speaking.

A compact and grizzled old man stood only feet away from her, tapping on a microphone.

"Good evening, and welcome! We have a lot to get to tonight, especially regarding the crab festival, so I won't take up too much of your time yammering. That reminds me, what do you call a crab that never shares its toys?"

There was a pained silence from the crowd, and then someone called out "Shellfish?"

"Bingo! Now here's one I betcha haven't heard. What did the crab say to the mermaid?" he asked, pausing only for a millisecond so that no one could steal his thunder. "Long time no sea!"

He cackled into the microphone, and Mr. Pilkington said, "Lord have mercy," under his breath.

"That's Captain Burch," Lucy told them, in a whisper. "He was friends with Mina. You might call him her, uh, well—*beau* is the word my generation would have used."

"They were dating?"

"Sort of," shrugged Lucy. "Mina was keeping him at a bit of distance. For his own good, she said. Doug Burch always did come on a little strong. I went to school with him."

"Hey, I recognize that name. That's the harbormaster, right? You kissed him on the front porch!" said Willa, suddenly enlightened. "And your mother grounded you for a month!"

"Really, Willa," Mr. Pilkington said.

"That was a long time ago," said Lucy, blushing.

Willa studied the captain. He was handsome, in a coarse, florid sort of way. She decided to try to talk to him after the meeting was over. Boyfriends and lovers, no matter how ancient, were always prime suspects when someone was killed. Mina may not have been serious about Captain Burch, but that didn't mean he wasn't serious about *her*.

"The first thing on the agenda tonight is the sidewalk on G Street," he said, reading carefully from a piece of paper.

"What did I tell you!" whispered Lucy, triumphantly.

"You'll be happy to know that the Council voted to get a quote from a local contractor. If it's within the town's budget for street repair, we'll proceed."

A roar of applause came up from the audience and Willa joined in, to be polite. Sidewalk maintenance was a big deal in Humbodlt Cove, it seemed.

"About time!" someone yelled, from the back.

"If you were so anxious to have it fixed," said Captain Burch, taking off his glasses to see who had shouted, "you could have done it yourself, Joel."

"You should be so lucky!" laughed the man, and everyone joined in, including the Captain.

To Willa, the entire exchange was baffling and not particularly funny.

"Settle down everyone," said Captain Burch, grinning broadly. "The sidewalk's not fixed yet, you know. Still plenty of time for the mayor to chicken out. Eh, Ian?"

There was a chorus of friendly boos, and Willa looked over to see Ian McKinley at the end of the row, smiling brittly at the joke. A sense of humor was not on his list of accomplishments.

"Next item of business is the crab festival. Irene! Irene Doyle, are you out there?"

In the back row, Irene raised her hand.

"Come on up here, darlin', and tell the people what kind of shindig you're planning. What's the matter, too shy? Didja hear the one about the shy crab, who couldn't come out of his shell?"

Irene stood but made no move toward the front of the room.

"I can tell everyone from here, thanks Doug. Stick that 'darlin' where the sun don't shine," she said, amiably.

Captain Burch laughed and Irene launched into a precise and orderly account of the Crab Festival Committee's plans for the event, which Willa gathered was an annual tradition. Dungeness crab was a delicacy, and people would already drive from pretty far away to get it, but Humboldt Cove went the extra mile for two weeks in early November, right at the start of the season. There would be live music, crab-eating competitions, a parade, and a host of food trucks and restaurant pop-ups.

"And we're gonna put the crab cakes tent on the north end of the town this year," Irene was saying, "so there's more room for the face-painting near the pier. I think that's all. Did I get everything, Harriet?"

She looked over at Harriet Snelling, sitting one row behind her.

"You said plenty, Irene," she said, repressively. "There's not much left for me to discuss."

Willa sensed the presence of a long-standing feud.

"I'm glad I was thorough," retorted Irene. "If anyone has questions or suggestions, the Committee is meetin' again in a week or two and you're welcome to come lend a hand. I think that's all, Doug. Back to you."

Doug Burch stood once more to address the crowd.

"Sign-ups for vendor booths will be down at Doyle's starting next week."

"That's right," Irene called out. "And don't bother comin' by before then, because I won't have the sheet ready."

"You heard the lady. Sign up next week, and not a minute before. And don't rush all at once, or you'll pull a mussel! Haw, haw, get it? Pull a mussel? What's next? Gary, you wanted the floor, didn't you?"

A paunchy man with a bristly gray and white mustache stood and walked to the front of the room. Unlike Irene, he was very anxious to take possession of the microphone.

Lucy elbowed Willa sharply in the ribs.

"That's Sheriff Poole," she breathed. "The one Mina was planning to run against."

Willa straightened up to give her full attention to the man, whose arrogant voice was somewhat undercut by a weak chin and big, brown eyes—like those of a dairy cow. He was one of those unfortunate creatures whose physical appearance did not match their personality. She had seen the same thing in a docile but extremely ugly bull mastiff. The most sinister appearance could hide sweetness of temper; in the Sheriff's case, mild and rather stupid features might be masking a nasty temper.

Willa's heart started racing, and she tasted something strangely bitter in her mouth. She realized, with a shock, that it was fear.

The Speech

"Good evening, everyone," the Sheriff began, looking directly at Willa. "It's nice to see such a full turn-out."

His gaze swept away immediately, but she had the uncomfortable feeling he was aiming his speech directly at her.

"I won't take up too much of your time. There are a few small items of county business to discuss. First off, I want to thank everyone who turned up for the highway clean-up last weekend."

"Next time, bring more donuts!" shouted someone, from the back.

The Sheriff allowed himself a sour smile.

"We appreciate the show of public support, as always. Second, be aware that we have evidence of increased crime in the area. If you've seen anything," he paused, rather unpleasantly, "*say* something, please. As you know, law enforcement can get tricky in the back hills. We depend on tips from local, upstanding citizens. It's everyone's duty to ensure the laws of the state and county are upheld. Anyone hiding information or abetting criminals will pay to the full extent of the law."

Next to Willa, Mr. Pilkington's body became alert.

"What do you want us to do about it?" asked the man who had commented on the lack of donuts.

"Keep your eyes on strangers—people who show up without an obvious reason or excuse, especially if they have a lot of money to throw around and no good explanation for where they got it. We've set up a tip line for that purpose. Don't hesitate to use it."

Again, Willa had the odd sensation that he was talking directly to her. Did the man really think she had come to California to start some kind of criminal empire? If so, she had to question his sanity in general.

In the back row, Sam Doyle raised his hand.

"Stop being so dang mysterious. What kind of crime are you getting at, Gary? Is it drugs again? Now that pot's legal, you guys don't have many legs left to stand on."

"I wish I could be more explicit," said Gary Poole, his eyes locked on Willa once more. "I will say that we are looking into a recent increase in smuggling activities up and down the coast."

"Smuggling? What kind of smuggling? How're we supposed to help you bust crimes if we don't know what kind of crime to look out for?" Sam protested, and there was a chorus of approving murmurs around him.

"Any unusual behavior should be reported directly to me," said Sheriff Poole, an angry glint in his eye. "On land or water."

Ian McKinley stood up from his seat in the front row.

"Everyone in Humboldt Cove knows their duty, and we look out for our own. Don't worry, Gary. We'll let you know if we see any criminal activity, whether it's drugs, theft, vandalism, smuggling, or anything else."

"Thank you, Ian. I knew I could count on you."

With a complacent look on his bovine features, Sheriff Poole handed the mic back to Captain Burch and returned to his seat. Ian McKinley was still standing, and the Captain seemed a little confused about how to proceed.

"Well now, it's getting on for seven already! Any other business before we wrap things up?" he asked, looking questioningly at Ian. "Mayor, you got something to say?"

Without quite thinking about the consequences of her actions, Willa shot out of her seat.

"Hello! Over here! I'd like to say something, if that's okay," she told the astonished Captain Burch, who nodded dumbly and handed her the microphone.

Outraged, Ian sat down and whispered something in his wife's ear.

Willa did not feel better about her decision when she caught a glimpse of Lucy's face beside her. The old lady had gone absolutely crimson with embarrassment, and even Mr. Pilkington looked nonplussed. Across the room, Brian smiled encouragingly at her, but the look on his face said *I sure hope you know what you're doing*.

Willa, who never knew what she was doing or why, took a deep breath.

"Hi, everyone! My name is Wilhelmina Lattner, and I just moved here to town. Many of you may have known my aunt, Mina Lattner. She lived in the pink house at the top of the hill—bright red hair, dachshunds. She loved this place and its history and I know I will too. I wanted to introduce myself and say how happy I am to be living in this community. And to let you know I'm not planning any—uh—demolition work on the McKinley house. I'm leaving it as is. Shoot, that's not what I meant—I'm not *leaving* it, per se—I plan to live there. Long story short, I'm staying in town, and so is the house, just as it is. I mean, I might paint it at some point. Bright yellow polka dots, this time."

Mr. Pilkington covered his face with his hands and there was a murmur in the crowd

"Just kidding," said Willa, growing desperate. "It'll be orange stripes. That's also a joke, by the way. I'll paint it an approved color. Um, thank you. It's nice to meet you all. Boy, do those crab cakes sound good," she ended, lamely.

Every eye in the place was on her, and while many people smiled kindly, the hateful look on Ian McKinley's face nearly froze Willa's blood. In the back corner, Harriet Snelling was openly laughing, showing each one of her yellow, pointy teeth. Willa felt suddenly afraid, surrounded by ogres and witches. Lucy was staring straight forward, and Mr. Pilkington was still covering his eyes, afraid to look. She looked in Brian's direction for moral support and saw Heidi scowling at her.

She's ill-wishing me, Willa thought, looking around the room hysterically. There was Doreen Whatsherface, sneering. The fat, sympathetic face of Justine Galway brought no encouragement, and her boyfriend's expression of deep compassion made Willa feel worse, if anything. Pity from the fish-guts man felt like a new low. The room began to spin dangerously, but just in time Jake Anderson caught her eye. He nodded, almost imperceptibly, and gave her a small thumbs up. She remembered to breathe again.

"Welcome to town, Ms. Lattner!" called the good-hearted Sam Doyle, after the silence had become excruciating.

"Welcome!" cried Justine and Dale, in unison.

There was a quiet echo of 'welcomes' and 'hellos' throughout the room, and Willa sat down, wishing she had never been born. Mr. Pilkington took one of her hands and Lucy took the other, but their encouraging squeezes did not make her feel better.

The meeting broke up shortly afterward. After Willa relinquished the mic, Captain Burch asked Ian McKinley if he wanted a go with the microphone, and was turned down.

"We've listened to enough speeches tonight," Ian said, pointedly.

Virtually squirming with humiliation, Willa tried to derive comfort from the fact that no one had said anything overtly negative about Mina, but that was a poor consolation.

I did plenty of damage to the Lattner reputation on my own, she thought, bitterly.

Who needed enemies when you could just sabotage yourself?

The Sheriff

People lingered in clumps afterward, discussing the festival or simply shooting the breeze.

"Good heavens," said Lucy, drawing Willa and Mr. Pilkington over to where Brian and Heidi were cleaning up the remains of the pastries and coffee. "I don't know what to say."

Brian grinned at Willa and handed her the last donut off the tray.

"Here," he said. "You need this more than I do."

Willa accepted the donut glumly.

"What was I thinking?" she said.

He placed a gentle hand on her shoulder.

"Don't beat yourself up. You were trying to get out ahead of the gossip. That took guts."

"I'm afraid you did more harm than good," said Mr. Pilkington, looking around the room. "This is not a friendly town."

"You two aren't seeing us at our best," Lucy assured him. "The look on Ian McKinley's face, though! You've made a dangerous enemy."

"Let him look all he wants, Ms. Garber," said Brian. "He'll think twice about messing with Willa again. And maybe she's started a new tradition! Open mics at the town meeting!"

"I didn't know it wasn't done," said Willa, miserably. "There was so much banter back and forth. People were calling things out from their seats! It seemed like a casual event."

After all, she thought, irritated, *if people can boo and shout insults from the peanut gallery, why can't I introduce myself?*

"There are unspoken rules in this town," Brian said, sweeping the last remaining crumbs off the table. "And an invisible hierarchy. The Doyles and McKinleys and Garbers can do and say what they want, and Captain Burch is always the moderator, so he gets free rein as well. We're not used to strangers making themselves at home here. But it's about time we got used to it."

Heidi glowered under her bangs at Willa and made a small, contemptuous sound that no one but Willa seemed to hear.

"Is the Sheriff always like that? What was he getting at, anyway?"

"Nothing," said Brian, rolling his eyes good-naturedly.

"He's one of those men who's always got a mission," said Lucy, chuckling. "Last year it was all about the marijuana farms up on Hagview Hill. Now he's off chasing some other hare."

"I thought it might have something to do with Mina," Willa began, exchanging glances with Mr. Pilkington.

Lucy shooshed her.

"Oh no, look out. Here comes Douglas. You'll have to say hello and pretend to laugh at his jokes. That's the only way to get rid of him."

"You could try kissing him again to shut him up," said Willa innocently, and Lucy gave her a playful smack.

Captain Burch approached the refreshments table, his hand outstretched.

"Well, well, well," he said, genially. "Ms. Lattner! Captain Douglas Burch, at your service. I'm thrilled to finally meet you. I'm not counting what happened back there as an introduction!"

"It's nice to meet you too," said Willa, trying to sound as if she meant it.

They were all acting like she'd committed the unforgivable sin.

"Your aunt never stopped talking about you," he said. "That is, if you're the author lady."

"That's me. This is my friend, Mr. Pilkington."

"Hey there, fella. Mina gave me one of your books to try, Ms. Lattner. Something about a pie that went around killing people. Still got it, if you want it back. Couldn't get past the first page."

Willa struggled for an adequate response. "I'm sorry to hear that," conveyed a concern far beyond what she felt. "Yes, I'd like it back," smacked of resentment. "Go ahead and keep it," opened her up to the humiliating danger of his insisting on returning it, unread. She settled on saying, "Oh," in a noncommittal voice.

"Speaking of pie, did you hear about the pie that won the beauty contest? It had the most a-peeling crust!"

Willa said something between *heh* and *hmm*—it was the best she could do for him.

"Planning to stay with us a while, Ms. Lattner?"

"Yes."

"Up in that big house, all alone?"

Willa took a slight, involuntary step back. The question was innocuous enough, but something about Captain Burch's hulking form and eager eyes was off-putting. And given what had happened this morning, the inquiry took on a rather sinister undertone.

"I'm not alone," she said, louder than she intended. "I've got Mr. Pilkington. And the dogs are excellent company. They raise the alarm at even the slightest hint of danger."

"Ah, the sausage dogs," he said, cryptically. "Say hello to Killer for me."

Guffawing, he said goodbye and lumbered away to talk to someone else. Jake and his parents, who had been standing politely off to the side, made their way forward. Lucy saw a friend across the room and excused herself, and Brian and Heidi had already disappeared out the back to load up his car with the remains of the plates, cups, and coffee things.

"Hello again," said Jake, shooting her one of his crooked smiles.

"Hello. Do you know Mina's attorney, Daniel Pilkington?"

"Not personally. I've heard a lot about you, though, sir. I'd like you both to meet my folks. Mom and Dad, this is Mina's niece—Willa. Willa, this is my mom Linda and my dad Bob."

Jake's mother, a vivacious woman of about sixty, gave her a warm hello, and his father shook her hand.

"We couldn't be more sorry for your loss," Bob said, sincerely. "Mina was always so good to B.J. And any friend of Mina's is a friend of ours."

"I thought you were very brave to speak in the meeting," said his mother. "Courageous! Like—like Joan of Arc! And your hair shining so brightly, just like armor."

"Uh..."

"Take it easy, Ma," said Jake, mildly.

"Settle down, B.J., she knows what I mean! How do you get your hair to do that, by the way?"

Willa felt her curls, tentatively.

"Do what?"

"Spring around like that," said Linda, leaning in. She grabbed one of Willa's curls and boinged it, happily.

"We've talked about physical boundaries," said Jake, pulling his mother back. "Ask before you touch, Mom."

"I want Willa to know she's welcome here!"

"By touching her hair?"

"Humboldt Cove can be a hard community to join," Linda said, ignoring him. "You go on being brave, hon. Welcome."

Bob and Linda drifted away, but Jake remained with Willa and Mr. Pilkington.

"Sorry about that," he said.

Willa waved it off.

"It's okay. Not the weirdest thing that's happened to me tonight. Can I ask you something?"

"Shoot."

"Everyone's acting like I did something crazy," she said, unable to contain herself any longer. "I just *introduced* myself, that's all!"

"It's not you," said Jake, firmly. "It's them. You acted like a normal person. It's the town that's odd—every last person here, including my parents. I heard about what happened this morning, by the way."

Willa frowned at him, her hackles rising.

"How?"

"You two have somewhere safe to stay tonight?" he asked, ignoring the question.

"We're going to bunk with my aunt's neighbor, Lucy Garber."

"My old biology teacher! Tell her hi for me. I'd stay there a few nights—at least until you can get a better security system. What did the burglar take?"

"Nothing much," she said, guardedly.

"Good," he said, with the same, crooked smile. "Keep it that way, huh?"

The crowd was dwindling, and Mr. Pilkington was just preparing to walk back up the hill with Lucy when they were approached by Sheriff Poole.

"Good evening," said the Sheriff. "I thought I'd introduce myself. Gary Poole, Klamath County Sheriff."

"Daniel Pilkington—Pilkington, Pilkington, and Gump."

"Willa Lattner," Willa said solemnly, resisting the temptation to add *big-nosed intruder.*

Sheriff Poole took a bite from the donut he was holding, watching her with the same intent stare Kyle bestowed on his ball before she threw it. She had a strange desire to run out of the room and see if he chased her.

"You're a very well-spoken young woman," he mocked, in a soft, dangerous voice.

Willa decided to disarm him.

"I instantly regretted my speech," she said confidentially. She had the satisfaction of seeing him blink. "Felt like an idiot!"

"How do you like your new home?"

Gary smiled at her but his mild, cow-eyes were distinctly unfriendly.

"What's not to like?" she replied. "The house is nice, and I don't know where else I could get a better view. I've got the harbor out one window and the Hags out the other. It's like being on vacation all the time!"

"Your aunt certainly liked to keep her eyes on the harbor," he said, still watching her through narrowed eyes.

"It's very pretty."

"You say you can see the harbor and the Hags?"

"Yep! And just a peep of what's beyond the cove to the south."

"An unobstructed view, then," said the Sheriff, finishing his donut and idly folding the napkin in his hand.

Willa watched, fascinated, as he continued to fold and unfold the paper square. It was an odd tic, and she found it disconcerting.

"You arrived in town rather soon after Mina's death."

"Her dogs needed care. And I was very interested in your Deputy's report," Willa said. "Do you agree with the Coast Guard's conclusion?

"Oh, yes. Deputy Anderson and I agree on everything, you'll find. A sad accident. She was fond of boats, your aunt. She took up fishing rather late in life," Gary remarked, meaningfully. "With a very expensive boat, too."

"Never too old to start a new hobby," said Willa.

"Do I understand correctly that you have taken ownership of The Three Hounds?"

"Part-ownership."

"And who owns the other part?"

"Brian Harrison."

"Mina Lattner made a lot of money from the bakery, as I understand it."

"What business is that of yours, may I ask?" said Mr. Pilkington, bristling.

"Everything that goes on in this county is my business. But I admit I am very interested in that particular little bakery. In fact, before she died, your aunt promised me access to her financial records, dating back twelve months."

Willa stared at Gary.

"Why?" she asked.

"For the purposes of an open investigation."

"Into what?"

"I'm not at liberty to divulge that."

Mr. Pilkington shot Willa a look that meant *shut up and let me handle this.*

"This is hardly the time or place to ask for evidence in a county investigation," he told the Sheriff, coldly. "My client will happily share the financial records for The Three Hounds when you present the proper warrant for that information. I assume you do not have one, or you would not try blindsiding her at a town meeting."

Gary looked at him, coldly.

"Mina Lattner promised me access. If anything, I'm trying to make things easier for your client."

"Nonsense. You're trying to intimidate her," said Mr. Pilkington, drawing himself to his full height. "With hints and threats. Are you investigating The Three Hounds or Mina Lattner herself?"

"That's private."

"So are the bakery's records, then. Come back with a court order and we will consider compliance."

The Sheriff shrugged, defeated.

"You'll be hearing from the county shortly. And if I discover you've tampered with the documents meanwhile, you'll be looking at jail time, Ms. Lattner."

Willa opened her mouth to comment, but Mr. Pilkington tugged on her sleeve and she stayed quiet. Gary turned and strode away, just as Brian walked up.

"I'm ready to go if you are, Willa. I think Ms. Garber's waiting for you outside, Mr. P.—she said you offered to escort her home. Geez, you two.

Why the long faces?" teased Brian. "Was Gary threatening to arrest you for intent to paint with polka dots?"

"No," Willa said, thoughtfully. "He was demanding the financial records for the bakery."

Brian's face grew still.

"He's still after those, huh?"

"It seems so. Why does he want them, Mr. Harrison?" asked Mr. Pilkington, giving the younger man a suspicious look.

"Darned if I know!" Brian said, throwing out his hands. "He pestered Mina for them before she died, but he got no change out of her. She knew the law. She laughed in his face."

"He said she promised him access."

"He lied, then," Brian said, bluntly. "Since she died, he's been asking me about it. Last week I told him, politely, to take a long walk off a short pier. I'm not handing that stuff over just because he wants it."

"Good man. But you really don't know why he's interested in The Three Hounds? I find that hard to believe, Mr. Harrison. Very hard to believe."

"It's true," said Brian, helplessly. "I don't have a clue why he wants them, and neither did Mina. We pay our taxes and all our licenses are current. Mina thinks it was a personal grudge. Intimidation tactics, to persuade her not to run for office."

"I sent everything to my CPA, Pilky," said Willa. "He said it was kosher."

The worry lines between Mr. Pilkington's eyes were becoming more pronounced.

"What kinds of things are smuggled in this part of the country?" he asked Brian. "Drugs? Guns? Wildlife?"

"Wildlife?"

"Er, ivory or—or redwood lumber? Or are we looking at human trafficking?"

"Lumber?" Brian repeated, not bothering to hide his incredulity. "Don't tell me you believe everything the Sheriff said during the meeting. Around here, we know better. He's talking about smuggling because he doesn't want everyone to know he's looking into a couple of big-shot cocaine dealers that set up on the hill last year. Everyone knows who they are and where they are, and keeps their distance. We've learned to read between the lines when it comes to Gary and his investigations."

"He seemed very interested in boats," Mr. Pilkington insisted. "And Mina's view down to the harbor."

Brian shrugged.

"Smokescreens. He hated Mina. He's just messing with your head."

"Where are these cocaine dealers you mentioned?"

"There's a big compound in the hills to the south."

"What does The Three Hounds have to do with drug dealers?" said Willa.

"Nothing!" said Brian, confidently. "That's how I know Gary's a jerk. Election mind-games."

"Hmm," said Mr. Pilkington, watching him.

He looked at Willa, and there was a warning in his eyes.

The Date

Lucy and Mr. Pilkington departed shortly afterward, arm in arm, but Willa and Brian stayed to help Sam and Irene Doyle stack chairs and lock up the community center.

They all left together at around seven thirty, and to Willa's disappointment, Brian asked the couple to join them at the Mexican restaurant for dinner.

"You don't mind, do you?" he asked, pulling her aside.

"Of course not," she lied, mortified that she had misunderstood the situation.

She really had thought it was a date.

"It will be good for you to get to know a few influential townspeople," he whispered, as they walked down F Street together, lagging a little behind Irene and Sam. "You'll need more allies than just me if you stay here."

Willa started a little at the word "allies." She turned to Brian, studying his face to see if the turn of phrase was purely accidental, or if there was a deeper meaning to it.

"Why do you say that?" she asked, sticking to a cautious approach.

"You had a forlorn look at the meeting," he said. "You're not alone here, but if we're going to stop people from spreading nasty rumors—or worse—you'll need more than just a good word from me and Lucy Garber."

"I need to tell you something," Willa said, making a snap decision. She thrust her hand into her purse and took out Mina's letter. "Read," she commanded him.

Brian read obediently, his eyebrows rising slightly higher at every line. By the time he finished, they had disappeared into his hair altogether.

"This is insane," he told her, wide-eyed. "I can hardly believe it! She *knew* she was going to be killed! She actually knew it!"

"Apparently."

"Everything makes so much more sense now," he said, excitedly.

"What do you mean?"

"The way she was acting the day she died. The things she said! And—well—shoot, hurry up, okay, because we need to catch up with the Doyles."

"This is a tad more important than tacos with the neighbors, Brian!"

He grabbed her hand and looked her deep in the eyes.

"Do you trust me, Willa?"

"I do," she said, honestly.

"Good," he said, dragging her into the restaurant. "Keep on trusting me, will you?"

When they arrived at the restaurant, they were seated immediately in a cozy corner booth. The waiter didn't ask Irene or Sam what they wanted to eat or drink, and his question to Brian seemed more of a formality prompted by Willa's presence than a real inquiry.

"You all must come here often," Willa said, after she had ordered a strawberry margarita and a plate of fish tacos.

"Fat Oscar's is the best around," said Sam, swiping a chip through a bowl of thick salsa and chomping down with gusto.

He was hogging the chips, but Willa felt too shy to reach across the table and pull the bowl closer. She eyed it now, hungrily.

"We're here every Friday night, and most Tuesdays as well," explained his wife. "And Mina practically lived here, poor soul. Oscar was devastated when she died."

She pointed to the back kitchen, where an extremely thin man was slicing avocados.

"*That's* Oscar?" Willa said, surprised.

"The first one was fat," laughed Sam, shaking crumbs from the now-empty basket of chips and calling loudly for a refill. "This is Oscar the third. They just keep getting skinnier. But the food has always been excellent, and it still is. Excuse me, I don't think Juanita can hear."

He stood and went to chase down Juanita, whoever she was. Irene smiled across the table at Willa.

"You must miss your aunt a lot," she said, kindly.

"I didn't know her that well," confessed Willa. "But I did like her. I'm very sorry she's dead. In such a terrible accident, too."

"It shocked us all," said Irene, growing serious. "Mina was a smart lady. Sam and I can't figure out what made her stay out so late that night. Doug—Captain Burch—couldn't make heads or tails of it either."

"What do you think happened?" Willa asked, sipping her margarita to hide the eagerness on her face.

"Our first thought was engine trouble."

"The Coast Guard says not," said Willa, quickly.

"So we hear."

"What do we hear?" asked Sam, sliding into the booth again with a fresh bowl of chips and salsa directly from the kitchen.

"We're just discussing Mina's accident."

"Accident my foot," began Sam, but he was muzzled by a look from Irene.

"What do you mean?" Willa demanded.

She had waited too long, though, for the question to be convincing.

"You don't think it's an accident either," Irene said, studying her face. "So the plot thickens! Why is that, hon?"

Brian took Willa's hand under the table.

"It's okay," he said. "Go ahead. Tell them. You said you trust me, right? So *trust* me."

There was silence at the table, as the other three exchanged significant glances with each other.

"You know something, don't you?" Willa said. "All of you. You need to tell me what it is."

"Why should we?" said Irene, softly.

"So I can *do* something about it!"

"It's about time someone did something about it," thundered Sam, slamming his fist onto the table and sending chips flying.

"Hear, hear," said Brian, beaming at Willa. "See, you two? I told you she would help."

"Can we trust her, though?" said Sam, half to his wife, and half to himself.

"Trust me with what?"

"We think there's more to Mina's death than meets the eye," confessed Irene. "And we've formed a coalition. Sam, me, Lucy, Brian, and Captain Burch."

"I think she was murdered," said Willa, bluntly.

"So do we!"

"And I intend to find who did it."

"Now that's more like it," said Sam, pushing the fresh chips and salsa her way. "Welcome to the club."

Brian got up from the table and went outside to make a few calls.

"He's assembling the Minions," Irene said, slurping up her margarita.

Willa stared at her.

"That's the name Sam gave us—the folks that are looking into your auntie's death. Mina's Minions. Lucy protested—said Mina'd have *hated* that."

Sam laughed.

"That's why I did it."

"We like to think that, wherever she is now, she is smiling down on our efforts."

"I bet she is."

"She wasn't a religious woman, but she was *good*. Really good. She's with the Lord, now, no matter what anyone says. She deserved a whole lot better than she got. The Minions are going to make sure whoever hurt her pays for it. Let justice roll down like waters," Irene said, suddenly solemn.

"—and righteousness like an ever-flowing stream," Sam added.

"Amen," replied Willa heartily, reaching for the basket of chips.

Brian came back in after a few minutes, beaming.

"Lucy wants us to come up to her place tomorrow morning. Doug's just over there in his usual spot," he said, pointing to the bar, where Captain Burch sat drinking tequila. "He's a little tipsy already—I suggest we hold off on additional murder talk until the group's all together."

"Deal," said Sam, as a waitress set down plates of steaming food. "These tacos ain't gonna eat themselves."

They stayed at the restaurant chatting until about midnight. Then Brian walked Willa back up the hill to Lucy's place. They went slowly, taking their time, savoring the conversation. Brian told her about business school, and his life afterward as a pastry chef at a fancy hotel in downtown San Fransisco.

"Why'd you come back to Humboldt Cove?" asked Willa.

"The lifestyle was glamorous, but it wasn't enough. I was unhappy. The truth is, I missed home. I moved back here, hoping to find a halfway decent job in Eureka. One day, I ran into Mina at Oscar's. She was looking for a new business opportunity, and we got to talking. Long story short, we pooled our money and expertise and opened The Three Hounds. The bakery has been more successful than I ever dreamed. Honestly, it was a match made in heaven—me and Mina."

"Yeah," said Willa, softly. "I can see that."

"She was a very special lady. But you know that. She trusted you enough to leave you the dogs, which says more than you know. You must have known her pretty well, huh?"

"Not as well as I would have liked."

He stopped walking and took her hand.

"Thank you for showing me that letter. That took guts."

"You can't tell anyone else about it. Not even Irene and Sam."

"My lips are sealed. But I think we'll be able to make some progress now. I want justice for Mina."

"Me too."

"I'm sorry I sabotaged our date."

"So it was a date?" she asked, feeling suddenly shy.

"Of course it was! And next time, it's just going to be you and me. No Doyles. No dogs," he laughed. "No lawyers. Just the two of us. I want to learn all about you, Willa Lattner."

"I warn you, it isn't pretty."

"I think it is," he said, looking at her meaningfully. "Did I tell you I've always had a thing for redheads?"

"No," she laughed. "Lucy Garber got there ahead of you."

"I've never dated a writer before. It must be amazing to create something from nothing."

"Have you read my books? When you do, you may change your tune. I don't try to *say* anything. There's no deeper meaning to any of it. It's just hijinks and antics. No one gets hurt but the bad guys, and that's very much offscreen. You're the one who creates something from nothing."

"When I bake a cake, I feel like God himself," he admitted. "But you make people come alive through your stories, and that's truly special."

Willa thought about Violet Valentine, that plucky young heroine who outsmarted criminals and the police, quipping heartlessly as she went, and stopping now and then to bake a chocolate cream pie. She smiled to herself. Once he read her books, Brian might change his mind about how special they were. How *was* she going to get Violet out of the latest scrape, anyway? Wallace was right, the last couple chapters of *Fatal Fudge* had more holes than a screen door...

"I think you were brave to come here," he said, and she realized he had been talking for some time now while she was musing on Violet's foibles. "You left everything behind to set up somewhere entirely new."

"I was actually living with my twin sister Wendy and her husband until about a month ago. The three of us were inseparable."

"What happened?"

"They moved overseas to be closer to his family. I was happy for them, of course, but I felt...unmoored. I didn't know what my new chapter would look like until I got the news about Mina."

"You must be lonely."

"A little."

"You don't have to be."

He smiled at her, and before she quite knew what was happening, he drew her close and kissed her. Then he walked her up to Lucy's doorstep and said goodnight.

Floating on a cloud, Willa let herself in with Lucy's spare key. She climbed the stairs quietly, so as not to wake any of the sleepers. *Murder talk withstanding, that was the best date I've had in a long time*, she thought, dreamily.

Her elated mood was somewhat dampened when she caught a glimpse of herself in the bathroom mirror and saw a large chunk of jalapeno between her front teeth.

Mail

To Jean Lattner

Mom,

Thanks for the email and for digging up that recipe for seven-minute icing. I appreciate you typing it out by hand, but what I really wanted was a picture of it—there are extra instructions in Grandma's handwriting on the back. Can you send me an actual pic of the front and back?

Take it with your phone, not your camera. Dad will show you how to attach it. And if you get a chance, can you send me your recipe for peach cobbler? You know the one I'm talking

about—there's a spice in it that begins with C.
It's NOT cinnamon. I want to say cardigan?

I'm doing well, and enjoying life with the dogs.
I haven't read the article on ticks and fleas
you sent yet but I'll try to get to it soon.
I figured out who their vet is and made sure
they've had all their shots, etc. They are very
good boys, they don't pee in the house, and all
three of them are fixed. I have decided to keep
them, so you'd better get used to the idea of
granddogs because you're going to love them!

I'm going to take your advice and hire a monthly
cleaning service. I know Sharon heard of a good
agency down this way, but last time I talked
to her she was getting mixed up between San
Francisco and San Diego so I'm not holding out
much hope.

RE: the insurance, YES I have an umbrella policy
now and NO, I don't know whether I have tsunami
coverage. I will find out as soon as I can.
Honestly, I'm not worried about it, and you
wouldn't be either if you could see the hill I

live on. I'd like to see a wave try to get up here.

Now for the uncomfortable bit. I have not talked to Steve. I will never be talking to Steve again, and I need you to let go of the idea.

I understand he's making advances towards Dad. He'll try to woo you over with his side of things if you let him. Rest assured, there is no "his side". He was a cheater and he thought he could get away with it. Well, he couldn't.

One more thing—I spoke to Wallace and *Fatal Fudge* will be released in January of next year. I can get advance copies for your book club if they're interested. I ended up using Sharon's fudge recipe and thanked her for it in the acknowledgments section—she'll get a big kick out of that.

Love,

Willa

P.S. If you call and I don't answer, it's not because I have been kidnapped and held for ransom. I've ordered a new cell phone, that's all, and it hasn't arrived yet.

The Captain

Willa awoke the next morning energized and excited to face the day, a mood buoyed by the smell of bacon and coffee wafting up from the kitchen downstairs.

She dressed quickly and made her way to Lucy's spare room, where Kyle, Killer, and Wags were waiting patiently to be released from their crates. Before they could begin their orgy of barking, she took them outside down the back staircase, let them do their business, and then slipped into Mina's house through the kitchen door.

"You fellas are going to have to stay here," she told them, and the look in Kyle's eyes nearly broke her heart.

Sometimes, he was almost human.

"Hey, it's not the way I want it," she protested, as though they could understand her. "But if you *will* insist on barking all the time, you're going to make yourselves unpopular. I'll be back in a bit to check on you. That's a promise."

She returned to Lucy's house, where the scent of coffee and bacon had become more pronounced. There was another smell in the mix now—something spicy and sweet.

Willa poked her head into the kitchen and saw Lucy standing over the stove, flipping sizzling slices of bacon. Mr. Pilkington was reading the paper at a small, round table and drinking coffee.

"Good morning, sweetheart," Lucy said. "Not exactly an early riser, are you?"

Willa looked at the clock.

"It's seven-thirty," she said.

"Exactly! I've been up since five. The early bird gets the worm!"

Willa opened her mouth to retort that seven-thirty was plenty early, especially if one preferred eggs and bacon to worms, but remembered her manners just in time.

"There's bacon, and strong, black coffee in the pot just over there, and I've got some blueberry muffins in the oven. We'll have a nice, relaxing breakfast before our council of war. Now that you and Daniel are in on our secret, we can get somewhere!"

Willa did Lucy's breakfast justice, raving over the muffins. Lucy sprinkled coarse sugar over the top of each one before it cooled, and the resulting creation was slightly crunchy, with caramelized edges and a cinnamon-forward interior, bursting with blueberries. Willa ate three of them before she knew what was happening.

"I'll give you the recipe, don't worry," said Lucy, anticipating the inevitable request. "They're pretty darn good if I do say so myself!"

Good enough to anchor an entire book, thought Willa, in a muffin-stuffed haze.

Bloodthirsty Blueberries? The Blueberry Beheadings? No, those didn't strike the right note. Violet Valentine books weren't gory. *The Muffin Murders*—that was more like it. Helping herself to a fourth muffin, Willa reflected that if she stayed in Humboldt Cove much longer, she'd gain about ten pounds and a dozen book ideas. She didn't mind the first at all if she could guarantee the second. Weight came and went. Books were forever.

"The Doyles mentioned that Captain Burch is part of the gang," Willa said, wiping crumbs off her lap. "Is that because he and Mina were buddies, or because he was the one to raise the initial alarm?"

"Both, really. He's been part of the—what did you call us?—the *gang* from the beginning. Gang! What word," said Lucy, pouring bacon grease into an old glass jar next to the stove. "That implies something negative, don't you think?"

"Al Capone!" said Mr. Pilkington, laying down his newspaper. "Tommy guns and molls!"

"I prefer to call us a club. Or, if you like, we are a league, and justice is our cause!"

"To justice," said Mr. Pilkington, holding up his cup of tea and clinking it against Lucy's mug.

"To justice," Willa repeated, sneaking another muffin.

Willa decided to take a quick trip into town before the gathering at Lucy's house.

She had been mulling on the probable size and weight of Mina's book. It didn't exist in the cloud somewhere—mere ideas on a screen. If Lucy was correct, Mina had banged the whole thing out on her ancient typewriter. That gave it a definite weight and heft. A stack of papers an inch or two thick was no needle in the haystack. If it had been in Mina's house, they would have found it already.

Willa's best guess was that Mina had given it to someone, either in person—or more likely—by mail. She'd had enough presence of mind before she died to send that letter to Willa. Perhaps she had disposed of the book at the same time. Shipped it out to a publisher, perhaps, or a trusted friend.

Willa told Lucy and Mr. Pilkington she'd be back in half a jiff and stopped by Mina's house to get the dogs. Mr. Pilkington followed her out to have a quiet word.

"I'm going to the post office to see if Mina shipped a package before she died," she confided. "You stay here and pump Lucy about town gossip."

"Good thinking. How was your date?"

"It was productive," she said, smiling. "Mina said Brian might prove a good ally. So far, she's been right. I showed him the letter last night."

"Oh," he replied, astonished.

"Just him—and I swore him to silence. It was the right move, Pilky. I know it was."

"It will be nice to have another ally," he admitted.

"Should we tell the others?"

"I think not. Mina only mentioned Brian. And speaking of Brian...I've been going over the events of last night in my head. Why does the Sheriff want the records from the bakery so badly, my dear? It has been weighing on me."

"I have to think it's an intimidation tactic. Brian and Mina aren't the type to fudge the ledgers or skimp on taxes."

He smiled, wanly.

"They're cook-bookers, not book-cookers! I agree. Mina was honest to a fault. And Brian is an upright young man with whom she trusted her business—that speaks volumes. But I have learned to listen when men like

Gary Poole talk. He has power here, whether we like it or not. If he wants those reports from The Three Hounds, there is a good reason for it. You say you sent them to your CPA?"

"Yes. He says the business was healthy and wealthy, with a good profit margin, large reserves, and an overall clean bill of health."

"I wonder..." said Pilkington, stroking his chin. "Have you shown them to anyone else? Any other experts?"

"I sent them to my brother-in-law—he's a pastry chef."

"And what does he say?"

"He hasn't written back yet."

"Reach out to him again. I have the uneasy feeling that something is amiss at the bakery. Our friend Brian is certainly innocent of theft or dishonesty, and yet he may know more than he's telling. Be careful, Willa—that's all."

"You be careful with Lucy, then," she teased him.

Mr. Pilkington removed his glasses, rubbing them on his shirt in a thoughtful manner. He put them back on and gazed at her earnestly.

"The danger is not coming from that direction," he stated.

"Is that your gut instinct?"

"Not precisely. A little cool logic. If this does hinge on Mina's book—and the break-in makes that the most likely possibility—neither Lucy nor Brian are viable suspects. Brian was actually staying in the house for a week or more after Mina's death. If he wanted to tear the place apart, he could easily have done it then. And as co-author, Lucy already knew what was in it! But I want to caution you against placing too much reliance on other people in town. Even those you think you know."

"Why the gypsy's warning, Pilky? Plain old stranger danger?"

"We will soon be meeting with a larger group, many of whom we do not know well. Lucy said the Doyles featured prominently in the book—and we don't know a thing about Captain Burch, apart from his dubious sense of humor and the fact that he serves as the harbormaster for Humboldt Cove."

"The ideal person to arrange a disappearance at sea."

"Exactly. So I don't think we should bring up the letter," he said, firmly. "That's a card we will keep hidden between ourselves and Brian."

"Agreed."

"And let me stress to you that while suppression of the book is the most likely motive for Mina's murder, we cannot know that for sure."

"We're on the same page, Pilky. But any more theorizing will have to wait for later," she asked. "The dogs are going to pull my arms off."

"Later," he promised.

The Humboldt Cove Post Office was located inside the tiny, three-room City Hall adjacent to Doyle's. Willa was hesitating outside, unsure whether to bring the dogs with her or tie them on a bike rack outside, when she heard a warning bark from Wags and a familiar voice behind her.

"Morning, Ms. Lattner!"

It was Captain Burch.

"Good morning," she said, politely.

The Captain's hearty, over-friendly manner was not to her taste.

"I thought we were all meeting up at Lucy's," he said, holding the door open for her.

"We are."

"So what are you doing down at City Hall at eight-thirty in the morning?" he asked, smiling at her with all his teeth. "Bring the doggies with you. We don't mind one bit, do we boys?"

Dentures, she thought, watching him beam down on the dogs. His teeth were all a bit too straight and white. She was reminded of the Cheshire Cat, a character she had always found terrifying. A smile without a face.

The Captain took a set of keys from his pocket and walked toward a small alcove in the lobby marked "Post Office."

"I was just stopping by on my way to Lucy's," he said.

"Oh," she said, nonplussed. "Are you responsible for the postal service here?"

"Yes ma'am! I share the job with a couple of the other city council fellas. We don't do a regular mail delivery service—the town's a bit too small for that—but most folks have a PO box here. Mail comes in around ten and last call for letters or packages is five PM. Come here at five-oh-one on a day I'm working, and you'll find the door locked and me drinking tequila at Fat Oscar's."

"I thought you were the harbormaster," she replied, awkwardly.

"So I am, most days. Share that job too, with a couple of the other sea dogs. Haven't worked on a trawler for close to ten years. I'm whiling away my retirement hawking stamps and sorting packages. Gives me a great insight into the inner workings of Humboldt Cove, let me tell you," he said, winking at her. "There are no secrets from this old codger. That reminds me, didja hear the one about the unstamped letter?"

"No," said Willa, with resignation.

It was no good trying to out-maneuver someone determined to tell you a joke. They'd find a way, no matter what, and you might as well grit your teeth and get it over with.

"Ah, that's okay. You wouldn't get it," he said, delighted. "Heh—you see? You wouldn't *get* it?"

He haw-hawed, very pleased with himself.

"How about this one—betcha haven't heard this one. Why are postal workers so inventive? Eh?"

"Uh..."

"Because we know how to push the envelope! Get it? Aw, you Lattners are all the same. No sense of humor," he said, good-naturedly. "So what can I do you for, missy?"

Willa eyed the avuncular old man, whom she suspected had been out drinking tequila at Fat Oscar's late into the night. He smelt strongly of Ben Gay and liquor. But he was part of Mina's Minions, and that changed things.

"I want to know whether my aunt mailed a package the last week of May," she said bluntly.

Subtlety was wasted on someone like Captain Burch. You had to say what you wanted in simple, declarative sentences and let the jokes wash over you.

His eyes grew wary.

"That's the week Mina died," he said.

He walked slowly behind the mail counter and powered on the computer.

"She came here around four-forty-five the afternoon of the twenty-fifth," he said, looking at the screen. "Two days before she...before she..."

Tears filled his rheumy eyes, bloodshot from alcohol, age, and ill health. Willa felt a growing liking and respect for the man.

"She looked scared to death," he said. "I never saw Mina scared before. Shoved a package and a couple of letters over the counter, and told me to make sure they went out at five."

"Did she say what was in the box?"

"No, and I didn't ask. Didn't do to pester Mina with questions. She'd tell you to go to Hades. But it was yea big," he said, indicating a rectangle about a foot long with his hands.

"Do you keep a record of where things are shipped?" she asked, hopefully.

"'Fraid not, Ms. Lattner. This package was important?"

"Possibly."

"Wish I could help," he replied, and she believed him. "You're a nice little gal. Lucy's been telling me all the nasty things people are saying about you, and I want you to know I don't believe it. Not a word. Any friend of Mina's is a friend of mine."

"Thanks," she said, and made a hasty exit before he could tell her any more jokes. "See you in a little bit."

She walked back up the hill to Lucy's, wondering what was in Mina's package, and where it had gone.

The 'gang,' such as it was, arrived at Lucy's at nine o'clock on the dot. Brian barged cheerfully into the foyer. He kissed Willa briefly on the cheek and then asked Lucy where the snacks were. Tutting, Lucy disappeared down the hall, Brian trotting after her.

"Come in," Willa said to the others. "It's nice to see you again!"

Captain Burch stood in the back of the group, holding his hat. Irene hauled him up next to her and shoved him through the doorway.

"Good lord, Doug, stop lurking there like the bogeyman and just go in! Lucy won't bite."

The Captain hurried down the hallway toward the kitchen, hot on Brian's heels.

"Painfully shy when it comes to Lucy, poor devil," said Sam Doyle. "They used to go steady, at one time. Didn't end well, or so I hear. It was Mina who pushed them back together—bullied them into being friends again. Mina could bully her way into the gates of heaven," he chuckled, and his wife slapped his arm.

"Not that she'd ever need to," she said, reproaching him with a look. "Mina was a saint, God rest her."

Amused, Willa shut the door and headed to the kitchen, where Mr. Pilkington was quietly sipping coffee and Lucy and Brian were helping everyone to cups of tea and leftover muffins.

So these are Mina's Minions, she thought to herself, wincing a little. Lucy was right. Mina would have hated that name. She tried to think of something less banal, and could only come up with *the Justice League*, which was definitely taken.

She caught a glimpse of the piece of plywood nailed to Mina's house out the kitchen window and her smile faded. The group didn't really need a name, as long as they fulfilled their primary purpose. They had better figure out who killed Mina, and why, before someone else got hurt.

The Minions

"First things first," said Lucy, once everyone was seated with a cup of tea or coffee. "The five of us have been running in circles for weeks without a thing to go on but intuition and common sense. Now that Willa and Daniel are here, we can finally get somewhere. I suggest we begin by asking what *they* think of Mina Lattner's death."

All eyes went to Willa, who had been trying to slyly grab another muffin without anyone seeing and was now caught red-handed.

"That's a loaded question," she said, her eyes darting to where her purse—letter and all—hung on a hook in Lucy's kitchen. "I thought her death was fishy from the moment I heard about it. I'm more interested in what made all of *you* suspicious."

The Captain cleared his throat.

"I raised the alarm, at first," he said, gruffly. "Mina was a recreational fisher—popped out on fine days and usually threw her measly little catches back! She wasn't after huge hauls like commercial trawlers, and she didn't love fishing enough to go out on a rainy night. When she didn't return, I got worried and called Sam."

Sam nodded.

"He sounded scared as heck, and it takes a lot to rattle Doug Burch."

"There was no reason she couldn't have made it back safe. If her engine quit, she'd have radioed me for help."

"So anyway," said Irene, "Doug told Sam, and Sam told me, and *I* started pumping Lucy about it. Lucy already had her hackles up, and she told me to ask Brian about it."

"Mina had been acting off for several weeks," Brian said, taking up the narrative.

"Off how?"

"Moody is the best way to describe it. She'd snap at me when she came into work."

"And I found her crying in the kitchen, the very day before she died," said Lucy. "She told me it was just her knee, acting up, but I knew something was wrong."

"She was depressed, plain and simple. So when I heard what happened—well, my first thought was that she'd killed herself," Brian told Willa, a little sheepishly.

"What?!"

"Excuse me," said Mr. Pilkington, highly offended on Mina's behalf. "Wilhelmina Lattner would never—"

"That's not what I think *now*," said Brian, interrupting the old man and holding up his hands. "But originally I wondered whether she'd arranged it to look like an accident."

"I told him that was a load of baloney," Irene said, busily pouring milk into her coffee.

"What made you so sure?" asked Willa, curiously.

Irene looked at Willa over the rim of her coffee cup for several seconds.

"The dogs," she said, finally. "She'd never have left them like that. Not without making arrangements."

"I should think not," said Mr. Pilkington.

"I set Brian straight on that at once. And since there was no other good explanation, we figured it must be foul play!"

"She had plenty of enemies," Sam said, shrugging. "Any one of 'em could have put her out of the way. If you ask me, Sheriff Poole's behind it. That man has been running the county like his personal piggy bank, and he couldn't stand the thought of a strong, smart woman like Mina Lattner muscling her way past him. I swear that man is dirty. He didn't want to let a sharp criminal prosecutor in after him. Losing the election was the least of his concerns. He was worried about jail time."

"What do you suspect him of?"

"Taking bribes," he responded, promptly. "Embezzlement. Racketeering. Money laundering."

"My, my," murmured Mr. Pilkington.

"Gary Poole is plenty dangerous, but I happen to think it's that Snelling woman," said Irene. "The Sheriff's not that dumb. He wouldn't get rid of a political rival by killin' her. He'd put up posters and run a smear campaign."

"Can you think of a reasonable explanation why Gary Poole would be investigating The Three Hounds?"

"Say what now?"

"Last night, after the meeting, he asked me for access to the financial records," Willa explained.

"He was bugging me about it too," said Brian. "But that was before Mina died."

"Did you hand them over?" asked Irene, with bated breath.

"Of course not! Mina didn't want to give him so much as a paperclip from the bakery, and I'm going to respect her wishes. He was just trying to find dirt on her. Still is."

"Like a cougar that won't let go of its prey," Sam said, disgusted. "Can you imagine trying to malign a dead woman?"

"I can imagine a lot about Gary Poole," said Irene. "But I'm sorry, hon, I don't see him putting his hide on the line by committing murder. Whereas Harriet Snelling is a piece of *work*, and I wouldn't put it past her to stick a knife in anyone who crossed her."

"You're just mad because she made the best crab chowder at the festival last year," snorted Sam.

"She cheated," cried Irene. "You know she did. No one makes better crab stock than I do."

"What do you think she did? Stole some bisque from one of those Michelin-star chefs in Napa?"

"She switched the ballots! I tasted *her* chowder. Like Campbell's Soup, only tinnier."

"Irene does make very good chowder," Lucy told Willa, loyally. "Big chunks of crab, and a little bit of bacon for flavor, and a mix of root vegetables. Potatoes, carrots, and—parsnips, is it, Irene?"

"Rutabagas," said Irene briskly, refusing to go down a culinary rabbit trail. "A woman who would cheat in a chowder competition is capable of anything, including knockin' Mina on the head and throwin' her out to the sharks. She's trying to run the crab festival this year. Lord, did you see the look she gave me last night? She wanted to be the one who talked at the meeting. I can't help it that Doug called on me first."

"She doesn't have a boat," said her husband. "How could she have drowned Mina from dry land, huh? Answer me that!"

"She could have rented a boat, Sam," his wife retorted. "And her sister Joan lives down in Trinidad, and Joan's husband is a commercial fisherman!"

"Does Sheriff Poole have a boat?" asked Willa, who sensed that a full-on marital tiff was impending.

"Everyone in this town has a boat."

"Oh," said Willa, startled. "Like who?"

"Sam and me, of course. The McKinleys. Dale Snood. The Parkers, and the Donaldsons, and little Ms. Twitterton, the piano teacher on G Street," Irene listed. "The Andersons have one. Lucy has one, of course."

"Just a little one," said Lucy, almost apologetically. "The harbor fees here are so steep."

"I've got one," said Brian, "but I dock it in Eureka. Can't afford to keep it here."

"Now, let's see. Doug has a boat, naturally," Irene said. "And so do some of the other guys at City Hall."

Captain Burch nodded, and Irene shrugged her shoulders at Willa.

"So really, everyone in town!"

"Well, who had their boat out the night Mina died?" Willa asked the Captain, directly.

"Sam and I were out earlier that evening," Irene said, answering for him. "We usually get our fish from the market downtown but George Lee was visiting his grandkids in Virginia that week. Dale Snood's fish stinks to high heaven, and the prices are too high in Trinidad and we didn't want to drive all the way down to Eureka for fresh salmon. People go nuts for it right at the start of the season, and we wanted to bag our limit so we'd have a few steaks to sell that week. We came back as soon as Doug told us the storm was comin', though. Returned to harbor around one-fifteen or one-thirty."

"Anyone else?" Willa asked.

"Bob Anderson was out until one-thirty," said Captain Burch. "He's an avid sports fisherman. Sheriff Poole is too—he went out earlier that night. He was back by twelve-fifteen."

"Hmm. And you talked to Mina at one o'clock?"

He nodded.

"Did you see Bob Anderson and Gary Poole when they returned? Personally, I mean?"

"Well, no," said the Captain, startled by this line of questioning. "But their boats were there, so they must have been."

"Someone else could have brought the boats back."

"I suppose so. But why would they? And where would Gary or Bob have been?"

"On Mina's boat, presumably."

"How would they have gotten off it again?"

Willa sighed inwardly. No wonder none of these people had figured out what happened to Mina. Their minds were too pure. She could think of a million ways it could have been done.

"Maybe there was a third boat involved," she said. "Or maybe you didn't talk to Mina at all that night. Maybe by the time you spoke, she was already dead."

"But I heard her voice, over the radio."

"Voices can be faked."

"Pardon me," said Mr. Pilkington, "but did you *see* her go out that night, Captain Burch?"

"What do you mean?"

"Did you see Ms. Lattner get on her boat and take it out of the harbor? Or did you make an inference because her boat was not in dock?"

"I saw her. With my own eyes."

"I'll vouch for him," said Brian. "I walked her down to the pier that night—she went directly there from The Three Hounds. Doug and I watched her get on the Old Girl and drive it out to sea. There was no one with her, so you can scratch that idea."

"Well, what do you think happened to her, then?" said Willa, crossly.

"I think she may have been poisoned," Brian responded, a serious expression in his blue eyes. "Given something in a drink that night, before she went out."

"Why didn't they find her body on board then?"

"There was nothing left of that boat," said the Captain, unexpectedly bursting into tears. "I went out with the rescue crew. I saw the wreck myself. It was horrible."

Brian placed a compassionate hand on Captain Burch's shoulder, holding it there until the man became composed once more. He looked up at Willa, and her heart melted.

"Where would she have gotten a drugged drink?" she asked him. "She was at the bakery with you."

"Heidi or I certainly could have spiked her cappuccino," Brian said, smiling at her a little sadly. "We had the opportunity. I can't speak for Heidi—though she's a sweetheart who wouldn't hurt a fly—but you'll have to take my word for it that I didn't slip Mina a Mickey."

"What was Mina doing there that evening?"

"She and I went over the books after closing sometimes. But she might have met with an enemy before she arrived."

"Has anyone talked to the staff at Oscar's yet? They'd know if she was there that night."

There was another uncomfortable silence, and Irene, Sam, Lucy, and Brian exchanged rather shamefaced looks. Willa refrained from sighing.

"Are those the only people who left port that night?" she asked. "Mina, Sam and Irene, Gary Poole, and Bob Anderson?"

"Yes," the Captain told her. "It was the first day of salmon season, and people take big risks when fresh salmon is involved. I'm surprised there weren't more folks out, honestly but I guess the storm warning scared them off. I did see lights from two or three boats in the distance, to the south. They must have put out from Trinidad. Or possibly Eureka, if they left port earlier in the day."

"We'll need to get information from the ports in Trinidad and Eureka then," said Willa, a little irritated no one else had considered that yet.

Mina's Minions indeed. They were all just playing detective.

"Okay, so let's think. Irene thinks the killer is Harriet Snelling, and Sam's money is behind Sheriff Poole. Brian thinks someone poisoned her here in town. What do you think, Lucy?"

"I think she met with an enemy at sea—possibly Harriet Snelling. I cannot go further than that."

"What's your theory, Captain? Who are you plumping for?" Willa said.

The big man went crimson and turtled down into the collar of his jacket.

"No idea," he said miserably. He added under his breath, so just she could hear, "But it's somebody we know. Has to be."

The meeting broke up soon afterward. Brian, Irene, and Sam went back to tend their respective businesses, and Douglas Burch returned to his office at the harbor. Deciding the dogs had been alone long enough, Willa went to Mina's house to catch up on a little neglected work while Mr. Pilkington took a nap at Lucy's. The final chapters of *Fatal Fudge* weren't going to edit themselves.

Her efforts to write fell flat, however. She checked her email as soon as she got home. There was nothing from her sister Wendy, which was disappointing enough. There *was* a pointed message from her agent, Wallace, who wanted to move up the deadline on her final edits. And much to her dismay, there was an excruciatingly long and rambling email from her ex-boyfriend Steve, which she forced herself to read.

She took a long shower to clear her head and tried once more to buckle down to a little serious work.

It was no use. She couldn't write convincing dialogue for Violet Valentine when the only voice in her head was that of Captain Burch.

It's somebody we know. Has to be.

Mail

To Steven Joyce

Steve,

Let's make this easy.

NO, I won't go to counseling with you. NO, you
can't have my current address. NO, I don't want
to meet for coffee next time I'm in Seattle.

I'm blocking this address. You may direct all
further communications to my lawyer. Or, better
still, why not forward them to your future
address by way of the fireplace?

Very sincerely,

Willa

Mail

To Wendoline Lattner-Santini

Wendy,

Hey.

My phone still hasn't arrived so I know you can't
call, but I am DYING here. I'd give anything to
hear your voice.

Steve wrote me the world's longest message.
Somewhere, in an alternate universe, another
Willa is still reading that email. It had the
quality of eternity about it.

You're going to love this. He wants me to go to therapy with him. I wish he had asked me in person, so he could see how hard I laughed. It's about six months and one affair too late for THAT, my boy. His sister knows of "someone really good" who deals with "situations like ours." I bet she does. Alicia hated my guts.

That ship sailed so long ago it's not even a dot on the horizon. I don't know how he got my email address, but now I have to change it AGAIN. This must be the third time since we broke up. The receptionist at my dentist's office thinks I'm a drug dealer.

If you return to the States and find that I have been institutionalized for my own safety, this is why.

I'm so angry I can hardly think, which is very bad news because Wallace is all over me to rewrite the end of the book. I got Violet into an odd situation with a horse and I can't wriggle out of it without unraveling the mystery entirely. He says the whole thing is too fanciful, but that never stopped me before!

She piloted a plane in the last one, if you'll remember, and nobody said anything about it.

Maybe this will be the book where I kill off Violet Valentine for good.

Wendddddddy.

I am falling apart. The dogs are great but they don't say much. I need my sister to hold my hand.

My date last night was weird, and then good, and then weird again. He kissed me goodnight, which was amazing—and it's been a while, as you know. But all the time, there was a chunk of jalapeno wedged between my incisor and my right canine. He MUST have seen it. There was no missing that thing. And he kissed me anyway, which is kind of sweet. Big green flag, right? I had almost forgotten what they looked like—Steve only waved giant red flags.

Please write back ASAP and tell me everything will be okay.

Love,

Willa

P.S. I don't have the heart to write another
message to G—can you ask him if there's a
non-dairy substitute for cream when making
ganache?

The Confidant

Mr. Pilkington came over to Mina's house after his nap and sat at the kitchen table with Willa, doing a crossword while she worked. Around one o'clock, she slammed down the lid of her laptop. She'd had enough of Violet Valentine to last a lifetime, and Wallace was going to have to deal with it—*Fatal Fudge* was what it was. If he didn't like it, he could drop her, and she'd thank him for it.

Kyle, who had opened one eye during her fit of pique, got up and began trotting out the kitchen toward the front door. Wags and Killer followed, and Willa decided she might as well go along for the ride. Kyle didn't often go anywhere on his own.

When she emerged into the hall, he was sitting patiently by the front door. The other dogs joined him there, staring at the door and wagging their tails.

"What is it, boys?" she asked, wondering if someone had left a package on the stoop.

She threw open the door to look and ran smack into Jake Anderson.

She let out a high-pitched scream and staggered backward, tripping over Killer and falling flat on her behind for the second time in as many days.

The dogs swarmed her, tails wagging and tongues out, and Mr. Pilkington came running down the hall as fast as his little cane would carry him.

"Hullo," Jake said, politely ignoring the fact that she was splayed in a heap on the floor, covered with anxious dachshunds.

He hauled her up without ceremony.

"I'm sorry to drop in without notice," he replied, picking up Kyle to stroke his silky ears. "Do you two have a minute to talk?"

"I suppose so," Willa said, helping Mr. Pilkington to the sofa. "Do you have more information about my aunt's death?"

"Not really. But I am ready to lay my cards on the table."

"What kind of cards?" inquired Mr. Pilkington, suspiciously.

"I understand if you're not in a similar position," he went on, ignoring the question, "and that's okay by me. Heck, if I were in your shoes, I wouldn't trust me either."

"Why not?" Willa said.

"You don't know anyone here, and you've got no reason to believe I'm a safe person to talk to. That's fair. We've barely met. I've got no reason to believe you're safe, either. But I'm not getting anywhere on my own. I want to offer up what I know, in case it helps. I don't expect a tit-for-tat situation unless you're open to it."

Willa looked at Mr. Pilkington, and he shook his head at her.

"We're not."

The crooked smile was back.

"Proof of intelligence. Are you at least willing to hear what I have to say?"

Willa decided it wouldn't hurt. They could independently verify everything he told them. If he was telling the truth, it brought them one step closer to solving the case. And if it turned out he was lying, well and good! That was data, and they needed more data.

"Fire away," she said.

"I still don't know how or why Mina died, or what caused her accident. Let me get that out of the way right off the bat. The only people who benefit financially from her death are yourself and Brian Harrison. I can't imagine that guy killing anyone, can you?"

He watched her keenly.

"No," she said. "I can't. He loved her."

"I went to school with Brian, and he's an okay guy."

"A stunning commendation," Willa replied. "So if you don't know why or how Mina died, what do you know?"

"I know who else had a boat out that night."

"So do we. Gary Poole, Irene and Sam Doyle, and your dad," she said.

Jake set Kyle down and picked up Wags, who had been waiting patiently for his turn on the coveted lap. Kyle trotted back over to Willa, laid down at her feet, and promptly went to sleep.

"You've done your homework," he said, approvingly. "You missed one thing, though. I was also out that night—with my dad."

Willa's eyes narrowed and Mr. Pilkington gave one of his little dry coughs.

"Captain Burch didn't mention that."

"Ah, you went right to the source, I see. Smart move. I thought you might have gotten your info second-hand."

"From whom?"

"This is a small town," Jake said, quietly. "And Irene Doyle doesn't have a discreet bone in her body. Everyone knows that she and Sam and Brian Harrison and Lucy Garber are 'investigating' Mina's death."

"They've formed a club," said Willa, smiling despite herself. "And the Captain's a member."

"They dragged him into it? I guess everyone's got to have a hobby."

"A hobby?" she repeated, faintly insulted. "These people were Mina's friends. They're trying to get some sort of closure for her."

"They're not doing a very good job," he shot back. "What do they know? What practical steps have they taken?"

Willa did not answer, partly because she had thought the same thing herself. His tone made her angry, though, and she realized she was becoming very protective of Lucy, Brian, and the Doyles.

"Relax, I'm not trying to run your friends down. Doug didn't mention I was on the boat that night because he didn't know. He was getting his dinner at Fat Oscar's when I boarded. When he returned, I was already in the cabin prepping for the fishing trip."

"Did you see Mina while you were out?"

"I wish I had," he replied, glumly stroking Wags' ears. "We went the opposite direction, up near the Hags. I didn't see Irene or Sam either. We did pass Gary's boat, briefly. But listen—Gary, Irene, and Sam were not the only people at sea that night."

"What do you mean? How do you know?"

"I'm friends with one of the guys down at the docks in Trinidad. He told me Harriet Snelling went out with her brother-in-law that evening—he's a commercial fisherman."

Mr. Pilkington looked up at him sharply.

"Why would Ms. Snelling go on a commercial fishing expedition?"

"I wondered that myself. It's interesting timing, don't you think? A working trawler is not exactly fun and games. And Harriet and Mina's feud is well-known and well-founded. Mina showed no mercy to the Humboldt Cove Patisserie.”

“What time did they come back in?” asked Willa.

“They were alerted to the storm around one o’clock and returned to port at two-thirty.”

“Did you ask for a full run-down of the people who went in and out of Trinidad that night?”

“Of course. No one else connected to Mina is on the list. Believe me, I checked multiple times.”

“How about Eureka or Crescent City?” she asked. “Does your network of buddies extend that far north and south?”

“Unfortunately, it doesn’t.” He looked and sounded so depressed that Wags began licking his face to cheer him up. “I’ve tried getting information from both cities, but no one will talk. They require a warrant to share that kind of information with a total stranger.”

“So get one, Mr. Investigator. You work for the Sheriff’s Department, don’t you?”

“It’s not that simple. The case has been closed. Gary told me to move on. I’ve had to do all my investigating off the record.”

Willa raised an eyebrow.

“Sheriff Poole told you not to keep digging?”

“Yes, and I know that looks bad—especially given the animosity between him and Mina. But we don’t have unlimited funding. I have to close a lot of cases I’d rather keep open.”

It definitely looks bad, Willa thought. *Funding or no funding.*

“What else have you got?” she asked.

"The most likely explanation for Mina's accident is the one we already have. She tried to get back to port—something happened to the boat, and the storm took things from there."

Willa made a contemptuous sound.

"*But*," he said, "I'm not discounting the possibility of interference at sea, though I can't figure out for the life of me how it would have been done. Mina wouldn't have let someone board her boat without a good reason. She may have been drugged before she went out, however. That could account for her death."

"Or maybe she had a heart attack or a stroke," sighed Mr. Pilkington. "Like myself, she was no spring chicken. Isn't that the most logical conclusion to draw?"

"Not," Jake said, thoughtfully, "if you knew about all the little accidents she had before she died."

"What makes you think we don't?" Willa retorted.

Jake's face froze as if an invisible wall had sprung up between him and them. When he spoke next, however, his voice was just the same; calm, cool, and friendly.

"I wasn't aware you two spoke that often," he said.

"She would call now and then," Willa lied. "She mentioned something about falling off a ladder."

"I see."

Jake's brown eyes watched her with a guarded expression. The wall was still up. Willa remembered, with a little shiver, what Lucy had said about bad apples at the sheriff's office.

"Anyway," Jake went on, "I've looked thoroughly into the poison angle. She didn't eat at any of the restaurants in town the night she died. I can't find anyone who saw her that day, in fact. She must have laid low at home.

She would do that, sometimes—nest at home for a whole day, working, and only stepping outside to let the dogs out."

"How do you know all this stuff?" Willa asked. "You say you were her law clerk, but that was a long time ago."

"Mina was a good friend," he said, and Willa noticed his hands were trembling, just as they had when he returned Mina's Tupperware the day before. "She encouraged me to keep trying for the bar, even after I gave up on law and came home to work for the county. Believe me, I'm not going to stop until I find out what happened to her that night. Even if she was murdered, as you so obviously think. Even if the killer is someone I know or like. And especially if the killer is someone *she* knew and liked—such as her beloved niece or attorney."

"And there it is," said Willa, sarcastically. "The real reason you're here. Why would we have killed Mina?"

"You inherited a giant house and a ton of money. I know what Mina was worth. You could build a swimming pool, fill it with cash, and swim around like Scrooge McDuck. And you, Mr. Attorney, might have been embezzling or otherwise mishandling her estate. If you were, I'll find out. And I suggest you don't get in my way."

"We wouldn't dream of interfering with an *official* police investigation," said Mr. Pilkington, caustically. "Let me make a suggestion in return. Stay out of our way. We will get justice for Mina Lattner, and your badge does not intimidate me, sir. I've prosecuted officers of the law before, and I will happily do it again."

"Touché," said Jake, laughing suddenly. "What motive are you giving me, out of curiosity? Why would I hurt Mina?"

"To protect your buddy, the Sheriff," said Willa.

"Protect him from what?"

"Being unseated by a better candidate."

"I would have been first in line to vote Mina in. So that dog won't hunt."

"What if the bad guy does turn out to be Sheriff Poole?" pressed Willa. "What will you do then, Mr. Investigator?"

"I'll arrest Sheriff Poole."

"What if the murderer is your own father?"

"What? Why would my dad want to kill Mina?"

"You tell me. The Anderson pride, perhaps?"

He stared at her for a long time.

"You've been talking to the resident Humboldt Cove historian, I gather? Ouch. I knew Lucy and Mina's book delved pretty deep into local scandal but I didn't know how far they dug."

Mr. Pilkington dropped his cane and it fell with a thud onto the carpet.

"The Anderson family does not come off well," Willa said, careful not to make eye contact as she bent down to pick up the cane. "Or so we hear."

Jake said nothing to this, and she thought he might be angry. When she looked over at him, however, she saw that he was laughing again. Killer and Kyle, attracted by the sound of laughter, jumped onto his knees, excitedly. He scooped them up and put them on his lap with Wags, letting all three of them lick his face.

"What is so humorous, sir?" demanded Mr. Pilkington.

"Yeah, what's the joke?" Willa said. "Ugh, sorry about that—Kyle! Wags! Killer! Down boys!"

The dogs ignored her.

"Let them be," Jake replied.

He let the dogs swarm him a little longer and then pushed them off, still laughing. They trotted back to Willa, tails wagging.

"Lucy Garber, bless her heart, is very proud of the heritage of Humboldt Cove."

"She's got a right to be," said Mr. Pilkington, leaping to Lucy's defense like the gallant old gentleman he was.

"No arguments here. Old Hezekiah Garber was one of a kind. Way ahead of his time, preserving all that pristine redwood forest. But not everyone cares where they came from. I've no doubt those ladies dug up some unpleasant stuff about my illustrious ancestors. So what? What's that got to do with me?"

Willa shrugged.

"Some people might think an unstained family legacy is worth killing for."

"Undoubtedly. But not me. Where is the book, by the way? Have you located it, yet?"

"No."

There was a brief silence.

"You two must be lonely," Jake said, unexpectedly. "It can't be easy being strangers in town. Especially when you're in mourning. And especially in a town like this."

"The burglary yesterday did not fill us with warmth for the community," said Mr. Pilkington.

"I can imagine. Hey—let's call a truce, just for one night. Why don't you come to my folks' house for dinner? Mom's making spaghetti. We might play Taboo or something afterward. Low key. You need cheering up, both of you. Afterward, I can go back to investigating you and you can go back to investigating me."

Willa hesitated. She didn't want to commit to anything, especially if Brian wanted to see her again tonight. Plus, Mr. Pilkington might be too tired to go out. And there were the dogs...

"I don't want to leave the boys here alone," she said, by way of an excuse.

"Bring them with you!"

"We wouldn't want to impose," Mr. Pilkington replied.

"My parents will be thrilled."

"I have plans tonight with Brian Harrison," Willa said, as a last-ditch effort to get out of it.

"And I am dining with Lucy Garber," said Mr. Pilkington, with finality.

"Bring them too! Ms. Garber, Brian, and the dogs. The more the merrier."

"Well..."

"I insist," he said. "There will be cookies. Mom's making another batch."

"Same kind you brought yesterday?"

"The very same."

"We're in," Willa replied recklessly, hoping Mr. Pilkington would approve.

She had a policy of never, *never* turning down a cookie.

The Baker

After Jake left, Mr. Pilkington looked at Willa.

"I hope you know what you're doing, my dear," he reproved her. "Accepting an invitation of this kind might prove dangerous."

"His parents will be there! I'm sure it's safe. I want him to think our guard is down. We'll go, eat some spaghetti, play a few games, and ambush him with hard-hitting questions about Sheriff Poole's investigation of the bakery."

"I wish we knew *why* Mina was killed," said Mr. Pilkington, with a little shake of his head.

"Me too. Right now we don't know if it's about the bakery, the election, personal spite, or the book! And if whoever killed Mina did it to suppress the book, why haven't they gone after Lucy as well? What's to stop Lucy from publishing it on her own?"

"We had a brief conversation about it this morning before you woke up. It seems no one knew she was helping Mina. They were keeping that part quiet."

"Why?"

"Because Ms. Garber didn't want her neighbors to think she was raking up scandals to make a profit. Her name wasn't going to appear on it at all."

"Jake Anderson knew Lucy was working on it," said Willa, eyes widening. "He said so."

"I noticed that," said Mr. Pilkington. "He should not have known that little fact—gave himself away. And then I gave *myself* away rather badly by dropping my cane."

"How many people knew Mina was writing a book at all?"

"The existence of the manuscript was common knowledge. Apparently, Mina brought it up in the last two town meetings, asking for voluntary contributions of old family records and letters. She let it slip that she'd found plenty of dirt already, making pointed references to town founders."

"She had no problem painting a nice, big target on her back," Willa said, wishing her aunt had cared a little more about what people thought of her.

"Hmm," said Mr. Pilkington. "It seems to be a family trait."

"Meaning I shouldn't have accepted an invitation from a potential enemy?"

"Meaning we should tread cautiously," he replied, and left it at that.

They returned to the kitchen, and Willa sat down at the table to give Violet Valentine another shot. The doorbell rang before she could even power her laptop on.

Sorry Violet, she thought, abandoning her computer to go answer the door. The dogs were barking, as usual, though since they barked equally hard at Lucy Garber and Ian McKinley, she couldn't use them as a reliable danger meter.

Sure enough, it was just Brian Harrison, looking a little put out at his reception.

"Geez, Killer," he complained, patting the fat dog's head, "give a guy a break. They must drive you nuts with all this racket, day in and day out. I thought I was going insane the two weeks they lived with me."

"I'm getting used to it," she said, grabbing the collars of all three dogs and muscling them into the laundry room. "What's up?"

"I had a quick break at the bakery so I thought I'd run up and see what you two thought of our get-together this morning."

Willa led him back to the kitchen and poured him a cup of coffee.

"Hi again, Mr. P. Oof," he said, sitting wearily on the bench seat. "Thanks. I needed this. I've been up since three-thirty."

"Insomnia?" said Willa.

"Bread," he replied, cheerfully. "It waits for no man. I usually come in around four or four-thirty, but poor Heidi's there at two-thirty most days, getting things going. The Three Hounds has never served day-old baked goods and we never will."

"You must have to go to bed quite early."

"I usually hit the sheets around nine o'clock. Pathetic, in a man of my age, but there's no help for it."

"But we were out until almost midnight last night!"

"Some things are worth staying up for," he said, earnestly.

She blushed. To hide her confusion she began speaking again almost immediately.

"To answer your question, I enjoyed my first meeting of Mina's Minions!"

"As did I," said Mr. Pilkington.

Brian groaned.

"Irene told you our name, huh?"

"I think it's sweet."

"No you don't," he grinned. "Don't try to fool me, Willa Lattner. I know you now, remember? Don't bother lying about the name or anything else! What did you *really* think of the meeting?"

He was still smiling, but there was a gravity to the question that made her stop and consider what lay behind it.

"It was interesting," she said.

"How so?"

"You and Lucy both kept a pretty low profile."

He darted a quick look at her and exhaled, as though he had been holding his breath.

"You noticed that, huh?"

"I gather there is not perfect confidence amongst the members of Mina's Minions," said Mr. Pilkington, putting his index fingers together and tapping them.

Brian studied the floor.

"I've known Sam and Irene my entire life—Captain Burch, too. I grew up with their kids, saw them at every ball game and piano recital. These people were our biggest supporters when Mina and I set up shop in town."

"But you don't trust them?"

Willa saw a flash of grief in his dark blue eyes.

"Whoever killed Mina must have known her well—been familiar with her habits. That narrows the field considerably. And I don't know if you knew this, but Mina was writing a book. About the town and local history."

"Was she?" said Willa, innocently.

"She was. And Sam and Irene have cause to resent it."

"You don't say," commented Mr. Pilkington.

"She talked about the book sometimes, down at the bakery. She said the Doyles, McKinleys, and Andersons would be embarrassed when the book came out."

"Interesting. Well, I already know how you feel about the Doyles and the McKinleys," said Willa. "How do you feel about the Andersons?"

He frowned in thought.

"I don't know them that well. I was at primary school with B.J. Anderson, their youngest kid. His parents are nice. She's a talker—comes in sometimes to try to bum the day-old pastries we can't sell. Their boat was out that night, which is suggestive. Strange night for everyone and their monkey to go fishing, don't you think?"

"I don't know what's normal and what's not in a harbor village like this," Willa said.

"It was rainy that evening, with a storm forecasted. Why were all these people so eager to get a little late-night fishing in?"

"It was the start of the wild ocean salmon season, right?"

"Yeah, and people do get a little nutso, but they could have waited a day or two for less choppy waters. Why did everyone go out that night?"

"Why was Mina out, if it comes to that?" Willa asked him, idly. She was surprised by the look in his eyes.

"I've been trying to figure that out myself," he said. "I'm not even sure why she owned a boat that nice. She only got into fishing very recently. Seemed like an odd purchase to me."

Willa stared at him and bit her lip.

"What are you saying?"

"I'm saying she may not have been fishing, that's all. I've been thinking about it since this morning, and I believe you're on to something. The Old

Girl may have been boarded from another boat. Maybe Mina went out on purpose that night for a rendezvous, somewhere private."

"Very private!"

"Exactly. And bad things went down," he said, and that flash of grief was back in his eyes. "Mina was one of the best women I ever knew, but boy did she make life hard for herself. I hate the idea that someone like Irene or Sam Doyle may have hurt her, but I don't think we can trust them implicitly—at least not yet."

"Indeed? I understood that Mr. and Mrs. Doyle initiated the murder squad," said Mr. Pilkington.

Murder Squad, Willa thought. *Now there's a good name.*

"Why would they draw attention to Mina's death if they were involved? Wouldn't it be safer to let things lie?"

"Maybe. But it might be an elaborate double-bluff. Mina was distraught in the days before her death, and now I know she was aware of her danger before she died. Can I see that letter again?"

Willa retrieved it from her purse.

"Yeah, see—right here. Her letter says not to trust anyone but me. She wouldn't have cared if Gary Poole or Harriet Snelling was out for her blood—she would have named them openly. But if the threat was coming from someone she knew and loved, like the Doyles..." he trailed off.

Or Jake Anderson, Willa added, silently. *Her loyal ex-law clerk.*

The thought made her sick.

What did she know of actual good in Jake's favor? Nothing but the fact that the dogs liked him. And what was the recommendation of a trio of dachshunds worth? They weren't picky about who they licked, as far as she could tell, and might fall for anyone who carried bones in their pockets. The evidence against him was piling up. He had been out on the ocean that night. He had the power and position to suppress evidence. They had only his word that he was investigating the death at all.

"Any plans for tonight?" Brian was asking now, and she forced herself to pay attention. "If not, we could go out again—just the two of us."

"I'm afraid so," she told him, wishing she had never accepted Jake's invitation.

His face fell.

"B.J. Anderson invited us to come over for dinner. He included you in the invite, if you're game."

"Me?"

"You and Lucy. You don't have to come," she said, nervously. "He's investigating Mina's death—did you know that?"

"No," said Brian, startled. "I thought the Sheriff's department had closed the case."

"They have. He's looking into it on his own—or says he is."

"Interesting. On what grounds?"

"He thinks the accident was a little sussy."

"Should we invite him into the Minions?"

"I don't think so. I don't know what to make of him. Right now, *I'm* his prime suspect," she laughed. "As the heiress. I want to pump him for more details tonight. Might be a good opportunity to make headway on the case."

"What the heck!" said Brian. "If it means having dinner with you, I'd go to a party given by Jeffery Dahmer."

"I hope it won't be quite *that* dangerous," said Mr. Pilkington, dryly.

"Whatever happens, we'll deal with it together, right?" Brian said, grinning at him. "Forget the Minions. You, me, and Willa are Mina's private revenge team."

The old man smiled back at him with approval.

"Mina was always up for a little revenge."

"It's settled, then."

"Go team!" said Willa, suddenly feeling happier than she'd been in a very long time.

Mail

To Craig Lattner

Dad,

Yes, there was a break-in at Mina's house yesterday. Remind me to smack Wendy over the head with a two-by-four because I told her not to tell you guys. I don't know why I bother. Things have a way of making it through the family grapevine no matter what I do.

Rest assured, I am fine. The broken window's been boarded up, so everything is safe from the elements for now. I've contacted a security company—you'll be glad to know the whole system will be set up by the end of the week. I'm paying out the wazoo for it since the house isn't set up for modern electronics, but I've got the money and I know we'll both sleep better at night if there are more than windows and one-hundred-year-old locks between me and the rest of the world.

Nothing but my phone was taken. The police are convinced it was just a little local hazing. They're probably right. I'm sleeping next door with Mina's neighbor, who's got all of Mina's spunk and none of her spicy language or backtalk.

Do you know if Mina had a literary agent, by the way? She and her neighbor were writing a book, and we can't find the manuscript or her notes. I'm wondering whether she sent it to a publisher or an agent already for proofing. Could you ask Grandpa if she said anything to him?

Before I forget, I'm seeing what I can only describe as CHEWING marks on the baseboards in my bedroom. Termites? Carpenter ants?

Please advise,

Willa

The Dinner

At five-thirty, after struggling for several hours to make Violet Valentine behave like a normal human being, Willa gave up. Today was not a good day for writing.

Every time she sat down to her computer, she'd been interrupted by a visitor or distracted by the dachshunds, whose favorite activity—other than sleeping—was tearing around the downstairs area, chasing each other and play-fighting. The "fights" always ended the same way, with Wags chewing one of Kyle's ears and Killer chewing the other. Kyle put up with this like a champ, though he sighed occasionally into his paws.

Willa had always assumed dogs were simple creatures who felt love, loyalty, anger, and nothing else. She was discovering now how ignorant she'd been. The boys were capable of complex thought, hidden motivations, and deep sadness. Kyle was certainly experiencing a state of genuine grief. What's more, Wags and Killer appeared aware of his sadness and did their best to cheer him up in the only way they knew how: romping, snuggling, and a whole lot of ear chewing.

Watching them snuggle down together now, Willa decided she didn't care what Jake said—she wasn't going to bring three dogs to his mom and dad's house without their express permission. She worried slightly about the possibility of the burglar's return but decided they'd be more comfortable in their own environment than shut up in Lucy's guest room for hours. It was bad enough that they had to sleep there.

She showered, taking more care than usual with her hair and makeup. Spaghetti and Taboo with strangers didn't make for the ideal second date, but she was going to make the most of it.

At six forty-five, she locked the house, leaving the dogs in the kitchen where they were most comfortable. She popped over to fetch Mr. Pilkington, who had gone to take a late tea with Lucy Garber.

"Good news," he said, rising from one of Lucy's flowered armchairs. "Ms. Garber has agreed to go with us!"

"I need to consult Linda Anderson about church matters anyway," said Lucy. "And it sounds like you're planning to do some investigating while you're there. Don't leave me out, that's all I ask! I don't want to miss even a minute of the fun!"

Fog was setting in, and the night was somewhat moist and chilly. They opted to drive into town rather than walking, since Mr. Pilkington's knee was acting up. Willa caught a glimpse of herself in the rearview mirror as she parked the car and groaned. Even the tiniest dose of salt air made her curls stand on end.

Thank goodness it isn't any shorter, she thought, trying to do a little last-minute repair before she exited the car. *Or I'd look exactly like Ronald McDonald.*

Willa helped Lucy and Mr. Pilkington out of the car and the three of them walked up the driveway to the Anderson's modest home, a ranch-style house on the southern end of town. The door opened before they were even halfway up the drive, and Linda Anderson came rushing out, hands outstretched.

"Come in, come in, come in," she gushed in one breath, and then went on without stopping, "and welcome to our home! Hello, Lucy. What a beautiful coat. Thank you for coming, Willa! Look how pretty your hair is—did you do it yourself? Tell me the truth, now: do you like spaghetti?"

Willa allowed herself to be herded into the house, tugging the hobbling old man along with her and trying to answer each question as accurately as possible without seeming too abrupt.

"Thank you—uh, no, I'm feeling good—thanks, yes, I do it myself—and I love spaghetti!"

"I am also quite fond of spaghetti," said Mr. Pilkington, kindly.

"Are you really? Oh no!" tutted Linda, who looked genuinely grief-stricken. "I decided not to make spaghetti last minute. I made meatloaf instead."

She watched them closely for signs of disappointment.

"Meatloaf is great," Willa said.

"I knew you'd love it!" Linda exclaimed, relieved. "B.J. says I make the best meatloaf this side of the Mississippi, but he just tells me what I want to hear."

"An affectionate son, then," said Lucy.

"Affection has nothing to do with it," said Jake, who appeared next to Willa and took her coat. "Good meatloaf is good meatloaf. I'd eat this meatloaf if it was made by Atilla the Hun."

Willa was arrested by the sight of a man sitting comfortably in an armchair in the living room. He rose when he saw her, and she felt a cold chill go up her spine.

"Do you know the Sheriff?" twittered Linda, leading Willa and the others further into the room. "Sit down, Lucy. This couch is very comfortable but so is that chair. It's got a firm cushion that's easy to rise from. And you're a nice height for the recliner if that's what you'd prefer, Willa. The footrest goes all the way up! Your nice friend Brian is in the kitchen with Bob, helping him toss a salad, but I'm sure he'll be out in a moment. Gary, have you met our guests?"

"I have," said Sheriff Poole, softly.

"Any luck with that tip line you were talking about?" Willa asked, brashly.

She perched herself on the edge of the couch. The recliner looked more comfortable, but the footrest did not lend itself to easy escapes. She was reserving the right to grab Mr. Pilkington and Lucy and flee if this encounter became too awkward. Brian could fend for himself.

"Perhaps," he said, coldly.

"Anything of use?"

"We look into everything that comes our way, Ms. Lattner. Every new lead. Every new arrival."

They stared at each other for a few seconds. Bob and Brian came in at that moment, and the conversation turned to the more mundane.

Willa was not sorry to discontinue her verbal game of chess with the Sheriff. She was beginning to think her aunt had underestimated the man.

It was a miscalculation Mina may well have died from.

Linda's meatloaf was remarkable, though Willa had not expected anything less from a woman who made such amazing cookies. When they finished eating, Linda and Lucy bustled away with the empty dishes, leaving the five remaining people to entertain themselves. Bob, Brian, and Gary began talking local shop, while Jake spoke politely to Mr. Pilkington about some of their mutual acquaintances in the Bay Area. Willa was beginning to feel rather out of it when she realized that Sheriff Poole's last remark was directed at her.

"What was that?" she said, embarrassed to admit she hadn't been listening.

"I was asking whether you had any previous experience running a bakery," he said, smiling at her in a ghastly way.

"None whatsoever," she said, smiling right back at him. "So it's a good thing I've got Brian. Is that why you want the financial reports from The Three Hounds? To see if we're running a tight ship?"

Mr. Pilkington grabbed his cane under the table and poked Willa's foot with it. She shot him an apologetic look.

"Interesting choice of words," Gary replied. "I'm curious why your aunt got into the pastry game, that's all. I thought perhaps it was a family profession."

"My brother-in-law is a pastry chef, but Mina never met him. Whose idea was it to go the donuts route, Brian?"

"Oh, Mina's—definitely. I was just along for the ride."

"And what made her think she could turn a profit selling bear claws and krullers to the local Sunday Schools?" asked the Sheriff.

"Market research," said Brian, calmly.

Willa noticed that Gary was folding his napkin into fourths, just as he had done the night before. The movement unsettled her, but she could not look away.

"I've researched the donut market myself," he said. "The margins are very thin. You must do a brisk trade in wedding cakes to break even."

"We do, though it was a tough sell at first. I kept telling Mina we would never make it big with a dozen jelly donuts here or there. She insisted we were doing well enough! We supply every church in town on Sunday morning, and Doyle's has a standing order for the donut holes they sell in the bakery department. Plus we cater every Boy Scout, Elks Club, and elementary school function from here to Trinidad. But she wasn't seeing the bigger picture. I finally convinced her to let me give cakes a try and that's when we brought Heidi in."

"Heidi Forrester," mused the Sheriff. "She's a transplant to the area, is she not?"

"She's the reason our wedding cakes are famous," Brian replied. "And one of the best decorators on the West Coast. Any other questions, Sheriff? Keep 'em coming."

"Gladly. What was Mina doing with the extra cash she made from your famous wedding cakes?"

"Investing it back into the business."

"I see. So you started making cakes so you could make more money so you could make more cakes—is that it?"

"That's how most businesses run," said Brian, shrugging.

"Your business is not like most business though, is it?"

"What's that supposed to mean?" asked Willa.

"Gary," pleaded Jake. "Come on. Let up."

"We're done discussing Mina Lattner and her business this evening," said Mr. Pilkington, firmly.

Bob Anderson cleared his throat.

"I hope you're planning to attend the crab festival, Willa," he said, making a nervous attempt to turn the conversation. "Mr. Pilkington, you should come up for it as well. I don't know if you've ever had fresh Dungeness crab, but you can't beat it."

"Mina Lattner must have been fond of crab," said the Sheriff.

"Why do you say that?" asked Willa, unable to tear her eyes away from his hands as they folded and unfolded Linda Anderson's nice linen napkin.

"She was always going out on that boat of hers. That's how she died, isn't it?"

"You tell me," Willa said. "How do *you* think she died? What do you think killed her, Sheriff Poole?"

"I asked first," he said.

They glared at each other, both breathing hard.

"Who's for dessert?" Linda cried, emerging from the kitchen with a large tray of cookies, followed by Lucy, holding a pot of steaming coffee. "I forgot to mention that I invited Ian and Patricia over for dessert and games."

"You didn't tell me Uncle Ian was coming," Jake said, his brows beetling. "That's kind of a large crowd, Mom."

"*Uncle* Ian?" said Willa, incredulously.

"Ian's my brother," said Linda, passing the tray of cookies. "I was a McKinley before I was an Anderson! We're shockingly inbred here in Humboldt Cove."

"That's a peculiar way of putting it," Lucy laughed.

Willa blindly took a cookie off the platter.

"So you grew up in my house?" she said.

"I sure did. And I can't say how happy I am that it's got such a wonderful owner! We loved Mina, and now we love you!"

Willa glanced at Mr. Pilkington and saw he was just as startled as she was. The Andersons now had a double motive for suppressing Mina's book, and as a half-McKinley, half-Anderson, Jake was rising to the top of the suspect list. Eating her cookie in a daze, her eyes wandered down the table to Gary Poole, who stopped folding his napkin when he caught her eye.

Instead, he crushed it into his fist, staring at Willa all the while.

The Dessert

T he doorbell rang, and Linda hustled out of the dining room, reappearing in a minute with Ian and Patricia McKinley.

"Do you two know our latest resident?" she cried out gayly, taking her sister-in-law's coat. "This is Mina Lattner's niece."

"Everybody in town knows her now," said Patricia. "After that wonderful little self-introduction at the meeting last night. Hello, again, Wilma."

"Willa," Jake corrected.

"We paid Wilma a welcome visit upon her arrival in town," said Ian, smoothly.

"How nice!" said Linda. "I haven't been inside that house for years. Mina told me I was welcome to come over and snoop around, but I never got a chance. I'd love to see it again. How's it looking, Ian?"

"Pink," said Ian, briefly.

"It was an awful shade of mint green when we were growing up," Linda confided.

"It was tasteful."

"It looked like a *booger*. And peeling all over! I was thrilled when Mina cleaned it up, and so was Mom."

"Mom was heartbroken."

"Mom was relieved to be rid of that white elephant—no offense, Willa, it's lovely now."

"I bet the neighbors don't feel that way," he said snidely. "How does it feel to live next to a hot pink house, Lucy?"

"There are worse things," said Lucy, pointedly.

Ian turned to Willa, with the pretense of politeness.

"How has your stay in Humboldt Cove been thus far, Wilma? I trust you're pleased with the town?"

"It's *Willa*. And I'm very pleased with what I've seen so far," said Willa.

"Your aunt liked it here."

"I believe she did."

"Enough to consider writing a book about the entire area."

"So I hear."

"It's a pity she didn't live to publish. The book was chock-full of interesting facts about this region—and my family. The McKinley forbears were shipping giants. We built up the wealth of Northern California almost single-handedly."

"That's a bit much, Ian," said Linda, uneasily. "All that is said and done now."

"You're in rare company tonight, Wilm—er, Willa. My great-great-grandfather founded the town, and Lucy's illustrious ancestor preserved the nearby redwood forests. He even discovered a rare butterfly, if I'm not mistaken."

"The Northern Bluestripe," said Lucy.

"Seeing a Bluestripe is on my list of things to do before I die," said Brian. "Lucy claims she's seen one but I don't believe her."

"I have so!" said Lucy, playfully. "Brian's been teasing me about that for at least fifteen years."

"Humboldt Cove has the best collection of rare butterflies in the western states, I believe. We boast a rich and fascinating history. Too bad Mina died before she could finish her book," said Ian, blandly. " I would have been so interested to read it."

"You may get that chance yet," said Willa, just as blandly. "I intend to finish it for her and find a publisher."

Ian blenched, and Patricia, who had been staring down at her french-tipped nails, looked up, astonished.

"Good for you," said Bob. "Linda and I will be first in line to buy a copy."

"Are you serious?" choked Patricia. "You really mean to finish it—and—and *publish* it?"

"Sure! I'm a half-decent writer."

"But you can't! You can't *do* that to us!" Patricia protested. "You don't know what was *in* that book."

"Sure I do. Interesting facts about the region."

"No, no, it's all lies about the McKinleys and Andersons—slander and libel."

"Quiet, Patricia," Ian hissed.

"What kind of lies?" Willa asked her, politely.

Bob whistled.

"Hoo-ee, I bet there are some stinkers in there about old Henry Anderson. I hadn't heard the McKinley dirt, though. What is it, Linda?" he asked, chuckling.

But Linda had gone into the kitchen for more coffee—though Willa thought that was probably just an excuse to get away. Patricia threw down her napkin and glared at her brother-in-law.

"You don't know what kinds of nasty things that woman was planning to say about—"

"Enough," said Ian, grabbing his wife's arm and squeezing it until she yelped with pain.

There was a long silence, during which even Bob seemed uncomfortable.

"I'm sure Ms. Lattner and her lawyer are very familiar with libel laws," said Gary Poole. "Aren't you, Ms. Lattner?"

"How about those 'Niners?" said Bob, desperately, and everyone began to make feverish chit-chat about San Fransisco's chances that year.

It was the first, last, and only time that Willa was happy to talk about football.

The rest of the evening was relatively calm. During dessert, Sheriff Poole talked only to Ian and Patricia McKinley. All three of them left as soon as the coffee cups were cleared.

Willa felt an almost palpable weight lift from her chest the moment they shut the door.

"Well!" said Linda, unconsciously echoing Willa's sentiments, "that's that, then."

"You should have told me Uncle Ian and Aunt Patricia were coming over," Jake groaned. "I wouldn't have subjected anyone else to it."

"They're harmless," said Linda, pooh-poohing him. "A bit stuffy, maybe, but oh well! Our guests didn't mind a bit."

She stared at Mr. Pilkington, who murmured something indistinct.

"How do you like the Sheriff?" she asked him, point-blank. "We love Gary to death, even if he is a little odd sometimes. He's been so good to B.J.—opened a lot of doors for him."

"What a character," said Bob, tolerantly. "Poor old Gary. We invite him over here about once a week, just to get him out of the house."

"He has a very distinct communication style," said Willa, trying to smile. "I almost felt like I was being interrogated."

"He's usually not that persistent," said Jake.

"Oddest thing I've seen in a while," his father agreed. "You missed it, Linda. The man was grilling poor Willa over the coals. And about nothing in particular. Donuts at first. And then boats, of all things! Talk about discussing rope in the house of the hanged! It's like he forgot how Mina—well, never mind. I'm sorry we put you in for that."

"I've had worse dinner conversations."

Not many though, Willa thought. The night hadn't yielded much actionable information, either. It would be a total waste if she didn't do something about it.

"Speaking of Mina," she said, taking a deep breath, "and her death, I hear you had your boat out that night as well."

"We sure did. We didn't know Mina was in danger, or we could've saved her. Biggest regret of my life."

"I say a grateful prayer every day that my boys came home in one piece," Linda said, fervently.

"We were in no danger," said Jake, with a hint of impatience.

"It's the Lord's mercy you two weren't dashed against the rocks and smashed to bits as well."

"Linda!" said Lucy, horrified. "For heaven's sake."

Linda realized what she had said a second too late, and her eyes welled up with tears of distress. It was clear she had a very tender heart.

"I blame myself," she sniffed. "I saw her only a day or two before the accident, and I had a *premonition*. I really did. I should have said something to her about it."

"You didn't tell me that," Jake said, running his hands through his hair until it stood on end. "Mom, I've been trying to trace all her movements that week. What time did you see her, and where?"

"How about a please, B.J.?"

"Please!"

"At the Humboldt Cove Patisserie," Linda replied, started by his intensity. "Don't get me wrong, the Three Hounds is *amazing*. Such flaky pastry—I'm in awe of you, Brian!"

"Thanks," said Brian, smiling kindly at her.

"Everything has real butter and high-quality chocolate all the way from Belgium! But it's a little spendy for everyday items. No offense."

"None taken! We use premium ingredients and charge premium prices."

"Exactly. So when I'm looking for basic bread rolls or *regular* donuts I'm still in the habit of going to Harriet's."

"Everything is cheaper there," Lucy concurred. "Though sometimes she forgets to take the labels off and it still says Safeway or Ralph's."

"Ah, but it's easier to get it from her than to drive all the way up to Arcata for it!" said Linda, and Lucy nodded in agreement.

"*When*, Ma? When were you at Harriet's?"

"It must have been right around seven-forty-five on the 25th. Or was it the 26th? The Patisserie closes at eight sharp, and I remember that I slipped in just in time, and Harriet was *not* happy. She closes early whenever she can get away with it."

"Not the best way to run a business in my opinion," said Lucy.

"I know, but it's *pointless* talking to her about it. Once, I hinted that the donuts were a bit stale, and she—"

"Ma!" cried Jake. "Focus up! What was Mina doing in Harriet's place? They did not get along, and there's no way Mina was trying to bum a few discounted pastries."

"Well, neither was I! I wouldn't *bum* anything," Linda said, austerely. "Whatever that means."

Brian winked at Willa across the table.

"I was hoping she would give me a deal on the cherry danish I saw in the window because I knew for a fact they were at least two days old. I was hosting Bible Study, and Doyle's didn't have a *thing* I could use except for Oreos and those fruit pies that come in the little green packages. You know, the ones with the goo inside that always make you feel pre-diabetic. Have you had those, Mr. Pilkington?"

"I'm partial to them myself," he admitted. "But they are quite sweet."

"I didn't want to serve Pastor Green goo-pies or sandwich cookies right out of the package…"

At this point, while she did not actually stop talking, she was forced to take a breath and the rest of the sentence became rather airy.

"…because she's so bougie—isn't that what the kids say? Everything's from the Pottery Barn catalog and she doesn't get her toilet paper from the Dollar General, you know? When she hosts, we usually have fancy things, either from the Three Hounds or that bakery down in Eureka."

"I know what you mean," said Lucy. "Hoity-toity. What's wrong with a little plain baking?"

"It's always some kind of fancy finger food. Sometimes she gets those frozen mini quiches from Costco and throws them in the oven after we get there..."

Linda became winded from trying to talk and breathe at the same time and was forced to pause.

"Hon," said Bob. "Try to stick to the point."

"The point? The point! Yes, well, Mina and Harriet were deep in conversation when I came in, and I was forced to interrupt them to ask about the pastries. I must have looked like an easy mark because the price Harriet quoted was twenty-five cents higher than what was actually printed on the package, if you can believe it! I pointed that out, and Mina laughed and told Harriet—well, I won't repeat it. But it was pretty rude."

"Rude how, Ma?"

"She implied that Harriet was scamming her customers. Harriet hit back right away and said if *she* was Mina, she wouldn't be so high and mighty about scams, and asked her if she'd had any conversations lately with the Sheriff."

"What did you think Harriet meant by it?" Willa asked, slowly.

Linda opened her eyes very wide.

"Nothing! Harriet is famously spiteful."

"She resents Mina for encroaching on her territory," Lucy explained.

"It's a free country, isn't it? Mina and Brian have brought a little class to the downtown section, which hasn't been nice since about the 60s, let's face it. Once the bakery went in, we got a bookstore there too."

"And Nancy Reed moved her resale clothing shop onto that street instead of having it rotting down at the very bottom of 13th and K, where no one ever went," Lucy added, helpfully.

"Harriet probably gets more business now than she did before, so she's got no real reason to resent Mina except for spite."

"So you don't think Mina was scamming anyone?" Willa asked.

"Of course not," said Bob, with firmness. "Linda's right. Harriet's nuts."

Willa gave Jake a sidelong glance and caught an expression on his face that made her uneasy. Linda rose from her seat and beckoned to her husband.

"C'mon, hon," she said. "Let's leave these five to talk. It's time for dishes. You wash, I'll dry. No, Lucy—don't get up. You've already done enough. Bob's on KP this time. Then we'll all have a rousing game of Trivial Pursuit, maybe? Unless you prefer charades."

She looked expectantly at Willa, who would gladly have undergone a root canal rather than play either game.

"Charades," she said, picking the lesser of two evils.

"Charades it is!" said Linda happily, and led her husband away.

As soon as they were gone, Willa pounced on Jake.

"Okay, spill it. What was Mina into?"

He colored.

"What do you mean?"

Willa clenched her jaw.

"I'm not dumb. It's obvious that Mina got herself into trouble somehow. Your friend the Sheriff thinks I'm knee-deep in whatever it is, or he wouldn't hint about criminal activities at town functions and reenact the Spanish Inquisition at otherwise innocuous dinner parties. This afternoon you claimed you were showing all your cards, but you're still hiding something big. Tell us what's really going on."

Jake leaned back on the couch and groaned.

"I don't know. I think Mina had stumbled into something bad, but I can't pin it down. I can tell you there are no official investigations of Wilhelmina Lattner open in Klamath County," Jake told them.

"Meaning what?" asked Brian. "She was under investigation elsewhere?"

"Gary's been working with the sheriffs in Humboldt and Del Norte on some kind of smuggling case. It's all very hush-hush, and he hasn't completely read me in—but Mina's name *has* come up."

"So it is smuggling," said Mr. Pilkington, meditatively. "Cocaine?"

"I swear I don't know. I'm not trying to play you guys. Gary's aware of my previous connection to Mina, and he's keeping me in the dark. This part of the coast, though, it's almost always drugs. Coke or heroin."

Willa's jaw clenched tighter, and she could actually feel her heart pounding in her chest—an unpleasant sensation.

"My aunt was not a drug smuggler."

"You didn't know your aunt very well," Jake said, almost defiantly.

"I did, though," replied Mr. Pilkington.

"So did I," said Brian. "And I'd bet my life Mina Lattner had nothing to do with drugs."

"Listen to me, will you? Whatever is happening here is dangerous. If you know anything—if Mina said anything before she died, or you've found anything in her house that might help, you have to tell me."

"We don't have to do anything," said Willa, grabbing her purse. "C'mon, guys. We're out of here."

"Please don't leave," he begged. "I'm extremely worried about you. Let's just say it out loud, okay? Mina was murdered. You all know that, and I know that. I thought that's where it would end, but I don't need to remind you that someone broke into your house yesterday, Willa. They were looking for something specific. What is it?"

Willa sat down, adrenaline still pumping. Her anxiety was sky-high. She closed her eyes and saw an image of Sheriff Poole, crumpling his napkin. She threw caution to the wind. They'd never get anywhere without taking a few risks.

"We thought it was the book she was writing," she said, trying to keep the panic out of her voice. "The one on Klamath County history."

He stared at her.

"Why would someone want that?"

"You heard your aunt and uncle tonight. They were vehemently against its publication. And you seemed pretty interested in finding it yourself," she retorted.

"Well, sure. I was helping her with it," he said, surprised. "With the edits. I wanted to make sure it got published. She was very proud of that thing."

Willa was close to tears, now. She felt muddled and scared and very, very full of meatloaf.

"Lucy didn't tell us you were involved."

"I didn't know myself," said Lucy, giving Jake a hard look.

He smiled, suddenly.

"Mina was having me polish it up before she showed it to you, Ms. Garber. Between you, me, and the walls, the book is terrible," he confided.

"Lucy said it was good," Willa stated. "Didn't you Lucy?"

"I haven't read it yet," the older woman admitted, with reluctance. "We outlined it together, but Mina wanted to write it herself."

"Mina was a brilliant lawyer and a clever politician but she couldn't write to save her life. When I clerked for her, I prepared all her written material. She gave me the raw manuscript about six weeks ago. It's the worst thing I've ever read. She couldn't spell, she didn't know how to use commas, and the thing was so boring I fell asleep on page three."

"I don't understand," Willa replied, perplexed. The meatloaf was sitting like a brick in her stomach. "You said it was chock-full of scandals, Lucy."

"It is!"

Jake shrugged.

"I never got that far. I was about a quarter of the way through when Mina asked for it back."

"Did she say why?"

"She told me she'd stumbled across more documents and wanted to revise one of the chapters. That was the last time I saw it."

Linda and Bob came out of the kitchen just then and they were forced to end their conversation. Upon reflection, Willa was not sorry. She feared they had been indiscreet enough with Jake already.

The evening wrapped up after they had played three excruciating rounds of charades and eaten about two dozen cookies, all told.

Linda sent them home with a dozen *more* cookies, and Willa left the dinner party feeling like she had a little too much to chew on.

The Deal

Brian had walked to dinner, but he accepted a ride home from Willa as it was raining fairly hard. The four of them drove back to Lucy's street in silence. Willa's mind and stomach were both significantly upset. She parked the car, turned off the engine, and sat in the dark.

"I don't know what to think anymore," she told the others.

"Nor do I," confessed Mr. Pilkington. "Smuggling rings and family scandals—books, letters, and threats. I can't make sense of any of it."

"At least we have an explanation now for why Jake is so interested in that book."

"We have an explanation, yes. But perhaps not *the* explanation. And you certainly revealed our line of thinking to him."

"It was a calculated risk."

"I never heard Mina was enlisting an editor," said Lucy. "She would have told me."

"I don't trust that guy," said Brian, grimly. "And I don't trust his relations either. No one is as ditzy as his mom seems. That whole family is dodgy."

"We cannot wait any longer," said Mr. Pilkington, with finality. "We *must* go to the police. Not here, perhaps, in Klamath County. But we could seek advice in Eureka."

"You said you'd give it until Friday."

"That was before I knew this might involve more than a personal grudge! If we are dealing with the smuggling and sale of cocaine, then I want out, and quickly. We are liable to get ourselves killed."

"Mina wasn't smuggling cocaine," said Brian, confidently. "The Sheriff is out of his mind if that's what he thinks."

"Of course she wasn't! But this seems to revolve around the bakery, somehow."

"It doesn't, though," he said. "It can't. It has to be something else. Jake—B.J.—whatever his name is, is trying to pull the wool over our eyes. Classic misdirection. He and Sheriff Poole want to keep our attention off the book."

"I agree!" said Lucy.

"Why would the Sheriff care about the book?" Willa asked, wearily. "None of this makes sense!"

"Hang on—what if the bakery stuff is a red herring to keep the *Sheriff* busy chasing imaginary smugglers until the Andersons and McKinleys can find the book?"

"I suppose that would explain it," Willa said, after a pause. "But—Jake says Mina was his friend. He seemed worried about us tonight. Genuinely worried. And call me crazy, but I kind of believe him."

"Talk is cheap," said Brian, cynically.

"It's a great mistake to believe what people say about themselves without independent verification," said Lucy.

"I concur. Mina is dead," said Mr. Pilkington. "She saw the danger coming and could not avoid it, which means her judgment of good and evil was critically flawed. Maybe she was his friend. And maybe he killed her anyway."

"That's horrible, Pilky."

"Life is horrible, sometimes. My best guess is that neither Sheriff Poole nor Jake Anderson are trustworthy. It's frighteningly easy for law enforcement to go bad, my dear. I want nothing more to do with this."

"Let's sleep on it," she said. "Please, Pilky? For Mina?"

"My greatest service to Mina would be preserving the health and safety of her niece," he replied.

"For me, then."

He stared straight out the windshield. It was beginning to fog over with condensation, as were Willa's glasses. The rain was pouring down, now.

"For you," he relented, finally. "But only for one more day. Do you hear? If we have made no progress by this time tomorrow, I'm talking to the police."

"Thank you."

He fixed her with a beady eye and a stern face.

"I'm serious, Willa. Twenty-four hours, and no more. Deal?"

"Deal."

"Sounds reasonable to me," said Brian. "One day and then straight to the police."

"Do not pass Go," Willa agreed, solemnly. "Do not collect two hundred."

They agreed to make the most of the next twenty-four hours, and Willa suggested they start the next day off by talking to Harriet Snelling.

"I want to know what she was hinting at that night in the Patisserie," she said. "And I want to know why she went out fishing with her brother-in-law."

"I wish I could go with you," Lucy said, regretfully. "I will be down at the town museum tomorrow, giving my normal weekday class on butterfly conservation."

"Pilky and I will pop in and try to catch the end of it," Willa promised. "I want to talk to a few other people from town—ask if anyone can remember seeing Mina before she got to The Three Hounds the night she died. But right now I think we'd better call it a night. It's freezing cold out here!"

Lucy slipped out of the car and hurried away. Brian kissed Willa goodnight and ran down the street toward his house in the driving rain, while Mr. Pilkington and Willa made a beeline for Mina's front door. The dogs went nuts when they were released from their crates, and between Wags' antics, Killer's attempts to convince them he hadn't already eaten two dinners, and Kyle's heartbreaking little tail wag, Willa decided she couldn't face taking them back to the cold little guest room next door.

"I'm going to risk sleeping in my own bed tonight. But you can go to Lucy's if you'd rather," she told Mr. Pilkington.

"No thank you. Whither thou goest, I will go, and whither thou lodgest, I will lodge," he replied.

"What's with the wedding vows? We're not getting married, Pilky."

"That part of the Bible is always misinterpreted," he lectured her. "It is not about romantic love. It is about friendship."

"I'll take your word for it."

"The long and short of it is, you're stuck with me. But don't worry. You're safe from my advances. Apart from the hair, you're not my type, anyway," he said, winking at her as he climbed the stairs.

Willa popped over to Lucy's to inform her they'd be sleeping at home that night after all. Lucy protested, but Willa overrode her, promising they'd call or come over at the first sign of trouble.

"No one's going to break in again," she said, as much to herself as to Lucy. "They wouldn't dare. And if they do, I feel sorry for them, that's all. I'm sleeping with three watchdogs, a butcher knife, and a canister of bear repellent."

She wished Lucy pleasant dreams and slipped out through the gate to the kitchen door, wishing she did have a can of mace or pepper spray. She grabbed the biggest knife in Mina's knife block, so as not to give the lie to her entire statement, and decided she actually would sleep with the dogs.

They'd bark, at least, if someone came in.

Donning her pajamas and robe and making herself a cup of chamomile tea—which she hoped would settle her stomach—she sat down at her computer again, determined to force Violet Valentine into submission.

Instead, she found a belated email from her brother-in-law, Guillermo, who had finally looked at the reports she sent over from The Three Hounds.

Happiness at finally hearing back from him swiftly turned to incredulity and fear, and she ended the evening by bursting into tears.

Mail

To Guillermo Santini

G,

When I hadn't heard from you in a few days, I got the bright idea to look in my spam folder and there you were! Sorry about that.

I don't know what algorithm dictates that some emails are innocent and others are suspicious, but it's clear it doesn't work very well. I found an email from Aunt Jean in here too, AND a coupon I really wanted, whereas my inbox contains nothing but ads and daily recipes from baking blogs I definitely did not subscribe to.

Your message has initiated a full-on panic attack and I want to talk to you in person about it. I don't have my new phone yet so maybe we could do a Zoom call?

I don't understand what you mean when you say the Three Hounds COGS are wrong. Maybe you got too excited, and forgot your English? That's a joke, of course. Your English is better than mine.

I looked up the acronym and came up with cost of goods sold, complete online gaming system, computer-oriented geological society, certificate of good standing, and something called the Central Ohio Ghost Squad.

WHAT ARE YOU TALKING ABOUT?

How could something be wrong? The business is making so much money. I checked all the numbers against the bank accounts and everything is accounted for, so it's not like someone is embezzling.

Please write back.

Willa

The Reports

At six AM, Willa awoke—stiff, exhausted, and emotionally frail. She fed the dogs, all three of whom had kept vigil with her during a sleepless night, and sat down to read Guillermo's email once more.

He kept using the same acronym: COGS. The COGS were off. He'd never seen COGS like that. She should certainly ask her partner about the discrepancy—likely a computer error—but curious, all the same. She should investigate the issue without delay.

As she re-read the email for the seventh time, Willa found herself out of temper with her brother-in-law. Why couldn't he say what he meant, in plain English? What was so "curious" about it all?

Guillermo never exaggerated, and he never cried wolf. The fact that he had encouraged her to look into it at all—let alone 'without delay'—spoke volumes.

Either Mina had been into something shady, and Brian didn't know about it, or Mina had been into something shady and Brian was up to his neck in it as well. Both scenarios were terrifying, and Willa nearly decided to pack her bags at once and get out of town before anything else went wrong.

As she was contemplating a hasty retreat, Kyle jumped onto her lap and commanded her attention. He looked into her eyes, woofed gently one time, and licked her cheek.

Don't go, was written on his face, plain as day.

Killer and Wags stopped play-fighting near her feet and looked up at her with the same, doggy intensity.

Stay with us, they seemed to say.

"You guys like me, huh?" she said, a lump in her throat. "That's great, but things are getting rough here, fellas. What am I supposed to *do*? What would Mina want me to do?"

Killer and Wags resumed their circle-running, and Kyle jumped into the fray now. They had said their piece.

It was up to her to figure it out.

"What are COGS?" she asked Mr. Pilkington, once he finally shuffled into the kitchen that morning in his robe and slippers.

He stared at her.

"You mean, like, the gears inside a machine?"

"No. The acronym, C-O-G-S."

"Oh, that," he said, his face clearing. "Cost of goods sold."

"Dang."

"You heard from your sister's husband, I take it?"

"Yes. He said the reports are 'off.'"

"How so?"

"He got very Italian and vague about it all," Willa said, grumpily. "I'm waiting to hear back from him."

Mr. Pilkington gazed at her with worried eyes.

"Willa, this is bad. Perhaps the Sheriff is onto something! And perhaps we should be more cautious with Brian Harrison."

"Mina was right about her accidents," she told the old man. "She was right about you. So she's right about Brian. I trust him."

"Be careful, Willa."

"I'm always careful."

"We must show him the email from your brother-in-law and ask him to explain."

"Very good idea. I was just heading that way, actually. It's time to hold Harriet Snelling's feet over the fire."

"Let me get dressed," he yawned, rubbing the top of his head where his hair was thinning.

"You look exhausted. Maybe you should stay in this morning."

"Nothing doing! We're taking equal shares in this investigation. And besides," he said, with dignity, "it's my duty to keep you safe."

Touched, Willa replied, "I appreciate the thought, but I can take care of myself. If something bad does happen, no one would possibly blame *you*."

"Au contraire. Mina Lattner would. And I'm far more scared of her than I am of you."

"No one's going to hurt me while I'm walking through downtown Humboldt Cove, Pilky! Stay here with the dogs—get some rest. I'll collect you later and we can catch Lucy's butterfly talk at the museum."

"I'm coming with you whether you like it or not. Though—ahem—I don't suppose you have a pair of tennis shoes I could borrow? My nice leather loafers are beginning to pinch—and I have noticed that our feet are about the same size."

"That's the rudest request anyone's ever made of me," Willa said, laughing.

"The truth hurts, my dear."

They set out from Mina's house around eight-thirty, leaving the dogs at home. Willa wasn't about to try taking them into the Humboldt Cove Patisserie again. Harriet might have a shotgun this time.

It was a chilly morning, and they were glad to reach the warmth of The Three Hounds, which smelled of butter and chocolate.

The bakery was empty of customers for the time being. Heidi looked up briefly from the cake she was decorating and nodded. Willa and Mr. Pilkington moved that direction, watching with fascination as she piped delicate, black and orange butterflies onto immaculate white fondant.

"That's stunning," Willa said, impressed despite herself.

"Remarkable!" added Mr. Pilkington. "Such dainty work."

Heidi peered through her long, dark bangs as if unsure what to make of them. She mumbled out a thank you and returned to her decorating.

"You have a real talent for this. Do you handle all the decoration?"

"Yeah. Brian bakes, and I decorate. He relies on me absolutely for that," she said, scowling down at the butterfly she was currently piping. "Our clients pay a lot of money for our cakes."

She said the words proudly, almost proprietarily. Willa got the message, loud and clear. They were Heidi and Brian's clients, and Heidi and Brian's cakes. This was Heidi and Brian's bakery, in other words. Hands off.

"Do you two need something?" Heidi said, with a return to brusqueness. "Because I have a lot of work to do."

"Two pain au chocolate and two coffees, to go."

Heidi pulled a couple of chocolate croissants from the pastry case. She bagged them up, handed them to Willa, and returned to her piping.

Willa bit into the croissant with enthusiasm, inadvertently squirting molten chocolate onto her nose. She grabbed a napkin to wipe it up, noting that Mr. Pilkington was nibbling his more cautiously to avoid the same mistake.

"You missed a spot on your right cheek," he whispered.

Willa scrubbed her face, grateful that Heidi had not witnessed the chocolate debacle.

"Do you mind if we ask you a few questions while we wait for Brian? It won't take long."

"I'm pretty busy," said Heidi, without looking up.

"I'm curious how well you knew my aunt."

"Mina hired me, if that's what you're asking."

"Did you know her before that?"

"No."

"Did you see her on the day she died?"

"What?"

"Brian said Mina was here that night—right before she went out on her boat. Were you there? Did you talk to her?"

Heidi's fingers fumbled, and the careful black outline she was piping around the largest butterfly shot out onto the pristine white fondant below.

"Look what you made me do! I'm going to have to wrap this again," Heidi said, hysterically. "And I'm already an hour behind. Will you just leave me *alone*?"

"Goodness me!" said Mr. Pilkington.

"I'm so sorry!" Willa said, truly repentant. "How can I help?"

"Shut up," Heidi hissed. "Just shut up and leave. Both of you."

Willa put her hands on her hips, fed up.

"Look, it's obvious you don't like me, Heidi, but if you can't deal with me in a respectful way, you should reconsider your employment here."

Heidi turned away, in silence.

"You owe it to me to be at least civil. All I'm asking about is the night Mina died. It's a simple question. Did you see her or not?"

"I don't want to talk about it."

"Why not?" demanded Mr. Pilkington.

"Leave, *please*," the girl began, her voice shaking.

Brian walked out of the back, and she snapped her mouth shut.

"What's going on?" he asked, cheerfully.

"Just having a friendly chat," said Willa. "I'm afraid I distracted Heidi and made her flub the decoration on this cake."

"Aw, it's alright," Brian told Heidi, after examining the marred fondant. "This is the smallest tier. We can rewrap it in no time, and it won't take long to pipe the rest of the butterflies. After that, is it ready to go?"

"Everything's ready," the girl said, staring at the floor.

"Because we need to get this on the road by six tonight, remember?"

"I remember."

"Hey," said Brian, turning to greet Willa.

He put his arm around her waist and gave her a quick peck on the cheek. Heidi burst into tears and hurried into the back of the bakery.

"What's with her?" he asked, bewildered.

"She doesn't like me."

"Sure she does!" said Brian, with all the confidence of the unobservant male. "What's not to like?"

"Plenty," Willa said, frankly. "She just told us to shut up and ship out."

"What do you mean?"

"She flinched when I brought up the day Mina died. She knows what happened—I'm positive. And it turns out the reports *are* off," Willa said, point blank.

Brian stared at her, dumbfounded.

"We went over this last night, Willa. Gary Poole is crazy."

"He may be shrewder than we think! I showed some of The Three Hounds reports to my brother-in-law, the pastry chef. He thinks there's something strange going on."

His eyes grew wide.

"Strange how?"

"I don't know," Willa admitted. "He hasn't been explicit yet. I'm waiting for a call from him."

"We wanted to give you a chance to explain," said Mr. Pilkington, stiffly.

"To be honest, Heidi takes care of all the reporting and ordering," he said, wringing his hands. "I'm not a detail guy. This is weird, guys. I don't know what to think."

"Just how well do you know Heidi?" Willa asked, in a low voice.

"I work with her every day."

"Do you trust her?"

"Hush," said Mr. Pilkington, making a little waving movement with his hand. "We don't want her to hear us."

Brian led them outside, and they stood on the pavement in front of the bakery.

"Of course I trust her," he said. "I've known her forever—since pastry school. Like I told Gary last night, she's the best decorator up and down the coast, and she came very highly recommended—brought a bunch of clients with her, too. High-rollers, who could afford to pay for big cakes. She really helped us to start thinking big."

"Maybe the Sheriff isn't looking into the bakery. Maybe he's really looking at Heidi, and her 'high-roller' clients. Did you ever think of that?"

"Not until now," he said, disturbed. "Look, Willa—she can't be stealing from us, if that's what you think. All the money is there."

"My brother-in-law says the COGS report is off. What is that, exactly?"

Brian scratched his head.

"It's just basic food service stuff, Willa. How much we spent on raw ingredients, how much we brought in from sales."

"How could that be off?"

"I don't know," he said, with determination. "But I'm going to find out. If Heidi has been doing something shady with my bakery, she's going to regret it. I'll dig into those reports as soon as I get back. Speaking of which, it looks like Harriet's in," he said, pointing across the street. "Are we ready? How should we play this? Good cop, bad cop?"

"No games," said Mr. Pilkington, with firmness. "We shall tackle it in a straightforward manner. Let me lead the way."

"Suit yourself, Mr. P.," Brian responded, grinning. "But I'd watch your back."

They crossed the road and entered the patisserie, where Harriet Snelling was pricing items in the front window.

"What do you want?" she snapped, as soon as they entered.

"Right down to business, I see," said Mr. Pilkington. "I admire that. What we want, dear lady, is information."

"I only sell cakes and bread."

"Allow me to introduce myself, since I did not have the opportunity last time we visited your delightful establishment. My name is Daniel Pilkington, and I am an attorney."

Harriet's eyes grew wary, and her tone became a shade more respectful.

"What do you want to know?"

"We are looking into the circumstances of Mina Lattner's death. I understand she visited your shop a day or two before she died."

"So?"

"Your conversation was overheard. You accused my former client of participating in a scam."

"Again, so?"

"I would like to know what you meant by it."

"No comment. Ask Sheriff Poole, if you're interested. That's all I'm going to say about it."

Mr. Pilkington gazed at her, hesitated for a moment, and then drew out his wallet.

"These cakes look very tasty," he said, removing a hundred-dollar bill.

He held the note out to her. After a moment's hesitation, she snatched it.

"Gary was having me watch the front entrance to the Hounds," she mumbled.

"Why?" asked Brian, astonished.

"He didn't say. Just had me write down everyone who went in and out. I kept a log for him."

"May I see it?" said Mr. Pilkington, holding out another hundred.

Harriet took the bill and walked behind the counter. She tossed a little notebook at him.

"Keep it," she said. "Sheriff's already seen this one."

"Thank you, Ms. Snelling. You've been most helpful."

"Anything else?" she said, looking hopefully at his wallet.

The patisserie must really be struggling, Willa thought, guiltily.

"Just one more thing. Why did you go out fishing with your brother-in-law the evening of May the seventh?" asked Mr. Pilkington.

She drew in a sharp breath.

"What do you mean?!"

"It's a simple question."

"Out!" she shrieked, pointing to the door. "I'm done talking."

Mr. Pilkington reached into his wallet again, but she picked up a broom and virtually shoved them out the door with it.

"No more questions," she said. "And don't come back!"

She slammed the door and locked it behind her.

"Well, well," said Mr. Pilkington, still clutching the little black book. "Now we're getting somewhere!"

The trio moved down the street toward the small town museum, walking and talking rapidly.

"So the Sheriff *is* investigating the bakery!" said Willa, excitedly.

"So she says. And she was willing to be bought when it came to this so-called investigation. But she did not want to talk about the night Mina died," said Brian. "That makes me think she knows what happened to her—or may even be responsible for sinking the boat! And maybe it has nothing to do with the book or the bakery!"

"The next step is to interview her brother-in-law down in Trinidad," said Mr. Pilkington.

"I can do that," Brian volunteered. "I have to go to Eureka later this morning anyway. I'll stop by on my way down."

"Fantastic. We will look through Harriet's book while you're gone, and we can meet again in the afternoon to compare notes."

They climbed the steps to the museum and immediately saw Lucy Garber amongst a small crowd of school children, cheeks pink with excitement. She was wearing an adorable little vest that read "Staff" and holding out a sheaf of flyers.

"Take one each," she was saying. "The coastal redwoods are known for many beautiful species of butterfly, including California Sisters, Mourning Cloaks, American Ladies, and Woodland Skippers. You should be able to find fifty species of butterfly in the museum, though some are hidden very carefully to make it more fun. If you can find all fifty, your teachers owe you ice cream!"

The crowd dispersed with their flyers in search of butterflies.

"Willa!" cried Lucy, happily thrusting one of the sheets in her hand. "Daniel! I'm so glad you caught the end of my little talk. Butterfly conservation is a subject very dear to my heart, and it's one of the chief purposes of the Garber Wildlife Foundation."

Lucy led them to a large case in the museum foyer, where several colorful butterflies were mounted.

"This is the very one discovered by Hezekiah Garber," she said, tapping the glass. "There have only been five other sightings since then."

"One of those was by you, or so you claim," laughed Brian. "I still don't know if I believe it."

"You are a stinker!" said Lucy, pinching his cheek. "This one needs watching all the time. He used to be a real troublemaker in high school—that's why I made him my lab assistant. To keep him honest and give him something useful to do!"

"She taught me everything I know about entomology," he said, affectionately.

"I like to think I've made a true lepidopterist out of him. Mina used to laugh at us, and say she preferred dogs to insects."

Willa and Mr. Pilkington exchanged brief looks. They were both of Mina's opinion. Four legs beat out six legs, any day of the week. But Lucy and Brian's passion was delightful—and so were Lucy and Brian themselves.

If they stayed in Humboldt Cove much longer, Willa had no doubt that she and Mr. Peanut would become avid butterfly enthusiasts as well.

The Package

Mr. Pilkington opted to stay at the museum for a while with Lucy, and Brian went back to work. Before Willa returned home to let the dogs out, she stopped at a few shops downtown to ask if anyone had seen Mina the night of may 6th. She drew a blank everywhere, though Justine Galway did give her one useful piece of information.

"You know Sheriff Poole?" she asked, beckoning Willa closer with one of her very long and very purple nails.

"Yeah."

"He was looking into Mina's shop. Asked me, Dale, and a couple of the other business owners in town to keep an eye on it."

"Did he say why?"

"Nope. So Dale and I told him to shove off. It's probably drug-related, and we're no narcs. Watch your back, girl—that's all I'm saying."

Willa showed her Harriet's book.

"Do you recognize any of the people listed here?" she asked.

Justine thumbed through the book and handed it back.

"I know most of the dealers up on Hag Hill. They ain't listed here."

Disturbed, Willa climbed the hill to Mina's house, determined to finally get some work done. Murder or no murder, she had to finish *Fatal Fudge*.

She spent a productive hour writing and then got up to give the dogs their lunch, noticing as she did so that she needed to water the back lawn. *And I'm almost out of milk*, she thought, writing a quick note to herself to buy more at Doyle's later that day. She was adding the final flourish to the "K" at the end of "milk" when something dawned on her.

She was adulting.

She, Wilhelmina Wendoline Lattner, was caring for other life, doing household chores, and thinking ahead about necessary purchases. And it wasn't so hard.

Over the last week, she'd argued an insurance claim, bought groceries, picked up dog poop, watered flowers, studied business reports, ordered a home security system, and sustained the life of three fellow creatures, all without assistance. She didn't need her sister, her parents, or her boyfriends to take care of things for her. She was capable of thinking and acting for herself. Who knew?

Well, Mina had known.

Mina had known it all along. She had taken Willa seriously, as a competent adult. And she'd trusted her with more than just the dogs. She had placed the burden of justice directly into Willa's hands.

Willa gulped. She desperately wanted to live up to Mina's trust, but now she had fewer than twelve hours to solve her aunt's murder before she turned it over to someone else. So what was the next move? It sure as heck wouldn't be to run. Lattners never retreated when things got tough. Lattners went in, guns blazing, and got results.

And sometimes got themselves killed, Willa added, uneasily.

The doorbell rang, but instead of shrinking with fear, she marched that direction, ready to meet whatever came her way—whether it was the creepy town mayor and his awful wife, or Sheriff Poole himself, come to arrest her.

"Bless my soul," she said when she opened the door and saw who was standing on the mat. "It's Mr. Peanut!"

"Pardon?" said Mr. Pilkington, confused.

"What are you doing at the front door?" she asked, kicking herself for the slip. "I thought you were still at the museum. Why didn't you come in through the back?"

"All will be explained," he asked, his eyes darting up and down the street. "Just let me in."

He was clutching a large package to his chest.

"This is from your aunt," he whispered. "My secretary found it on her desk this morning and shipped it here via FedEx. She called to let me know."

Willa whisked him inside without another word and waited, breathless, to see what Mina had sent. He thrust it toward her now.

"I didn't want Lucy to see me enter through the back gate," he said, his voice shaking. "She came home about half an hour ago, while I stayed in town to do some shopping, but you know her, she's always peeping through the windows. We should look at this alone before bringing her in."

Willa opened the box, feeling a bit shaky herself. Within was a stack of papers about two inches thick. The top sheet read "*Klamath County California: A History, by Wilhelmina Lattner.*"

She gasped.

"The book! Finally! But I don't understand," she said, closing the box again so she could read the address. "Why did this take so long to get to you?"

"I don't know," he said, worry lines between his eyes. "I am quite unable to account for the delay."

"It's postmarked four weeks ago. She must have sent it before she died."

"That much is obvious," he said, dryly. "I did not suppose she rose from the dead to wait in line for stamps at the Post Office!"

Willa rummaged in the box, and found a long, white envelope, with the words "To Pilky" scrawled in large, generous letters on the front.

"May I read this?"

"Please do," he said.

Willa opened the envelope and drew out one sheet of paper.

Dear Pilky,

You will be surprised to get this, and I hope the shock isn't too much for your heart. Or perhaps that is exactly what I hope! The afterlife may be grand, but I'm sure I miss the company of my oldest and dearest friend.

If by some miracle I am still alive when you receive this, hang on to it for me. I'll tell you the whole story over a cup of coffee and a donut. If I'm dead, I need you to undertake an important errand on my behalf.

Please send or hand-deliver this package to my niece, Wilhelmina Lattner the Second. (I can't think why women don't go by seconds and thirds, just like the men, and I'd rather like to start a trend.)

She will know what to do with it.

All my love,

Mina

The Manuscript

"**G**ood grief," said Willa, stunned. "What makes her think *I'll* know what to do?"

Mr. Pilkington laid his mug on the table and tapped his long fingers together, thoughtfully.

"I believe my friend saw a certain similarity between herself and you," he said.

Willa scowled.

"We're both unmarried, career women. Is that it?"

"No, no. That is not what I meant at all! Mina's strong personality and fierce intelligence were immutable—married or unmarried; career or no career. Jobs and relationships are not characteristics, my dear girl. They are simply accidents of fate, like the color of your eyes or the city where you were born. What you two share is something deeper. She identified in you a similarity of *mind*."

"She didn't know me!" she cried.

"That is not true," he said, gazing at her intently. "She knew you from a child, did she not?"

"Well, yes. She was around a lot when I was growing up. Before my grandmother died."

"And she followed your adult career with keen interest."

"Read my books, you mean?" she smiled. "I guess you could call that following my career."

"Your aunt was no fool," he said, quietly. "If she says you will know what to do with this book, then *you will know what to do with this book.* That said," he added, "I will help you if you'll allow me. Shall we divide and conquer? I will read the first half, you read the second?"

"That's as good a plan as any," said Willa, gratefully. "Come on now, Pilky. Let's get started!"

By two, they had each made their way through approximately one-fifth of their assigned sections. It was slow-going, back-breaking labor—every word of it. Jake was right. It was one of the worst things Willa had ever read.

Pedantic, over-wordy, and riddled with typos, it read like a hybrid civics textbook and a third-grade English composition.

Willa pushed valiantly on through three chapters on the complex mechanism of land claim filing protocols—in which Mina spelled every fourth word incorrectly—until she had a splitting sinus headache. Next to her, Mr. Pilkington struggled through a particularly brutal chapter called "Gold Assaying: A Detailed Overview." His eyes were watering and he was rubbing his temples.

"Anything?" she asked, pouring him a fresh cup of coffee.

"Nothing. Oh dear. I knew Mina had a rather dry style of writing, but I wasn't prepared for this."

"She couldn't edit herself," Willa agreed, "There's a whole, pointless section here about the exact science behind telegraphs. She spelled telegraph ten different ways, incidentally, and didn't get it right a single time. How did she survive in her professional life?"

"Clerks, my dear," said Mr. Pilkington.

Willa thought of Jake and gulped.

"Have you gotten to any actual history?" she asked, peevishly. "I haven't seen anything about the founding families of Humboldt Cove. It's all land filing protocols and unnecessary science lessons."

"I'm afraid I've been stuck in a chapter about the chemical composition of gold ore for the last hour," he replied, looking so bummed about it that Willa burst out laughing.

"Look at us! We're fading fast. We need to take a break before we end up in the insane asylum."

Mr. Pilkington laid down the page he had been reading and gratefully accepted the last of Linda's cookies.

"I cannot imagine why Mina thought it necessary to put this book into my care," he said, shaking his head. "I see no scandal here."

"We haven't gotten to the good parts yet," Willa groaned. "There's a whole pile of letters, notes, and journals here, too."

She picked up an old leather diary that had belonged to Hezekiah Garber and flipped through it, glumly. Mr. Pilkington coughed.

"I rather wonder if there are any good parts," he replied, and then stared out the window over Willa's kitchen sink. "Do you have a gardener?"

"I know the yard is getting a little brown," Willa sighed. "I'll take care of it later today."

Killer, Kyle, and Wags began barking furiously at the kitchen door. Willa stood and walked to the window. She was just in time to see a glimpse of sleeves and trousers, before whoever it was ducked inside the shed.

"Oh, I see—you're right, there's someone out there," she said, nervously. It was chilly in the kitchen, but she was beginning to sweat. "Mina may have hired a gardener I don't know about."

"She did it under the table then," said Mr. Pilkington. "I looked at all her recurring payments before transferring the estate to you."

"Lots of people pay for household chores under the table."

Mr. Pilkington set his lips into a prim line.

"Mina Lattner never did an underhanded thing in her life. If she owed taxes, she paid them."

"Then who the heck is in my shed?"

They stared out the window together, neither of them breathing, while the dogs continued snarling at the door.

"Maybe it's the housebreaker again," Willa said, wishing she wasn't sweating quite so profusely.

She'd be sopping wet before long. She made a split—and rather foolish decision.

"Call 911," she ordered Mr. Pilkington. "You'll have to run upstairs to get reception. Fourth-floor linen closet."

Ignoring his astonished expression, she opened the kitchen door and let the dogs out.

They sprinted toward the shed, yapping as only dachshunds can yap when they are angry. Willa understood now why they had been bred to hunt and kill badgers. They were ferocious, ruthless, stubborn animals, and beneath their cute, hot-dog exteriors lay the hearts of wolves.

Backed by the dogs, Willa felt reckless and invincible. She threw open the shed door expecting to see—she did not quite know what! A giant, perhaps? An ogre? A prison escapee, complete with striped black-and-white uniform?

Instead, she encountered the defiant and embarrassed face of Ian McKinley.

They stared at each other for a full ten seconds with no sound, no movement—as though someone had pressed pause on a TV show. Then, all at once, there was a chaotic, jarring resumption of noise and motion.

"Call them off! Call them off!" Ian shrieked, as Killer jumped up, snapping at his hands, and Kyle bit through his jeans and drew blood around the ankles.

"Down boys," Willa commanded, trying to sound authoritative.

The dogs trotted meekly away and stood at her side, hackles still raised, teeth still bared. She bent down to hold their collars.

"It *bit* me," Ian said, watching as blood began to stain through his left sock. "It actually bit me!"

Willa looked up at Ian, still holding the dog collars.

"It's a he. His *name* is Kyle, and you have exactly five seconds to tell me what you're doing in my shed."

"Or what?" he said, trying to regain the upper hand.

"Or I sic Kyle on you again," she said, bluffing her hinder off.

She had no idea why the dogs had listened to her the first time, but she doubted it would happen again.

"Do that and I'll sue," he said, growing cocky. "And I'll kick that little wiener's head off for good measure."

"Trespassing *and* threats of bodily harm!" said Willa. "Keep it coming, Ian. When the police arrive I'll have a nice selection of things to charge you with."

"Police?" he repeated, disconcerted.

"My lawyer is inside, talking to them as we speak. Mr. Pilkington!" she hollered. "Mr. Pilkington!"

The little man came cautiously out, trembling and leaning more than usual on his cane.

"The Sheriff is on his way," he said.

Willa saw the tension on Ian's face relax immediately and bit her lip with irritation. Like Ian, she had no belief in Sheriff Poole's ability to behave impartially. Ian looked down at his left foot, where the red stain was rapidly spreading.

"Good," he said, haughtily. "I'm glad he's coming. There are protocols for dealing with animals that attack humans, you know."

"Sir!" replied Mr. Pilkington, appalled by this piece of effrontery.

Willa took a more practical approach.

"Sic 'em, boys," she said, letting go of Killer, Kyle, and Wags.

It was worth it to see the look on Ian McKinley's self-satisfied and rather stupid face.

The Intruder

While they waited for the Sheriff to arrive, Willa managed to muscle the dogs back into the kitchen and shut the door. Out of sheer human decency, Mr. Pilkington brought Ian a handful of paper towels to staunch the bleeding.

Sheriff Poole pulled up in front of the house a few moments later, accompanied by Jake Anderson. Willa almost wilted in relief when she saw him. She didn't care what the others thought. She was beginning to like the Deputy. He had common sense, if nothing else.

"What's going on?" demanded the Sheriff, striding through Mina's back gate and into the garden.

Jake followed him. He took off his hat, nodded at Willa, and gave his uncle a pained look.

"What are you doing here, Uncle Ian?"

"This woman and her dogs attacked me," Ian replied, promptly.

He held up a few blood-stained paper towels as proof.

"Is this true?" Gary asked, scowling in Willa's direction.

She scowled back at him.

"Certainly not! This man was trespassing on my property. He broke into my tool shed. The dogs were trying to protect me."

"I can vouch for that," said Mr. Pilkington, standing as straight as he could with the support of his cane. "Ms. Lattner and I noticed the presence of an intruder in the backyard. She went—quite bravely, I might add—to investigate the matter, bringing her dogs with her as a precaution. They naturally defended their mistress. My client and I are pressing charges of trespassing, breaking and entering, and—"

"Threats of bodily harm," Willa added, cheerfully.

"—threats of bodily harm on this man."

"Breaking and entering?" Ian protested. "The shed was unlocked, and furthermore—"

The Sheriff ordered him to be quiet, though Willa suspected it was less an official reprimand to a perpetrator than a warning to a friend.

"Which one of you did he threaten?" asked Jake.

"Kyle," said Willa.

"And where is he?" asked the Sheriff, looking around as though he expected someone called Kyle to materialize on the spot.

"Inside."

"Well, let's get him out here to speak for himself, shall we?"

"Kyle is one of the dogs," explained Jake, a smile twitching around the corners of his mouth.

The Sheriff relaxed immediately.

"I see," he said. "I think we can discount the threats, then. People say hasty things when they're frightened."

Ian nodded.

"Three dogs were set upon me with no warning and no provocation! I was terrified. I could have been killed."

"No provocation?" said Mr. Pilkington.

"Three dogs loosed on one man," the Sheriff said, scratching his chin. "That's a bit extreme. I've heard you accuse him of no worse than walking into an unlocked shed. What had this man done to warrant an attack on his life?"

Jake stifled a laugh.

"Do you have something to add, Deputy?"

"They're *wiener* dogs, sir," he said, making his face a blank. "The three of them probably weigh thirty pounds between them."

"They bit me," said Ian, shrilly.

It was clear to Willa that Sheriff Poole was losing patience with the whole matter.

"What were you doing in Ms. Lattner's shed?" he asked Ian.

"Looking for something my father left there before the house was sold."

"A likely story. Someone broke into my home yesterday. I have a pretty good guess who it was now, Mr. McKinley. What did you do with my phone?"

Ian began to look genuinely frightened.

"That wasn't me," he said. "Gary, you've got to believe me!"

"Where were you yesterday morning?" Willa pressed.

"I don't have to tell you that!" he said.

"If you weren't here tearing my aunt's office apart, you must have been somewhere! Where were you, Mayor?"

"I'm not answering any questions from you, you upstart, heartless, soulless hussy! You're exactly like your aunt. Messy hair, big attitude, without a shred of decency or family feeling, and no sense of the *history* of this town—"

"Enough," said Jake. "You may not have to tell her anything, Uncle Ian, but you sure as heck have to tell me."

"I'm not saying a word! Not a single word!" cried Ian, going on to say quite a bit. "You should know better, B.J. I'm ashamed of you, and your mother will be too."

"Don't talk about my mother," Jake said, dangerously.

"If you want to go around defending uppity spinsters who come to bulldoze our community and trash our history with their big-city morality and their intellectual snobbery—"

"Hey!" said Willa.

She wasn't sure if he was talking about her or Mina but she didn't appreciate him calling either one of them a spinster.

"Tell us where you were yesterday morning, and be quick," said the Sheriff, losing patience with the whole thing.

"Home with Patricia."

"Can she vouch for you?

"Certainly."

I bet she can, thought Willa, bitterly.

"Very well then. Why didn't you ask Ms. Lattner's permission to look in her shed?"

"I tried knocking," he said, "but no one answered."

"I've been home for hours," Willa retorted.

"I apologize for trespassing, Wilma," he said, through gritted teeth, "but I assure you I meant no harm. You'll be hearing from my lawyer about the damage your dog did to my leg."

"I wouldn't, Ian," said Gary, seeing the gleam in Mr. Pilkington's eye. "Are we done here?"

"No! I'm pressing charges against this man," said Willa. "He broke my window! He stole my phone and probably took some of my aunt's personal papers."

The Sheriff's eye narrowed.

"You have no proof of that."

"Okay, fine. When I get the proof I'll charge him with theft. For now, I'm happy to stick with trespassing on my property, entering my shed, threatening my dog, and whatever else applies."

"You are within your rights to do so," he said, coldly. "Deputy Anderson will stay and attend to the paperwork. Ian, you're free to go for now. We'll be in touch once the charges are officially filed. Actually, you're in no state to get home on your own. I'll take you downtown," he said, dragging the limping man away.

"Welp," said Jake, "you have a certain flair for trouble, 'Wilma.' I'll give you that."

"Trouble seems to follow me wherever I go in this town," she sighed.

They stayed outside while Jake took their official statements. Willa felt awkward about not inviting him in, but she wasn't taking any chances—not with that manuscript and the research strewn all over the kitchen table. Not when she was this close to figuring out what had happened to Mina.

"Yoohoo!" they heard, and turned to see Lucy Garber, returning from a run.

"Is everything alright?" she asked, her eyes darting from Jake's uniform to Mr. Pilkington's dark suit. "Why, Daniel—you're shaking! Has something happened, Willa?"

"You could say that," said Willa, opening the back gate to let Lucy in. "Ian McKinley just broke into my shed!"

A variety of emotions passed over the old woman's face.

"That can't be," Lucy said at last, though uncertainty marked every feature. "There's nothing in Mina's shed but some broken pots and a lawnmower."

"He must have been looking for the book," Willa said.

Lucy gasped.

"But that would mean he was the housebreaker! The McKinleys have a troubled past, I grant you, but Ian would never sink that low."

"Oh yeah? He called me a hussy, Lucy."

"And an uppity spinster," Jake supplied, grinning at her.

"Ian's awful. And it's not like his ancestors were any better. What about all those slave ships you mentioned?"

Lucy shushed her, with agonized eyes.

"Quiet, Willa—not in front of—oh for heaven's sake!"

She stifled a sob and then broke down into tears.

The two men stared at Willa, unsure what to do. There was a brief silence, punctuated by barking from the dogs, who heard a new voice outside and wanted to put in their two cents.

Willa put her arm around Lucy and said something inane, like "There, there." Lucy drew in a deep, shuddering breath.

"It's okay, Lucy. Really. I'm fine."

"I don't know what's happened to Humboldt Cove," she sobbed. "First Mina is killed, then you get robbed, and my neighbors are acting like strangers. Oh, won't those dogs *ever* stop barking? They don't give me or anyone else a moment's peace! Yapping and yapping until I feel like I'm going crazy."

"We'll figure it out," said Willa, with more confidence than she felt. "And the boys are just a bit upset at the moment. I'll hush them up."

Lucy hurried back to her house, crying. Willa turned to shrug at Jake and caught an absent, almost calculating look in his eyes that chilled her blood. He noticed she was looking at him and the expression cleared, but she could not forget she had seen it. He was definitely up to something, and the thought was demoralizing. She had enjoyed their little sparring matches. He wasn't Brian, of course. There was only one Brian. But he wielded a certain rough charm of his own.

"We'll question Ian about the burglary," said Jake, after he had asked for a few more details. "I suspect my aunt Patricia will back him up a hundred percent, though. Your phone is long gone, and the most he'll get for entering your unlocked shed is a slap on the wrist."

"Are you sure you're not covering for him because he's family?" she asked, cooly.

"I'm giving you an honest assessment of the situation. I don't think it's safe for you to stay here. Can you keep sleeping at Lucy Garber's for a while?"

"I can, but I won't," she said, flushing red. "I'm not going to let a goon like that frighten me. He can't say boo to a ghost—not really. He was afraid of *Kyle*."

"I'd be afraid of Kyle too—he's got sharp teeth! But I recommend putting yourself out of harm's way, Willa."

"It sounds like you're trying to get me out of my house."

He stared at her, hurt.

"You should know me better than that by now."

"No, Jake. I don't know you at all. I appreciate your concern, but Mr. Pilkington is staying with me," she said, putting her hand on the old man's shoulder. "We'll be fine."

"I shall do my best to protect you, my dear," he said gallantly, and she smiled at him.

If it came to that, she was pretty sure who would be doing all the protecting, and it wasn't Mr. Peanut. She caught Jake's eye and could tell he was thinking the same thing.

Once he finished taking their statements and hinted at an invite for a cup of tea inside (which Willa politely squashed), he left, giving Willa a quizzical, backward glance over his shoulder.

Willa shook her head briskly. She had been indiscreet, lured by meatloaf and chocolate chip cookies into confiding more than she intended. There would be no more dinners at the Andersons or chats over tortilla chips with the Doyles. Mina was right. There was no one she could trust in Humboldt Cove but Brian, Pilky, and the dogs.

The dogs were nearly frantic when they finally went back inside, and it took several minutes of petting and cuddles to calm them down.

"Shall we keep going on the book?" the old man asked, looking down at Mina's manuscript with resignation.

Another forced march through Mina's terrible prose was daunting, but Willa nodded. They only had a few hours left to solve the mystery before they'd have to take it to the police.

"It's now or never," she said, glumly.

Mail

To Guillermo Santini

G,

So there really IS trouble afoot at The Three Hounds Bakery? Dang it, G. You're only supposed to tell me what I want to hear. That is your sacred duty as a brother-in-law.

I appreciate your attempt at a mini-lesson on restaurant reporting, but it was WAY too technical. The only thing I gleaned is that you think our cost of goods sold percentage is too low and our income is too high, given the number of employees and what we're selling. And it's the wedding cakes that are off the most, yes?

I had my CPA look at the financials for
The Three Hounds, and everything is good. No
funny business with taxes. He said we're even
overpaying slightly, out of caution. So I'm
going to require a little more convincing that
something is wrong. And I need it in clear,
comprehensible English.

Write back as soon as you can. Better still, call
me. You can try reaching me at The Three Hounds
after three PM today. Wendy has the number.

Willa

P.S. Not to be dramatic, but this is literally
a matter of life and death. CALL ME.

The Assistant

Mr. Pilkington spent the afternoon plowing through the book, while Willa returned emails, paid bills, and occasionally tried jumping back into her portion of Mina's manuscript. She couldn't concentrate, though.

"What do you think Guillermo means about the wedding cakes?" Willa asked her companion, for the millionth time.

It was old ground. They'd gone over Guillermo's email and The Three Hounds' records several times now. Mr. Pilkington sighed.

"Let me see the reports again, though I fear we're beating a dead horse."

She pushed her laptop screen toward him, and he peered nearsightedly at it.

"I wish I understood restaurant management better," he said. "I know enough about profits and loss to tell that the bakery is very successful, but I have no idea how much marzipan is too much. Sheriff or no Sheriff, this may all boil down to a simple computer error! Have you tried calling your sister or her husband again?"

"I've taken your phone up to that stupid linen closet about fifty times. They aren't answering. I've left your number, though."

"You must press Brian about it this afternoon—preferably when that young lady is not around to overhear you. Be careful, Willa. She may be very dangerous."

"Shoot!" Willa cried, springing up from her seat and knocking poor Kyle onto the floor. "I forgot! I have to be down at the Three Hounds in like five minutes. Are you coming?"

"I think I'll stay and make more progress on the book," he said.

"Okay. If Wendy happens to call your number, direct her to the bakery."

Mr. Pilkington nodded, but the movement was slow and painful, as though he were exhausted beyond measure.

"I feel bad leaving you like this," she said, remorsefully. "Take a break from reading while I'm gone, at least."

"No, no," he said, removing his glasses and wiping his eyes. "I can stand a lot you know. I was in the Korean War. A mere manuscript can't break me."

"This one might."

"You may not believe this, but I am enjoying myself, in a way. I do feel close to Mina again. There is, hmm, a *flavor* of your aunt in these words. The merest whiff, of course. But even dry bread is a feast for a starving man."

"You must really miss her."

"Indeed I do."

"I thought Lucy might be starting to fill that hole in your heart," said Willa, smiling at him.

"Ms. Garber is a delightful woman, but there was only one Mina Lattner. See here, my dear—you will be careful, won't you? If Heidi is up to funny business it may not be safe to confront her—even with Brian as backup."

"What if it isn't Heidi? Or a reporting error? What then?"

"What do you mean?"

"What if it's Brian, Pilky? Or what if it was Mina, all along?" Willa replied, forcing herself to say it. "Selling cocaine or—or smuggling—or whatever is going on there."

"Mina Lattner would never have done anything illegal," said the old man. "She was absolutely straight. You'll have to take it from me since you didn't know her."

Maybe you didn't either, Willa thought uneasily, as she walked out the door.

Heidi was still piping butterflies in the corner when Willa entered The Three Hounds. She jumped at the sound of the bell over the door.

"Sorry," said Willa, penitently. "I didn't mean to startle you. I'll keep out of your hair."

"You need to leave," Heidi said, approaching her almost hysterically. She made a frantic shooing motion. "Get out of Humboldt Cove. You and the old man."

"Why?" said Willa, shocked by the intensity on the girl's face.

"Leave. Please! Leave and don't come back, or I can't answer for the consequences," whispered Heidi, close to tears.

"What's going on here? Are *you* the reason the Sheriff's been on my back ever since I got to town?"

"You don't know anything. Get out while you can," said Heidi, fiercely. "Unless you want to end up like your aunt."

The phone rang just then, and Brian emerged from the back.

"Can you get that?" he asked Heidi, and she hurried away, accidentally bumping into him as she went.

He rubbed his arm, watching her go with a puzzled expression.

"Geez, is she okay?" he asked Willa.

"She's scared," said Willa, softly. "She threatened me, Brian."

"What?!"

"She told me to get out of town while I could. I'm convinced she killed Mina, or she knows who did. We need to pin her down on those dodgy reports—shake it out of her before *she* skips town."

He rubbed the back of his head with his hand, looking distressed.

"Slow down, Willa. I just got back from Eureka. I haven't had a chance to look at the reporting in detail, and I don't even know what we're looking for!"

Before Willa could answer, Heidi marched back into the cafe portion of the bakery and said, "The call's for you, Ms. Lattner."

"You can take it there," said Brian, motioning to a phone on the wall behind the register.

He sat tactfully at a table to wait for her, sipping coffee and looking out the window.

"Hello?" she said.

"Um, yes, we're looking for the owner of the most successful bakery in Northern California," replied a familiar voice.

"Wendy," cried Willa.

"Wills! I'm so glad we caught you."

"We?"

"Ciao bella!" said another familiar voice. "I, too, am here. We are on the speaker phone."

"It's just speaker phone," laughed Wendy. "You're always dropping rogue 'the's' in there."

"Save the lectures for when *you* can speak Italiano as fluently as I speak English," he said. "Do you have *un minuto* to talk about those reports, Willa?"

"Is it bad?" Willa asked, feeling a familiar knot in the pit of her stomach.

"Can anyone hear you?" said Wendy. "You're kind of *whispering* in a creepy way."

"Yes, so I can't talk long. What's the deal?"

"Guillermo thinks someone is either very incompetent or deliberately perpetrating fraud."

"Dang," said Willa, fiddling nervously with the phone cord. "You're sure?"

She wished Brian wasn't right there listening, so she could be more explicit.

"The large wedding cakes are dodgy as heck," Wendy responded, bluntly.

"How so? And keep the business jargon to a minimum."

"How's this for simple? The bakery isn't using anywhere *near* enough ingredients to make cakes that size. And there aren't enough hours in the day to produce that many cakes along with everything else you're selling. Not with two employees. You sent Guillermo six months of COGS, labor, and inventory reports, Wills. We've got them open in front of us now. In may, you produced one two-tier, one three-tier, and *four* five-tier wedding cakes," she said. "The two and three-tiers are okay—looks like one went to a wedding in Arcata and the other to Eureka. They vary in flavor, filling, and decor, as you might expect."

"So?"

"So all the five-tier orders are the same. Lavender-lemon cake, with rose-flavored filling and lavender buttercream. Plus two lavender sheet cakes. Plus a groom's cake—also lavender. Must be some kind of package deal. We're talking enough cake to feed hundreds and hundreds of people."

"Well, maybe they all went to the same enormous wedding," Willa whispered.

"They went to four separate locations on different days," Guillermo chimed in. "Four weddings, Willa. Identical orders. Five-tier lavender-lemon cake, two sheet cakes, a groom's cake. I see at least two of the same orders every month for the last six months. Each retails at seven thousand dollars."

"Is that a lot?"

"Would you pay seven thousand smackeroos for a bunch of cake?" asked Wendy.

"No, but some people might."

"Have you ever had lavender cake with rose-water filling? It's like eating soap, Wills. That's weird enough in itself. But listen, the two and three-tier cakes range from two hundred to seven hundred bucks a pop, depending on the flavors and fillings."

"So the five-tier cake packages are overpriced? Is that what you're saying?"

"Well, *I* think so. But there are brides who'll pay anything, and if they think they're getting a good deal, that's on them. We just checked out The Three Hounds website," Wendy went on. "You don't offer the five-tier cake package on your order form, so they must be available only upon request—that's all very upscale and boutique and it's fair play. When you buy a Rolex, you're paying for the name, right? The same can be true for cake. And some people like floral aromatics."

"I, myself, am fond of them," said Guillermo, seriously.

"You also like goose liver, my love. Still with us, Wills?"

"Yep."

"Okay, so far, so good. The problem is that The Three Hounds isn't *making* those five-tier cakes, sis. You're just selling them."

"How do you know?"

"You are not buying enough supplies to make that much cake," said Guillermo.

"Maybe we have a lot of ingredients in storage."

"You can't stockpile milk, butter, and eggs. Not unless your customers like rotten baked goods."

"So what do you think is happening?" Willa said.

Guillermo and Wendy conferred briefly, and Willa shot a nervous look at Brian.

"Still there?"

"Yep."

"Okay, so here's what we think. If your taxes are above board, and your bank account looks okay, it's safe to say the money is real, even if the cakes aren't."

"What does that mean?"

"The Bakery is selling *something*, Willa," said Guillermo, solemnly. "Ask your partner what he is baking into those five-tier cakes because it isn't lavender, butter, and sugar."

Willa wrapped the phone cord tighter around her fingers, feeling like she couldn't breathe.

This was bad. This was very bad. She realized she hadn't inhaled in over thirty seconds, and drew in a gulp of air. No wonder Heidi was afraid of her own shadow. No wonder she panicked when Willa brought up the night of Mina's disappearance. She must be using the cakes to cover the sale of drugs to those dealers up in the hills above town...

Brian flashed her a dazzling smile from across the room. She saw the butterfly tattoo on his right shoulder peeking out of the sleeve of his t-shirt as he waved.

"Wendy, are you still there?" she asked, realizing she hadn't spoken for a full minute.

"Still here, Wills. Are you okay?"

Her sister sounded deeply concerned.

"No," she said. "No, I'm not."

"Will you be?"

"I don't know," she said bleakly, and hung up the phone without saying goodbye.

The Cakes

Willa hesitated by the phone, unsure what to do next. Brian smiled over at her.

"Good call?" he asked.

She pulled herself together, forcing a neutral expression onto her face.

"Very," she said. "I finally heard from my twin sister! Sorry about the interruption, but I've been trying to talk to her for days."

"How's Rome treating her?"

She walked slowly over to the table where he was sitting and pulled up a chair.

"She's great, thanks."

"What's wrong, then?" he asked, and then he grinned, enlightened. "I see. Your sister wants to know I'm on the up and up, right? The grilling of the boyfriend! So, what does she want to know? I have great credit, no debt, and a lot of money in the bank. Never been married. College degree, MBA. I own my house. Never been in jail."

"That's not it, Brian."

"She wants the lowdown on my former girlfriends, eh? Well, that's a short conversation, Willa. I haven't dated much. I guess I've just been waiting for the right girl to come along."

He took her hand and looked into her eyes.

"I'm glad I waited."

"Uh, that's not what I meant," Willa said, reluctantly withdrawing her hand. It was taking every ounce of her self-control to stick to the main concern.

Think about Mina, think about Mina, she told herself. It was hard to think about anything else when Brian Harrison was looking at her, though. Those eyes.

"So what's wrong? You're not breaking up with me, are you?"

Willa blinked at him. Breaking up? That seemed a little dramatic.

"I've figured out what's wrong with the reports," she whispered, leaning in.

"What is it?"

"We aren't using enough ingredients to make the big wedding cakes."

"What do you mean?"

"We aren't ordering enough raw ingredients to sell the big cake packages. You know, the five-tier lavender and rose cakes. We sold several of them last month."

"That's a very popular package."

"Is it? I have a hard time believing that many different brides ordered seven thousand bucks of soap cake, Brian," she said, impatiently.

"Lavender and rose are hip flavors right now."

"Did you take the orders? Did you talk to those brides yourself?"

"No, Heidi handles all the orders—she meets with the couples who are getting married. And she deals with our vendors."

"Exactly," she said, meaningfully. "She isn't purchasing enough to fill the orders she's taking. And you guys aren't using enough ingredients to deliver the finished product."

"That can't be true. I make the cakes, Willa. I made the cakes for the order we're shipping today. I'd be the first to know if I didn't have enough ingredients."

"The books say otherwise."

"Maybe Heidi's reporting is sloppy," he said, hopefully.

"Or maybe she's pulling one over on you! She just threatened me, remember? Told me to get out of town if I didn't want to end up like Mina. It's hard to misinterpret that."

"Are you sure that's what she said? That doesn't sound like her."

"I know what I heard! The bakery is profiting heavily from these cakes, Brian," Willa said, frustrated. "We're getting paid for the five-tier packages, month after month. So either people are accepting smaller cakes than they ordered, or we're not selling them cake. Heidi's prepping one today, right? Is it one of the lavender-rose deals?"

"Yeah," he said.

"Let's go check it out, together. If it's just cake, then there's a simple mistake somewhere. A reporting error."

"Heidi won't like it."

"So?"

"Your energy makes her nervous. Whatever this is," he said, waving his hand in a circle in front of Willa's face. "This edgy vibe you're giving off. I've never seen her make a mistake like she did this morning. We don't have time to fix more piping errors."

"She's nervous for a reason! We're getting close. I promise I won't say anything to spook her. I'll be as quiet as a mouse," Willa persisted.

Brian raised a brow.

"You're Mina's niece, alright. She wouldn't hear anything she didn't want to hear either."

"I'll take that as a compliment."

Brian led Willa back into the kitchen, where Heidi was putting the final touches on the last butterfly. She turned her back to hide a tear-stained face.

"Looks like she's finishing up the last tier," Brian explained, with artificial cheerfulness. "Now she can pop it in its box, all ready to go."

"You don't stack the cakes here?" said Willa.

"Of course not," he laughed. "Have you ever tried transporting a multi-tiered cake? It would topple over at the first bump in the road. No, we package them separately so they arrive at the wedding venue safe and intact. Then we spend an hour or so setting up the cake on-site. It's a very delicate business, Willa. Requires a steady hand and nerves of steel."

Heidi's hands were far from steady as she lifted the butterfly-adorned cake. Willa counted the boxes that were lined up along the stainless steel counter. One, two, three, four...*five*.

"Five tiers!" she said. "That's a lot of cake."

"It's one of our most popular packages," Heidi said, without turning around. Her hands were openly shaking now.

"Careful, Heidi," Brian warned.

"I'm being careful!"

"Can I see the other layers?" asked Willa.

"No," said Heidi. "I've already boxed them."

The phone rang, and Brian excused himself to answer it. Willa watched in silence as Heidi finished taping up the last box.

"These packages are several thousand bucks, right? Seems like a lot of money for cake," she remarked.

Heidi whirled around.

"The butterfly cakes pay my salary and line *your* pockets with money, so—"

"What did you call them?" Willa interrupted.

"Nothing," said Heidi, turning beet red.

"You said butterfly. Is that because of the decoration or the lavender? Are the five-tier cakes always piped with butterflies, or can people order flowers or other designs?"

Heidi ignored her. She began picking up the boxes, one by one, and taking them to the walk-in freezer.

"Where are the sheet cakes that go with this order?" asked Willa, persistently, just as Brian strode into the back.

"That call was for you, Willa! You're a popular gal today. You can take it out there. Here, Heidi, let me give you a hand with that..."

He hurried over to assist Heidi. Leaving them to it, Willa returned to the front of the bakery and picked up the receiver.

"Hello?"

"Hey Wills! It's us again."

"I can't really talk."

"Yeah, we gathered that when you hung up on us," said Wendy. "You sound awful, Wills. Listen to me, because this is important. I know you like cute-bakery-owner-guy, but Guillermo says any restaurant manager worth their salt is checking COGS and inventory reports every week."

"I know what I'm saying," Guillermo chimed in, with conviction. "I have worked everywhere. Steak houses, coffee shops, bakeries. It is the same all over. An experienced pastry chef would see the discrepancies immediately."

"Mina didn't catch it," explained Wendy, "because you guys are paying taxes and bringing in an enormous profit. That's usually all the business owner cares about. But your profit margin is way, *way* too high—even for the most successful patisserie. It's sussy as heck. And it's the chef's business to know how many ingredients you have and how many you use."

"Couldn't his assistant be fudging things in the system?" she asked, whispering into the receiver.

"Is cute-bakery-owner-guy dumb?"

"No."

"Does he come to work every day?"

"Yes."

"Is he doing any of the baking?"

"All of it."

"Then he knows about it. Talk to him."

"I was afraid of that," Willa said, gutted.

"We're extremely worried about you, sis."

"I can take care of myself."

"You can't even boil water, Wills."

"I can do a lot more than you think I can. Love you. I'll keep you posted."

She hung up and her fingers formed themselves into tight fists, as she fought a fierce internal struggle.

Mina had told her to trust Brian. It was almost the last thing her aunt had said. But if Wendy and Guillermo were right then he must be involved, at least peripherally...

Willa went around in circles, trying to make sense of it. She felt an almost visceral need to get home to the dogs, where she knew what she was dealing with, at least.

Brian returned to the front of the bakery and beckoned her back to their table.

"I can't believe I'm saying this," he whispered, "but you're right, Willa. While you were on the phone, I checked those boxes. There's only cake in one of them."

"See!"

"Heidi's definitely up to something. We need to think this through, though, because I don't want to scare her off. One of us should follow her when she makes the delivery—see where she's really going."

"What? No, Brian. That's crazy. We need to call the police."

"The Sheriff won't believe a crazy story like this. We need to bring him the proof. Here's the plan. I'll wait until Heidi packs up the van, and then I'll get in my car and follow her out of town..."

Willa felt like she was suffocating. Brian was talking but she couldn't hear him. She looked at his handsome, smiling face. His brilliant blue eyes. His deep voice—sometimes amused, sometimes tender—still chattering away at her now.

She sat very still, trying to pull her wits about her. They had proof now that this was all tied to Heidi. To Heidi and those dodgy-as-heck five-tier cakes, covered in intricate piped butterflies...

Butterflies. Willa zoomed in on Brian's shoulder tattoo and flinched. It was no good. No matter how many mental loop-di-loops she went through, she'd never be able to convince her protesting intellect that Brian wasn't involved.

She couldn't rely on Mina's letter or Mina's gut anymore. She was on her own, for the first time in her life.

No Wendy. No Guillermo. No Mom or Dad to pull her out of a bind. It was up to Willa alone to decide. She forced herself to think about every interaction she'd shared with Brian and felt a faint chill creep over her heart. What did she know about Brian Harrison, after all?

He *had* come on pretty strong, right away. Asking her out almost immediately after meeting her. Kissing her on their first date. And why?

He didn't know her. Not really. But he liked her! She was sure he did. He had actually kissed her knowing she had a giant piece of pickled jalapeno in her teeth. Huge green flag, just like she'd told Wendy. If that wasn't true, disinterested love, what was?

Oh no, Willa thought, as the humiliating realization dawned on her.

How could she have missed it? It was so obvious.

No one would kiss a stranger with food stuck in their teeth. Not unless they were desperate. And Brian *was* desperate, she realized, watching across the table as he continued talking—desperate to keep her hooked. He smiled, gazing into her eyes as he fed her Blarney, as sure of her now as he'd ever been. He'd played her easily.

She looked down at her arm, where goosebumps had begun to form.

Real friends handed you a napkin when there was shmutz on your face. Real friends told you when your fly was down. Mina may have trusted Brian, but Willa sure as heck didn't.

She had to move forward, then. But to where? And who? To Lucy? Maybe, but she might have a hard time believing her star pupil was rotten to the core.

Mr. Pilkington, then? He was the world's biggest sweetheart, and he had shown himself willing and able to back her up. He was so old, though...

Who else was there? The Doyles? The Captain?

Willa had a sudden mental image of Jake Anderson cooly telling her there was chocolate on her mouth.

She hesitated a moment, and then began rummaging through her purse, looking for the card Jake had given her the first day they met.

"Have you been listening to a word I said?" Brian asked pleasantly, and it took every ounce of Willa's willpower not to scoot her chair away from him.

"I need to make a call," she said. "Can I use your phone again?"

"It's your bakery too," he said, smiling tenderly at her. "So it's your phone."

Ten minutes ago, that smile would have melted her into a pile of goo. Now, it merely irritated her. His teeth were too straight.

"You said you baked the cakes that are going out today, Brian."

"Well, I did, but—"

"Twenty minutes ago you sat right where you are now and swore you had made enough soap cake to fill the order. Did you bake the cakes, or didn't you?"

"It's complicated," he began.

"How's this for complicated? The first day I came you told me you handled all the ordering. Do you remember that? You said you picked the restaurant management software. You said you ordered on Mondays and Thursdays. Today, you're acting like Heidi calls the shots. So which is it?"

"Calm down, Willa. You don't quite understand how a food service business operates, that's all. Let me explain it to you. The chef is more like a footsoldier. He fills the orders. It's the decorator who plans everything out—"

"Make up your mind, Brian."

"There are very simple explanations for all of this."

"I doubt it," she said. "I've had enough of whatever this is. I've been dumb, but I'm not this dumb. Thanks for the coffee. I'm going home."

"What about the plan to follow Heidi? Why are you giving up so soon, right when we're about to get justice for Mina? I really think if we trail Heidi, we can crack this case..."

"Thanks but no thanks. Have fun with your cakes and your butterflies. I'm out."

"*What* did you say?" he asked, reddening.

"You heard me," she said, and left before he could reply.

The Discovery

Willa practically ran back up the hill toward Mina's house, not daring to turn around until she reached the summit, in case Brian was following her. She wished now that she had called Jake from the bakery while she had the chance. It would have been awkward, but she could have pulled it off.

There was no time to lose. Brian might follow her up here any minute. She would grab Mr. Pilkington and the dogs and hightail it out of town. She'd take Lucy with her too, if she could convince the old woman to go. They could use Mr. Pilkington's phone to call the police once they were safely out of Humboldt Cove. With a little shiver, she wondered what people were really buying with those butterfly cakes. Guns? Drugs? Whatever it was had been worth killing for.

Willa opened the gate to Mina's back garden and stopped short. The kitchen door was wide open.

"Mr. Pilkington?" she called, terrified.

There was no human reply, but Killer and Wags bolted out of the door, barking at her, and she followed them into the kitchen.

Mr. Pilkington was lying face-down on the floor, blood seeping from a wound on the back of his head. Kyle stood guard beside him, anxiously licking his face.

Willa threw herself down on the floor beside him, feeling for pulses. The old man's hands were warm, and though his pulse was weak, his heart was beating still. Limp with relief, she turned him over. His glasses were broken, and there was a long cut down his nose, but the main injury seemed to be the blow to his head. He did not respond to her voice.

She looked around. There was broken ceramic on the floor from Mr. Pilkington's teacup, but the manuscript and all of Mina's notes were gone.

"Shoot, shoot, shoot," she said, her panic rising as she realized Brian could not have been responsible for what happened here.

He'd been with her the entire afternoon! *Heidi was in the back though*, she thought. He must have given her instructions to come up here and fetch the book, and…

She shook her head. That didn't make sense at all! Brian was laundering money through the bakery. Why would he care about this pointless old book? Maybe Mina had stumbled on something while doing her research—some kind of hideout for smugglers? A sea cave used by pirates for stolen goods? Willa made a frustrated sound. Those theories were worthy of the Hardy Boys, but they had no relation to real life.

She searched the unconscious man's pockets but his phone was missing. She had no way to call for help.

"Lucy!" she cried, kicking herself for not thinking of it sooner. "Stay here," she told the dogs, "I'm going for help."

With almost preternatural understanding, Killer and Wags lay next to Mr. Pilkington, one on either side, ready to attack if necessary. Kyle left his post and followed her out the door.

"Go back," she told him, but he set his ears back, and trotted after her more quickly, if anything.

Dachshunds did what dachshunds pleased, and Kyle was coming with her whether she liked it or not.

"Lucy!" she hollered, letting herself in the side door to the Garber House. "Lucy! Are you there? I need help!"

There was no reply. Willa yelled Lucy's name a few more times, but the only response she got was from Fluffy, who sauntered down the stairs to see what all the racket was about, gave Willa a bored look, and hissed at Kyle. The hiss was a mere courtesy—a social nod to the age-long animosity between dogs and cats. She could not have looked more indifferent. Kyle tucked his tail between his legs, hackles raised.

Willa remembered, with relief, that Lucy had a landline in the kitchen. She was running toward the back of the house when she heard the sound of hysterical barking.

"Quiet, Kyle!" she commanded, without stopping. "Leave Fluffy alone!"

The barking became more agitated. She whirled around, hoping she wouldn't have to physically intervene in a cat-and-dog fight, and saw Fluffy licking herself, unconcerned, on top of Lucy's hall table. Kyle was barking at the door that led to the basement.

"Fluffy's not down there right now, you goof," she said. "Look, she's right there."

Kyle kept barking and began ramming his little head against the door. The sight was so disturbing that Willa froze, unsure how to proceed.

"What is it, boy?" she said. "Is it Lucy? Is she hurt?"

Maybe she had fallen down the stairs, bringing the laundry up. Willa opened the door and peered down a dark, narrow stairway.

"Lucy, are you down there?" she called.

Kyle burst past her, hurtling down the stairs so fast his back legs couldn't keep up. He stumbled down the last three steps, landing on his back, and scrambled up. Willa flicked on the light switch and ran down the stairs after him.

The basement was large, and cluttered with the cast-off furniture and unwanted impedimenta of a hundred years. Lucy's modern washer and dryer sat in the corner nearest the stairs, but the rest of the space was vast, dark, and full of forgotten memories and cobwebs.

Willa followed the sound of Kyle's barking and found him next to a small closet door.

"Lucy's fine," she scolded him. "There's nobody down here but rats. Come on, boy. We're leaving."

Kyle suddenly stopped barking, his body stiff—his ears perked toward the door. In the stillness, Willa thought she heard something too. A faint scratching sound.

"Lucy?" she said, slowly turning the handle.

It was locked.

Swearing under her breath, she tried it a few more times and then knocked, hardly knowing what she expected. The rats and roaches weren't likely to let her in. There was a swift knock in reply, however.

Someone was definitely inside.

"Hang on, Lucy! I'm coming!"

She considered trying to break the door down but changed her mind after a cursory examination. This was the product of another era—solid oak, well-crafted, and unlikely to yield to her shoulder. She sent up a desperate prayer for help and spied a gleam of silver on the ledge above the door. She snatched it down and unlocked the door.

Kyle nosed his way in and trotted toward a dark, huddled shape in the dimmest corner of the little closet.

A voice—hoarse with disuse but oddly familiar—spoke through the darkness.

"Who's a good boy? Who's the best boy in the world?"

Willa stared, shocked almost beyond belief, as Kyle flung himself ecstatically into the arms of a dirty, disheveled old woman. But it wasn't Lucy Garber.

"I knew you'd get here eventually," croaked Mina Lattner, triumphantly. "What *took* you so long?"

The Showdown

"A unt Mina?" Willa gasped, unable to take it all in. "Good lord! *Aunt Mina*?!"

"In the flesh," said the old woman.

"But you're dead," said Willa, stupidly.

"No, I'm not! But I'm likely to be soon if we don't skedaddle out of here. Where are we exactly, if you don't mind me asking?"

Willa helped her aunt stand on trembling legs.

"Lucy Garber's house. In the basement."

"Well, I'll be a monkey's uncle. I'm surprised she had the gall to use her own house. I always knew she was a little crackers but she must be absolutely barking mad. No offense, Kyle."

Kyle wagged his tail at her happily.

"Lucy did this to you? But why?"

Willa's own legs felt like jello now, and she was having difficulty supporting both her aunt's weight and her own.

"Didn't you get the book from old Pilky? Or did he let me down?"

"It was lost in the mail for a few weeks," Willa explained, her head spinning. "I only got it this morning."

"Oh, that explains it then. You haven't had a chance to read it yet, I take it?"

"Just parts," said Willa, evasively. "Mr. Pilkington and I were splitting the job. I haven't gotten past your deep dive into gold assaying."

"Fascinating, is it not?"

Willa rolled her eyes into the darkness and helped Mina out the closet door.

"If you had read further, you would have found the chapter on Hezekiah Garber."

"I know all about Hezekiah," said Willa, impatient with her aunt's slow pace. "Please try to go faster, Mina. We need to get out of here."

"When you've been starved for weeks and kept in a dark room by yourself, you can lecture me about pace," Mina said, tartly. "I'm eighty-five, for Pete's sake. I'm going as fast as I can. And you don't know jack squat about Hezekiah Garber."

"He founded the town," Willa said, leading Mina by the elbow and almost weeping with frustration.

They weren't going to get out in time. Lucy might show up at any moment, and they'd be trapped down here.

"And?" said Mina, as though coaching a recalcitrant child on its history lessons.

"And—I don't know! He stuck out the claim here through a hard winter and was a champion of ecology and women's rights. It doesn't matter right now, Aunt Mina! Please try to move faster."

Willa wished Kyle was big enough to help her push Mina along. What she wouldn't have given for a Saint Bernard right now!

Mina's legs were giving out, crippled by near starvation. Willa propped her upright against a post in the middle of the basement and contemplated her next move. Maybe she should return Mina to the closet and come back with reinforcements. Or she could leave her here with Kyle as her bodyguard and borrow one of the neighbor's phones. Either way, she'd never get the woman up those stairs—not in her weakened state—and whatever she decided it had to be quick.

Gently, she lowered Mina onto the ground by the post.

"I'm going to go for help," she said. "You're hidden from the door here. Keep quiet and still, and I'll be right back."

Mina shook her head.

"Your heart is in the right place, Willa, but I'm afraid it's too late for both of us," she said, pointing up the stairs to where Lucy Garber stood glaring down at them.

Kyle sat on Mina's lap, growling ferociously in Lucy's direction.

"Lucy!" Willa cried, figuring her best bet was to act dumb.

She had the smallest sliver of hope that Mina was wrong—that Lucy knew nothing about what was happening. There was no response. Willa could not see Lucy's face, backlit as she was by the bright light from upstairs.

"You'll never believe what I found down here!"

"You must think I'm very stupid. I am not. So whatever big move you're planning right now," Lucy said, shutting and locking the door behind her, "I'd reconsider. You're going to die either way, but we can make it hurt if we want to."

"We?" said Willa, her heart sinking.

So the Doyles or the McKinleys *were* involved. Who else would be aiding and abetting Lucy to suppress the book? Willa stuffed down a wave of fear and looked around for something she could use as a weapon. Her eyes were adjusting to the light now, and she could see that Lucy wasn't carrying anything—no knife, no gun. If she acted quickly, she could throw the old lady off balance.

What would Violet Valentine do? she asked herself, half in jest. The answer was always something brave and dumb. She saw a broom lying next to Mina and bent over to pick it up.

How's this for dumb, Violet? she thought.

"I wouldn't if I were you," Lucy said, amused.

"I have no trouble believing *you* wouldn't, Grandma Moses," Willa replied, picking up the broom anyway, and grabbing a nearby jug of Windex for good measure. "But I would."

Behind her, Mina chuckled.

"Shut up, Mina," snapped Lucy. "And try to have a little common sense, Willa. I told you we could make it hurt. You should know by now that I mean what I say."

"What's this we stuff, Lucy? I don't see anyone over there. Do you have an invisible buddy or are you getting senile?"

"Who knows you're here, Willa?" Lucy said, briskly, ignoring the insult. "Did you call anyone from town? Truthful answers will earn you a pleasant death. Lie to me, and you will not enjoy the next twenty-four hours."

"Stay there," Willa muttered over her shoulder to Mina. "I'm going to rush her."

"Forget the Windex. Go for the big guns. Here's some lye. That outta sting," Mina whispered.

Willa set down the blue fluid and picked up the nearly full bottle of undiluted sodium hydroxide that Mina shoved in her direction.

"Be careful," Mina said, making her voice ring out now. "Watch your back, Willa. She's old but she's evil."

"And *you* are an interfering know-it-all!" Lucy shrieked.

"Guilty as charged!"

"You obnoxious, red-headed hag! Coming to my town, throwing your money around, taking down the price and dignity of this neighborhood with your awful pink paint!"

"You're just jealous because Douglas Burch has been making sheep's eyes at me," Mina taunted her, calmly. "You're mad that I stole your boyfriend! Admit it!"

"You are a human parasite," said Lucy, her voice shaking with anger. "Buying old property as if you had a right to it—"

"Hey!" said Willa. "Wait a minute, I've heard that before."

"So've I," said Mina. "Well, I'll be darned. You don't by any chance write Op-Eds for Humboldt Cove Gazette, do you?"

"That's it! That's where I heard it! But the article I read was over ten years old. It goes back *that* far, Lucy? So you're the reason Mina has a bad reputation in Humboldt Cove!" Willa said, enlightened.

"I don't need anyone's help to ruin my reputation," Mina laughed. "I always thought Ian wrote those articles but they do smack of Lucy Garber. Weak, cowardly, and mean. You're a jealous old witch, Lucy."

"You took something I loved," said Lucy, nastily. "So I took something you loved. You'll never see your precious lawyer friend again, Mina. I killed him."

Mina shrieked and tried to stand up, but Willa whirled around and motioned her to stay put.

"Pilky's okay," she whispered. "Let me handle this."

Mina slumped back down, relieved, and Kyle stood next to her, wagging his tail fiercely.

"What exactly is going on here, Mina?" Willa asked, so that Lucy could hear. "Why is this crazy old lady whacking inoffensive lawyers on the head and holding prominent townspeople in her basement? Is this really all about that history of Klamath County?"

"Of course. She's cuckoo-bananas, my love," said Mina. "I was washing dishes in my kitchen one night when Lucy barged in holding a frying pan and smacked me with it! Last thing I remember is Kyle licking my face after I hit the floor. When I woke up again, I was in that closet there, bruised from head to toe, and Lucy was holding a butcher's knife. She told me she'd slit my throat if I didn't tell her where the manuscript and my research was. So I told her to go right ahead and do it."

Mina laughed, and her voice was so raspy and parched she sounded like a dying donkey. Kyle stopped barking momentarily and licked her face.

"The amazing Lucy Garber didn't have it in her to kill an old woman in cold blood. Thought she'd starve me out. As if a little bread and water treatment would intimidate me."

"Wait, what? What about your boat?"

"What *about* my boat?"

Kyle began barking as only a dachshund could bark—shrill, persistent, and furious.

"You were on your boat the night you disappeared," Willa hollered, over her shoulder. "Don't you remember?"

"I haven't been out on the Old Girl since the third week of June."

"Wow, Lucy must have really conked you one."

"I would remember taking my boat out," said Mina, irritably. "I did no such thing."

There was a sudden, heart-stopping pounding noise on the door down to the basement.

Oh thank God, Willa thought, once her heart started beating again. *Someone's come to help.*

"Down here!" she yelled, while Kyle barked hysterically. "Help! Help!"

Lucy walked calmly up the steps and unlocked the door, and Willa's heart sank. The others must have arrived. Lucy's mysterious "we."

The door swung open, but instead of Irene and Sam Doyle, or Ian and Patricia McKinley, the silhouette of Brian Harrison appeared at the top of the staircase.

The Garbers

Willa felt almost physically ill with surprise and dismay. She could not quite believe it was Brian, even when he flashed her one of his famous smiles. She blinked, trying to take it all in. Brian and Lucy. They made quite the unusual crime duo.

"What are you doing here?" she said, flatly.

"Nice to see you too," he said. "Did you think we'd let you go once you figured it out? This isn't one of your stupid books."

"I thought you hadn't read my books."

"I've met the author. You're stupid enough to think I liked you. I date models, Willa. Not four-eyed clowns. Do you even *comb* that hair?"

"Come over here and find out."

"Quiet, both of you!" Lucy snapped again. "What took you so long? They're being very difficult."

"I'll take care of it. Have you ever been badly burned before, Willa?" Brian called out, pleasantly. "I've got oils at the bakery that will melt your skin and knives that can slice a chicken clean to the bone."

Willa breathed deeply and gripped the handle of her broom. She heard Kyle growling beside her and took heart.

"I'm sure you do. But we're not at The Three Hounds, are we?"

"I should have killed you then."

"Yeah, you should have. For crying out loud," said Willa, stamping her foot. "What is going on, here? The two of you are giving me whiplash. First I thought this was about smuggling, then I thought it was Mina's stupid book, and now it turns out it was The Three Hounds all along? I can't believe you two are working together. Didn't you ever learn to say no to drugs, Lucy?"

"Drugs?" repeated Mina.

"Brian is laundering drug money in and out of The Three Hounds," Willa explained. "Though I have no idea why Lucy is helping him. Didn't you figure that out already? Isn't that why you're down here?"

"*That* is not what I figured out. And this is about my book, I assure you."

"Zip it, both of you," said Lucy. "I'm in no mood for shenanigans. This idiot is behind on today's shipment already, and if we don't get a move on we'll lose the sale."

"See?" whispered Willa, turning around.

Mina gave her a puzzled look.

"Heidi's getting it out now," said Brian, carelessly. "We won't lose the sale."

"And yet they've already called to express their displeasure at the delay," Lucy snapped.

"How is that my fault? Heidi got behind, and I had to spend most of the day keeping Willa busy. She kept asking questions about the reports—"

"Why did you give her access in the first place?"

"She asked me for the financials! What was I supposed to do? It would have been more suspicious not to give them to her."

Lucy whacked his arm.

"You could have altered them, you idiot."

"Ow, *geez*," he said, in an injured voice. "Lay off!"

"Doctoring the books is fraud 101," Willa said. "Didn't they teach you that in business school? I'm disappointed in you, Lucy. You should have picked a better partner. When did you two start your joint life of crime, anyway? Have you been smuggling drugs in and out of this coast since Brian was in high school? Is *that* why he was your TA? To help you make crack or cook meth?"

"Quiet," ordered Lucy. "Stop talking nonsense. If you cost me this client, Willa Lattner, I will keep you alive for months, letting Brian slice away at you one bit at a time, until you beg us to kill you."

Willa's blood froze in her veins and she wavered.

"Baloney!" said Mina, unexpectedly. "Words. Nothing but words! I've never seen such a silly pair of criminals. If they had even a lick of sense between them, they'd have killed me days ago."

"You tell 'em, Aunt Mina. You know what I see?" said Willa, backing up until she could feel Mina's hand reaching up toward her own.

The physical touch gave her courage.

"What do you see?" asked Mina, stoutly.

"One arrogant coward and one old hag."

"Fancy that! I see the same thing. It's three to two."

Brian laughed.

"Three? You can't seriously be counting that wiener dog amongst your assets."

"He's smarter than you are. Let's be real, guys. I'm on to you both now. You can't use Mina's business anymore, and you can't hide behind your rich dealer friends or Heidi's high-roller clients. Your only hope—both of you—is to leave town now and never come back."

Brian laughed again and moved closer.

"You have *no idea* what's going on, do you?"

"You told me she had figured it out," Lucy snapped.

"I thought she had!"

He drew nearer.

"Keep coming and *I* will make it hurt," Willa muttered, uncapping the jug.

If she could lure him closer, she'd throw the lye in his face and whack him with the broom and Kyle could attack from the floor...

"Stop this at once," ordered Lucy, in a commanding voice. "She's baiting us, you idiot. Step back and let's think this through in a calm and rational manner."

Brian ceased advancing and went obediently back to her side.

"Go upstairs and get my hunting rifle," she told him, irritably. "The key to the gun safe is hanging in the kitchen, and there are bullets in a little box at the back of the junk drawer."

"I don't think I should leave you," he said, uncertainly. "She's dumb but she's nuts."

"I can handle it," said the old lady, drawing herself up proudly. "I'm a Garber, aren't I?"

"Yeah, and you never shut up about it," said Willa, rudely.

She felt a tug on her jeans and looked down.

"Keep her talking," murmured Mina. "This hinges on the book. Trust me."

Willa nodded. She had no idea what was going on, but she trusted Mina.

"You're distantly related to someone who used to be rich and powerful, Lucy," she said. "Whoop-de-freaking-do."

"I am directly descended from Hezekiah Garber," said Lucy, shrilly.

"What did old Hezzy do that was so special? Part the Red Sea? Cure cancer?"

"He was a great man! He founded Humboldt Cove!"

"So?"

Lucy stared at her, eyes popping from her head, lips trembling with fury.

"He built this entire region by strength of character alone, and the same great blood flows through my veins."

"This is pointless," said Brian, looking up toward the door. "Just let me get the gun, will you?"

Lucy grabbed his arm and held him fast. She was only five feet tall to his six feet or more, but she was used to being obeyed.

"Forget your dried-up old ancestors for a minute. Who are *you*, Lucy?" Willa said, shouting to be heard over Kyle's yapping. "A kidnapper?"

Lucy did not lessen her grip on Brian's arm, but she used her other hand to wave impatiently in Willa's general direction.

"The Garbers rise to meet their circumstances, no matter how messy."

"We don't have time for this!" Brian whined. "I told you it was a mistake to keep Mina alive, and now look what's happened! If you had just listened to me in the first place—"

"Shut up," said Lucy, sharply. "Pull yourself together. You're a Garber, for heaven's sake. Act like one."

"He's a *what*?" said Willa, her ears perking.

"A Garber," said Mina. "They're blood relatives."

"You're kidding me. How?"

"Lucy got pregnant out of wedlock when she was sixteen. Probably with Captain Burch's baby, though I've never confirmed it. Poor old Doug. I'm surprised you didn't figure it out already. The birth certificate is with all the other Garber research I sent you."

"Shut up!" screamed Lucy.

"The whole thing was hushed up," said Mina, conversationally. "She adopted the baby girl out to a family in town. I don't think Doug ever knew."

"Quiet!"

"Anyhoo, Brian is Lucy's grandson."

"He can't be," said Willa, in disbelief.

"Look at their chins!"

Willa peered through the darkness of the basement. Lucy and Brian did indeed share the same bright blue eyes and prominent chin. She wondered how she had never spotted it before. That explained why they were working together, perhaps, but she didn't feel any closer to the truth about what was really going on.

"Why don't they tell anyone about it?"

"Because Lucy's an old fuddy-duddy. Didn't want to admit she had a little oopsy early on. But Brian's a Garber, alright. She trained him to be just like her—groomed him since high school to follow her footsteps."

"Well, well, well! What would Hezekiah Garber say if he could see his offspring now?" said Willa. "How would the great man feel about liars, cheats, and murderers?"

"He was a liar and a murderer himself," said Mina. "So he'd probably have been proud as punch."

Kyle leaped off Mina's lap, howling and yapping in turns.

"Shut up, shut up, *shut up*! Don't you dare say another word about Hezekiah! Will someone please make that stupid dog be quiet?" said Lucy, hysterically.

"A murderer, huh?"

"No!" Lucy shouted.

"Yes," said Mina, with a maddening calmness and certainty that seemed to drive Lucy mad. "I told you this was about the book, Willa."

Brian pulled anxiously at Lucy's arm.

"Who cares? It's time to get a move on, Gran."

Lucy whirled around and slapped his face, hard.

"Good grief, Lucy," said Willa, contemptuously. "For once I agree with Brian. Who cares? Maybe Hezekiah Garber was a great man. Maybe he was a murderer. I don't know. Never met the man, haven't researched him, couldn't care less. I'd never even heard of him before I moved here."

"How dare you?! Hezekiah Garber was renowned everywhere for his charity, his power, his goodness—"

"Renowned *everywhere*? He founded one tiny town in the smallest county in California. He was a blip in history, Lucy, and now he's a pile of dust in the Humboldt Cove cemetery. If you kidnapped my aunt just to protect his memory, you're out of your mind. I'd respect you more if this *was* about drugs."

"Make her stop," Lucy screamed, pushing Brian toward Willa.

"She's got that whole thing of chemicals," he complained, rubbing his face where she had slapped him. "What if she splashes me?"

"You'll wash it off in the tap, idiot. It's just lye—it's not going to melt you."

"*You* go over and get splashed then, Gran."

Lucy slapped him again, harder this time.

"Don't you *dare* talk back to me," she said. "Do as I say, this instant."

Chastened, Brian began moving toward Willa and Mina.

"I knew a woman once who had lye burns on her face," said Willa, reminiscently. "Her right eyeball got it too. She didn't get to the ER in time so she wears a patch now, like a pirate. Your face is so pretty, Brian. Too pretty for a man. I'd be happy to help you out with that. Some women like a few battle scars. Even four-eyed clowns."

"Just let me get the gun, will you?" Brian said to Lucy, uneasily.

They argued while Willa shouted insults about the Garber bloodline and Kyle barked his head off. For a while, all was utter chaos.

"Stop it, all of you," said Mina, her voice cracking.

No one listened.

"Quiet!" she said, tugging on Willa's pant leg.

Willa paid no attention. She was trying to calculate how close Lucy or Brian would need to be for her to throw the lye. She wanted to do maximum eyeball damage.

"Shut up and listen!" thundered Mina, and everyone was startled into obedience.

Even Kyle was quiet, though the sound of barking continued above them, along with the heavy tread of many footsteps.

"Help! Help!" yelled Willa again, at the top of her lungs—hoping against hope it wasn't just Heidi, come to check on Brian and Lucy. "Down here!"

There was a second or two of absolute silence. Then the door splintered open, and in ran Killer, Wags, and Jake Anderson, followed by Sheriff Poole, several other officers, and a bloody but conscious Mr. Pilkington, holding an ice pack to his head.

"Wahoo!" shrieked Mina, exuberantly. "Now that's an entrance!"

"Hands up," said Sheriff Poole, to Lucy and Brian.

Lucy screamed with anger and tried to charge her way out of the basement, but Gary grabbed her arm and held it fast. Brian reluctantly put his hands up. Mr. Pilkington hurried down the stairs, followed by the dogs.

It was hard to tell who was more eager to get to Mina—Killer, Wags, or the gallant old Mr. Peanut.

"You made it just in time," Mina called from her position on the floor—in control of the situation, as usual. "And I mean *just*. Next time move a little quicker. Gary, I've never been glad to see you before but I could kiss you now."

"Never thought I'd say it, but it's nice to see you too, Ms. Lattner," said Sheriff Poole, tipping his hat to her. "Deputy, take care of her, will you? I'll call an ambulance."

The Sheriff and his officers led the furious Garbers upstairs.

"Alright Mina?" said Jake, approaching the old lady.

He helped her to her feet. She embraced Mr. Pilkington with one arm and drew Jake in with the other, while Wags, Killer, and Kyle frisked around her ankles.

"I am now! *Good* boys," she said with approval, directing her comments to dogs and men alike. "Very, *very* good boys."

Mail

To Wendoline Lattner Santini & Guillermo Santini

Dear Lattner-Santinis,

I know you're extremely concerned about the "goings on" here in Humboldt Cove because I came home at one AM to roughly five thousand emails from Mom and Dad. Thank you, Wendy, for raising the alarm. It will take me weeks to calm them down now.

I won't get my new phone for a day or so, but I'll try hopping on a video call as soon as I can. I'm likely to be tied up tomorrow morning at the police station. Yeah, that's right. I caught a couple of murderers this evening.

I jest, of course. I caught zero murderers. But I did help catch two kidnappers! And when we are done with them, they'll have assault, robbery, and attempted murder on their rap sheets as well.

The Three Hounds was being used as a front for some kind of smuggling. We're not sure what yet. I hope it's something reasonably innocuous like pot, and not automatic weapons or heroin or…or…

Nope, the other alternatives don't bear thinking about. I'm already going to have a heck of a time getting to sleep tonight.

Thanks for raising the initial alarm, G. You are blessed among brothers-in-law. May your bread always rise and your pastry cream always set.

Sadly, things are over forever between me and cute-bakery-owner-guy. We might have overcome some obstacles, but I really soured on him when he threatened to cleave me in twain with his chicken-boning knife.

Oh! I haven't said anything yet about Aunt Mina. What's that song we used to sing in Sunday school? *God's not dead, NO! He is aliiiiiive.*

Mina and God have at least one thing in common in that she's also ALIVE. Barely. But the old girl has some fight left in her. I just got home from the hospital, where she was laying down the law to the charge nurse about something or other.

Turns out, she never went out on her boat that night. She was next door the whole time, rotting away in the basement. And she survived with barely a scratch! The doctors were incredibly impressed. She's dehydrated, malnourished, and weak, but they say it's nothing a few days of IV fluids and a little physical therapy can't cure. That's a testament to the Lattner fortitude and physical strength.

Speaking of which, I'm so tired I can't stand up. Off to bed with me. More details to come.

Willa

P.S. I love you both very much, but do you
see what happens when you leave me alone for
a second? Kidnapping! Smuggling! Death threats!
And I've loved every minute of it. Stay in Rome
as long as you like. I'm going to be just fine.

The Ally

"I still can't bring myself to believe it," said Mr. Pilkington from his comfortable seat on the window bench in Mina's kitchen.

Two days had passed since the showdown in the basement, and Mina had just been released from the hospital. She sat next to her lawyer now in her robe and slippers, both of them sipping tea and nibbling on Linda Anderson's cookies.

"Believe what?" said Willa, curiously.

She pulled up a chair, making room for Jake Anderson to sit next to her. Wags and Killer were curled up in the corner by the fireplace, fast asleep, while Kyle lay protectively on Mina's lap.

"Any of it, frankly! I cannot imagine how a nice, sane woman like Ms. Garber could have lost her head so entirely. Kidnapping an innocent woman, and for what?"

"To stop me from publishing the book, Pilky. We've been over this."

"I don't particularly understand it either," Willa admitted. "I thought this was about drugs!"

"It's all in the manuscript," said Mina, sternly. "Haven't you finished it yet?"

Willa, Jake, and Mr. Pilkington exchanged furtive glances.

"Not yet," Willa said, hoping she'd never have to. "All I know is that Hezekiah Garber owned the land on which Humboldt Cove was built, and founded the town."

"He was a pillar of the community, a champion of women's rights, an ecologist, a philanthropist, and a noted lepidopterist—though I have always found the latter more creepy than admirable. Catching poor wild butterflies and pinning them to boards? The actions of a sociopath! Anyway, old Hezekiah was a great man and he certainly founded the town of Humboldt Cove. But that was only after he stole the land from Henry Anderson, who staked the claim here originally and never left it for a minute!"

"No kidding?" Jake whistled.

Willa munched a cookie.

"Hang on, now. Lucy told me Henry Anderson abandoned the claim."

"That's what she was brought up to believe. But it's a downright lie. Henry claimed the land. He mined it faithfully and found gold. And he was foolish enough to tell Hezekiah about it in a saloon near Eureka. Got him a knife in the back one winter's night, and an unmarked grave."

"But Lucy said Henry went east and died in jail somewhere!"

"Lucy said, Lucy said!" Mina scoffed. "She said a lot of things, didn't she? We certainly found news reports about Henry Anderson, but they were planted by Hezekiah Garber, who owned the newspapers! For years, he even wrote letters to poor Henry's wife, pretending he was Henry and saying the most awful things."

"How do you know?"

"Lucy let me poke around the books and newspapers in her attic, and one day about two months ago, we found a set of Hezekiah's journals at the bottom of a musty old trunk. The man thought he was Pepys, I suppose. Recorded everything, quite cold-bloodedly, from his breakfast meats to his many sins. Names, dates, details—all of it extremely damning. Lucy was horrified, naturally. She begged me not to print it, and we argued for some time. Eventually, she gave in and gave me her blessing to proceed. I believed her, fool that I was."

"Why did you send the manuscript away, then?"

"The accidents," said Mina, sipping her tea thoughtfully. "There were too many accidents, all in a row. I began to suspect they had something to do with the book. Ian and Patricia McKinley came to talk to me about it the day I finally shipped it to Pilky. They ambushed me as I was coming out of the garden shed—I had been potting a few late tomatoes—and asked when the book would be published. Ian has known for years about the original source of his family's wealth. He asked me, point blank, if I was including anything about James McKinley's shipping business prior to 1860. I told him I was and he made a fuss. That afternoon, I found the macadamia nuts in my peanut butter, and I wondered if Ian and Patricia had paid a visit to the kitchen before confronting me in the back garden. The timing was right."

"If you thought Ian was trying to kill you, why didn't you talk to the police about it?"

"You know about my feud with Gary Poole. He wouldn't have listened. Besides, he'd been asking the oddest questions lately about the Old Girl and drug smuggling, of all things."

"*Drug* smuggling?" said Jake.

"Well, some kind of smuggling or trafficking. I thought he was trying to find dirt on me ahead of the election. As if I would be involved in drug running! But some people will believe anything. I think he got to Harriet

Snelling, by the way. She invited me over the week things came to a head and began hinting around. She seemed to think she'd be in a position to buy The Three Hounds off me! Told me I'd better sell while I could!"

"Did you ask what she meant by it?"

"I didn't think it deserved the compliment of rational attention. Besides," she smiled, "your mother was in there at the time, listening with all her might. I knew if I said anything the entire churchgoing community of Humboldt Cove would hear about it."

"True."

"With everyone behaving oddly, I couldn't pin down who was behind the accidents. But once I found those macadamia nuts, I decided they meant business, whoever they were. That afternoon, I went into the bakery, and Brian Harrison gave me the oddest look—as though he was surprised to see me, even though we had a definite appointment. *That* really scared me. I began to wonder about him. Gary Poole had been after me for weeks to give him records from The Three Hounds, and I was willing! Nothing to hide on my end. But Brian kept persuading me to hold out. On principle, he said. After that odd look, though—well, I started suspecting the accidents weren't about the book but about the *bakery*. I hurried home and wrote the letter to you, Willa. And I sent the book to Pilky, just in case I was wrong."

"Why didn't you say who you were suspicious of?" Mr. Pilkington asked, rubbing his eyes wearily. "It would have saved quite a bit of heartache. We didn't know whether your 'death' was about the book, the bakery, or personal spite!"

"Turns out it was about all three," Jake laughed. "But you would have saved us a lot of time if you had been more explicit, Mina."

"Innocent until proven guilty! That's the basis of our justice system. I was a very respected criminal prosecutor, remember? Accusations *I* make carry outsized weight, and I was terrified of causing harm to an innocent person. Besides, I knew Willa'd figure it out. She's got brains, even if she doesn't always use them."

"Thanks," said Willa, sarcastically.

"Don't mention it. Anyhow, it was a stroke of luck I sent the book and the journals away when I did," said Mina. "The first thing Lucy did was tear my house apart, looking for them. And was she furious when she couldn't find anything! She and Brian almost came to blows about it."

Willa picked up Kyle and scratched his belly. He was a new dog now that Mina was back—cheerful, perky, and full of energy—but he retained a strong affection for Willa. He had spent most of the evening happily trotting back and forth between them, sniffing hands and switching laps.

"I heard bits and pieces of their quarrel through the closet door. *What do you expect us to do now?* Brian asked her, very angry. *It was supposed to look like an accident!* He wanted to kill me right then and there and hide the body. *Not until we find the book*, she told him. She said she had a plan. Then they moved away, and I couldn't hear anything more."

"She had a plan alright," said Jake, shaking his head. "Fooled us all. All it took was a little clever sleight-of-hand. That night, Brian went down to the harbor and struck up a conversation with Captain Burch. It was drizzling, so Lucy put on Mina's raincoat—they're much the same height—and hurried out onto the dock. Once her back was to them, Brian pretended he'd just noticed her. He pointed her out to Doug and said something like, *look, there's Mina—she must be going fishing.* Then he stepped outside and called her name, and Lucy waved at him without turning around."

"Risky! What if the Captain spotted it wasn't Mina?"

"There'd be no harm done. Brian would laugh and say he needed his eyes checked, and they'd have tried something else. But they got lucky. Captain Burch was fooled, and he made the perfect witness. He would—and did—swear he'd seen Mina go out that night. He was even convinced he spoke to her! Lucy did her best to imitate Mina's turn-of-phrase, and any dissimilarities in their voices could be put down to radio interference."

"One old hag sounds very much like another, eh?" said Mina, laughing.

"You said it, Mina. I didn't. Brian said goodbye to the Captain and drove like a bat out of hell down to Eureka, where he took out his own boat and met with Lucy at a prearranged spot just south of Humboldt Cove. They swapped boats, and Brian took the Old Girl as close to shore as he could. He rigged the throttle so the boat would accelerate toward the rocks, and then jumped off and swam to Lucy. They sailed back to Eureka and docked his boat as though nothing had happened."

"How do you know all this?" said Willa, admiringly.

"Brian flipped on Lucy the minute we separated them. He's trying for a lighter sentence since she's the one who actually kidnapped Mina."

"And hit me!" said Mr. Pilkington, rubbing the back of his head painfully.

"She was trying to kill you if that makes you feel better."

"Why would that make me feel better?"

"Because she wasn't very good at it," Jake said, his eyes twinkling. "Sometimes it's nice to revel in the incompetence of evil people."

"They should have killed me when they had the chance," Mina said, contemptuously. "I would have told them where the book was if torture was applied! But they thought they could starve me out. They gave me half a cup of water a day and five Saltine crackers, just to make sure I'd stay conscious enough to talk."

"You held out very bravely," said Mr. Pilkington, patting her arm with affection.

"I've no doubt I *would* have Pilky, but after a week or two of that, Heidi Forrester began slipping me extra food, bless her heart. Her conscience was bothering her. She's not the first girl to be duped by a handsome devil like Brian Harrison," she said, glancing shrewdly over at Willa, who blushed and hung her head. "I never quite trusted him, for all his charm and wit. Well, that will teach me not to listen to my gut."

"Why on *earth* did you tell me he would make a useful ally?" Willa said, exasperated with her aunt. "Geez, Mina. You almost got us both killed."

"It was a grave miscalculation," said Mr. Pilkington, shaking his head sadly.

"What's all this?" asked Jake.

"Aunt Mina wrote me a letter saying she'd been murdered and that I shouldn't trust anyone in Humboldt Cove except the dogs and Brian Harrison."

"I said no such thing!" said Mina, indignantly.

"Maybe Lucy whacked you harder than you thought," said Willa. She grabbed her purse from its hook in the corner, took out the letter, and thrust it into Mina's hands. "See, right there!"

Mina did not bother looking at the paper. She threw it on the table, and Jake picked it up to read it.

"See? She said I might find an ally in Brian Harrison!"

Jake looked up from the letter and exchanged glances with Mina.

"I said you might find an ally in *Brian*," Mina said, sharply. "I certainly did not say Harrison. And I specifically told you not to trust a soul *in Humboldt Cove* except the dogs. Brian Harrison lives just down the street! Your reading comprehension is very poor, Willa."

"Well, who the heck is Brian then?" Willa snapped.

"You never looked at my card, did you?" murmured Jake.

With a sinking feeling in her stomach, Willa fished through her purse to find the card. She stared at it, did a double take, and swore under her breath.

"*Brian J. Anderson*," she read. "*Deputy Sheriff of Klamath County*. Brian J.?"

"Brian Jacob," said Jake, smiling. "B.J."

"Oh for Pete's sake..."

Willa looked at her aunt, still laughing like a hyena, and felt—not for the first time that week—that Mina had a lot to answer for.

The Butterflies

"*Y*ou're Brian?"

Jake's crooked smile was back.

"Well, technically. I was christened after my dad's dad. My grandpa was around a lot growing up, so I went by B.J. or Jake in my family and at school. I thought I'd try my real name out at law school for a change, but it didn't feel like me. I'm only Brian to the people who knew me during those years."

"Brian is a fine, strong name," scolded Mina. "If you're going to use your middle name, you should at least call yourself Jacob. It's more dignified."

Willa felt as though she could gladly strangle both of them.

"Why didn't you tell me your name was Brian?" she demanded of Jake, unreasonably.

"I didn't know Mina mentioned me in a letter," he said, gazing at her with mild brown eyes. "Plus, you didn't trust me further than you could throw me."

"Well," she said, softening, "I changed my mind about that. I actually thought about calling you from the bakery, but Brian was right there listening, and I had already shown all my cards. It's a miracle I made it back to Mina's house, let alone over to Lucy's basement. And I still don't know how you figured out where we were!"

Jake reached for another cookie.

"A combination of luck, gut instinct, and a little help from Mr. Pilkington and the dogs. Killer and Wags sniffed you out immediately."

"That's a lot of words to say nothing at all," said Mina, scoffing. "You'll make an excellent lawyer."

Jake laughed.

"Coming from you, that's high praise. The truth is, I became very suspicious of Lucy Garber after we found Uncle Ian in the shed."

"Ian McKinley was in my shed?" said Mina, brows furrowed. "What was he snooping around there for?"

"Gary wormed the whole story out of him. He was setting up cameras in the backyard. There's one in the shed pointed at the kitchen window, by the way. I need to grab it before I leave today."

"What?!" said Willa and Mina, together.

"He's been watching me?" said Willa, feeling her skin crawl.

"Not in a Peeping Tom capacity," Jake assured her. "He had a half-baked notion he could gather dirt on you—catch you doing some illegal remodeling—and report you to the state historical resources commission."

"What made him think I would harm the house?" Willa said, disgusted.

"Not what; who. Lucy Garber told him—in confidence—that you had plans to knock out some of the walls and tear down the crown molding."

"Why?"

"She wanted to run you out of town."

"So she was the one spreading rumors about me? All while pretending to be my only ally in town? That two-faced little sneak!"

"Classic wolf in sheep's clothing. She covered her mischief by pretending to help you out. Mom says Lucy cornered her one day down at Doyle's to discuss 'poor Willa Lattner' and all the awful things people were saying about you."

"Listing them out in great detail, I suppose," Mina snorted.

"Yep. And then declaring *she* didn't believe a single word of it, but there was no smoke without fire. Meanwhile, Brian was doing the same thing. Between them, they hit the whole town, got my aunt and uncle and a few other people riled up, and did a lot of damage to your reputation."

"So it's their fault Ian broke into the house!"

Jake looked at her.

"Who said he was the housebreaker?"

Willa gaped at him.

"You did, just now! You said he was planting cameras in the yard."

"And that's all he said," Mina stated, crisply. "Really, Willa, for a writer you lack the ability to parse language correctly. Precision of speech is very important, whether in conversation or writing."

Willa opened her mouth to say something uncomplimentary about Mina's precision in the written word and caught the eye of Mr. Pilkington, who shook his head ever so slightly at her. She remained silent.

"It was an honest inference, Mina," said Jake. "Ian was trespassing."

"And he was wandering all over the house without permission that night he and Patricia stopped by."

"Well, snooping is all he did. The housebreaker was Brian Harrison."

Willa stared at him.

"That can't be," she said, flatly. "He was at the bakery when it all went down."

"You talked to him?"

"Well, no," said Willa, thinking it over. "I asked Heidi if I could grab a quick word, and she said he was busy in the back, trying to get some sourdough in the oven."

"She was covering for him. He watched you leave that morning from Lucy's house, and then he broke in."

"Why?"

"To look for the book, of course!" said Mina.

"That doesn't make sense. Brian lived here for several weeks after you 'died,' Mina," said Willa. "He had plenty of time to look for it then."

"He knew the book wasn't in Mina's house. He was looking for *this*," said Jake, holding up Mina's letter, which he still held in his hand.

Willa scowled.

"That's impossible. He didn't even know about it then. I kept it secret."

"You left it lying around, though," Jake laughed. "I saw it myself on the kitchen counter the first morning I came here. Mina has very distinct handwriting. Lucy spotted it as well, and she panicked and told Brian. They were worried about what Mina may have told you before they kidnapped her, and wanted to find out what you knew. They were furious when they couldn't find it. "

"I put the letter in my purse before I went out," said Willa, slowly.

"That's why they took your phone—to check it for voicemails or emails from Mina. They were convinced you were hiding something."

"Well, they needn't have bothered breaking in. I showed the letter to Brian voluntarily only a few hours later. Sorry, Aunt Mina."

"You did your best," said Mina. "Next time read my instructions more carefully."

"I don't think that would have helped. I liked and trusted both of them. I didn't know Brian was bad news until Wendy and Guillermo told me the pastry chef must be involved. And I would *never* have believed it of Lucy until I saw it with my own eyes. She told me she was your best friend!"

"You shouldn't believe what people say about themselves without verifying it."

Willa began laughing, helplessly.

"What?"

"Lucy told me the exact same thing."

"I've got to hand it to her—she's smart as a tack. And I always thought her bugbear about heredity and personal character was old-fashioned nonsense," said Mina, meditatively. "But I'm beginning to think she was right."

"About what?"

"Genetics. Character traits being passed down, and so on. That whole clan has got an evil streak."

"I never suspected her myself," admitted Jake. "Not until the day we found Uncle Ian back in the shed. That's when Lucy finally gave herself away."

"I don't remember her saying anything in particular," said Willa, frowning in the effort to recall.

It had been a very stressful day.

"Nor do I," said Mr. Pilkington. "She seemed to be a very charming and concerned neighbor."

"She said the dogs never stopped barking at her," Jake replied, simply.

"Good lord," said Mina, raising an eyebrow.

Willa stared at them.

"So what? They bark at everyone in town. They're always barking."

"Are they?" said Jake, meaningfully.

Willa paused to think.

"Well, they barked a lot the first day I came."

"Who was in the house with you?"

"Just Mr. Pilkington...and Brian."

"Ha!" said Mina.

"They were rowdy with Lucy the first day I met her, outside the house. She told me not to worry about it—she said they barked at everyone, and Mina had never been able to train them properly."

"And you believed her?" said Mina, horrified. "Cover Kyle's ears so he can't hear you."

Willa thought over the last week, in detail. The dogs hadn't barked at Irene or Sam Doyle. They hadn't barked at Justine Galway, or Heidi, or Mr. Pilkington, or Jake.

"Dachshunds are extremely intelligent," said Mina. "They can smell a black heart just as easily as they can sniff out a pig ear."

Kyle looked up at her and gave a small woof of corroboration.

"It's remarkable, but true," Jake agreed. "So as soon as Lucy mentioned it, I knew something must be inherently wrong with her. I came back up here later that afternoon, determined to have a private word with you about it. I found Mr. Pilkington just regaining consciousness, with Killer and Wags attending him. He'd been left for dead, and that was good news for us, because Lucy didn't bother hiding her face."

"I let her in when she knocked. And of course, she saw the book at once and recognized it. She sat down to chat for a moment or two and then asked me whether she could borrow one of Mina's frying pans. I sat here and watched as she picked one out. She walked toward me, holding it," he said, with a little shiver. "And that's the last thing I remember."

"The woman has a frying pan fixation!" said Mina.

"She was busy hiding the papers in her safe upstairs when you came in looking for help, Willa."

"How did you know I was at Lucy's house?"

"I didn't," said Jake. "But they did," he went on, pointing at Wags and Killer, still fast asleep in their basket in the corner. "I called Sheriff Poole as soon as I found Mr. Pilkington. I knew Lucy would be desperate, and I didn't want to try to bring her in on my own. The dogs were restless while I was waiting for backup, so I let them outside to do their business. They sprinted towards Lucy's back door, barking madly. Just then, Gary arrived with the other officers and we followed the dogs. The rest is history."

"Thank God you got there in time," said Willa.

There was a long pause, while everyone contemplated the unpleasant alternatives.

"What's going to happen to Lucy and Brian?" asked Mina.

She looked into her coffee cup as though indifferent to the answer, but her delicate, blue-veined hands trembled slightly.

"I don't know for sure," Jake said. "Lucy has wisely kept her mouth shut, so it will come down to her word versus Brian's for many of the charges. The good news is that Brian sang like a canary the minute he was out of her sight, and we've gotten quite a lot of information from Heidi Forrester as well. I've spoken with the DA about going easy on her. She's cooperated with us fully so far, and she'll get brownie points with the judge for feeding you all those weeks."

"Poor little thing," said Mina, unexpectedly. "She'd come in, silent as the grave, slip me the food, and hurry back out again. Her better angel was fighting for her, but it was an uphill battle against the charisma of a devil like Brian Harrison. I can't believe I ever liked the man. What a chump I was to partner with him! And all along he was using my business and my money to—to—" she paused, perplexed. "Well, what the heck was he doing with The Three Hounds?"

"Yeah!" echoed Willa. "What were they smuggling in those butterfly cakes? Cocaine? Heroin? Meth?"

Jake grinned.

"Butterflies," he said, with a little shrug of his shoulders.

Mina, Willa, and Mr. Pilkington stared at him, equally astonished.

"Beg pardon?" coughed Mr. Pilkington.

"Believe it or not, there's a black market for exotic butterflies—dead or alive. Transporting them from Central or South America by plane can be risky, so they're often brought in by sea. Brian and Lucy worked as mediators between buyers and sellers. He'd take his boat to an agreed-upon rendezvous spot and receive the specimens. Then she'd find an interested collector and negotiate a purchase price. The buyer would pay by purchasing a special wedding cake package."

"Are you telling me," said Mina, her lip curling in distaste, "that they were baking live butterflies into those cakes?"

"No, no. They'd mock up fake cakes from styrofoam and cheap sugar icing, and hide the butterfly amongst the boxes. There was usually one real cake, for show, but it was just flour, butter, and sugar—no insects."

"Plenty of lavender, though," said Willa, gagging.

"The lavender-and-rose theme was a bit of a joke on Brian's part, I gather. Dessert only a butterfly would enjoy."

"He said butterflies were his spirit animal," Willa said, unsure whether to laugh or cry. "He had that tattoo on his shoulder and everything."

I should have known he was a jerk the moment the words 'spirit animal' came out of his mouth, she thought.

"Local law enforcement has been coordinating for months to shut down this butterfly smuggling ring. They knew specimens were coming into Humboldt and Klamath Counties, and a careful look at the bank statements of known collectors showed a commonality—a purchase of wedding cake from The Three Hounds Bakery. Sheriff Poole thought Mina was behind the whole thing. He recruited Harriet Snelling and a few other shopkeepers to watch the business for him. When Mina went missing, he assumed she had been taken out by a rival or killed over some dispute. After Willa showed up in town and the shipments continued, he became extremely suspicious of her."

"No wonder I was so unpopular around town," Willa mused. "Half the people thought I was here to tear down a historical relic and the other half thought I was illegally trafficking butterflies."

"Gary Poole is an unmitigated moron," said Mina, with contempt. "As if I would involve myself in something as dangerous and unethical as wildlife smuggling!"

"He was just doing his job, Mina. Your name was on the business license for the bakery," Jake pointed out, reasonably. "And you did own an expensive, brand-new fishing boat."

"I'm learning to fish in my old age," said Mina, defensively. "Is there a law that says an old lady can't own a flashy boat? I'm still mad as heck they ruined it. The Old Girl was my baby."

"Why did Harriet get so mad when we asked her why she was out fishing that night?" Willa asked. "She practically swept us out of her shop!"

"Take it from an old prosecutor—there are only three things that motivate bad behavior in humans," said Mina, shrewdly. "Anger, money, and sex. With Harriet, my money is on the latter."

"You're kidding," said Willa, making a face. "Her?"

"You should be burned at the stake for a witch, Mina Lattner. You're right, as usual. Harriet's been having an affair with her brother-in-law," said Jake. "They went out that night for a little hanky-panky. She was terrified it would get back to her sister."

"One moment, please," said Mr. Pilkington, who had been doing his best to follow the conversation's many twists and turns. "Forgive me for belaboring the point, but am I to understand that Ms. Garber was involved in these, er, illicit smuggling activities?"

"They were her idea!" Jake replied, "The Garber money ran out a long time ago, and she had no intention of selling the family home. She's a big deal in the butterfly community, and she had all the clout of the Garber Wildlife Foundation behind her. It was easy for her to find serious collectors with big pockets. She persuaded Brian to come back to Humboldt Cove. The two of them decided a bakery was the perfect front—and a celebrated prosecutor was the perfect partner! Who would suspect Mina Lattner of criminal behavior? It was worth sharing half the money to shelter in your big, virtuous shadow."

"I suppose we would have gone on for years like that if I hadn't found that old diary."

"You signed your death warrant, there—though it was Willa's decision to find and finish the book that really made them panic. Lucy felt reasonably safe until then. She was angry that Mina wouldn't tell her where it was, but she felt safe in the knowledge that no one else cared about it. Willa presented a definite threat."

"There's one thing I still don't understand," said Willa. "Why did Lucy and Brian agree to be part of Mina's Minions?"

"I'm going to kill Sam Doyle for that," muttered Mina. "There are so many better names they could have used."

"Right?" said Willa. "The Murder Squad!"

"The Revengers!"

"The Bloody Buddies," Mr. Pilkington suggested, and was instantly met with withering looks from aunt and niece.

"You've met Irene and Sam Doyle," said Jake. "Forces of nature. And Captain Burch is no slouch. The three of them might have made actual headway on solving your case. It was safer for Lucy and Brian to join up and muddy the waters."

"Why did Brian tell me about the Minions at all? Why take that risk?"

"It was obvious to both him and Lucy that you were suspicious about Mina's death. They brought you into the Minions because they wanted to keep an eye on you."

"Will you stop saying Minions?" Mina groaned. "I feel silly enough! Those two made an absolute fool of me, and I'm heartily ashamed of myself. But I'm more eager than ever now to finish my book. That'll cook Lucy's goose," said Mina, with satisfaction. "I'll round out the chapter on Hezekiah Garber by telling the story of my own kidnapping. It will be a bestseller!"

Willa, Jake, and Mr. Pilkington exchanged looks again. Mina was in for a rude awakening.

"Of course," Mina went on, self-consciously, "I'll need a good editor. You can punch up the dull bits, can't you Willa? Add a little of that mystery writer's flair? My prose might be a *bit* dry at times."

"Just a bit," said Willa, trying not to smile.

"Well, I stick to the facts, whenever possible. The good thing is, we won't need to embellish anything. When pride and arrogance meet vanity and greed, the sparks fly on their own! Lucy and Brian have practically written the last chapters for us. Horrible, rotten, prideful—both of them. And bug lovers, to boot.”

“Ugh, what a family!” said Willa.

“Indeed. And now we’ll make the Garber family name known up and down California.”

“I’m not sure I want to put a target on my back, Aunt Mina. Lucy threatened to have Brian melt my *skin* if I messed with them, remember?”

She shuddered.

“I remember. But when you and I are done with them, they’ll rue the day they messed with either of the Wilhelmina Lattners!”

Aunt and niece looked at each other and smiled.

“What a family,” echoed Mr. Pilkington, softly.

Woof, said Kyle.

Mail

To Wendoline Lattner-Santini

Wendy,

It was lovely to hear your voice, even for a little while. I'm extremely excited that you and G are coming out to visit Humboldt Cove, if I did not make that clear by the series of screeching noises when you told me the good news.

Tell G, by the way, that I am taking Italian lessons so he can't swear under his breath in 'Italiano' anymore and expect to get away with it. Tell him I'll rat him out to his mother AND his priest.

I have some updates. Mina and I talked it over and decided that I should stay with her while I'm researching my new book. She offered to give me the entire third and fourth floors for my very own! She knew I couldn't bear to leave the dogs OR the house OR The Three Hounds, even though I didn't technically inherit any of them. We've agreed to share custody until she dies for real.

Personally, I can't see her ever dying. The Grim Reaper wouldn't have the NERVE to take her. She gets this look on her face when she's irritated that could peel paint clean off the wall. I like her tremendously. Almost as much as I like you.

I like you so much that I took your advice and called Steve to hash it out. We had an actual conversation about the infidelity and the break-up that was not covered in five layers of sarcasm. It lasted hours and it was the worst thing that has EVER happened to ANYONE. But in the end, we both got some closure. He understands that it is over.

More importantly, I understand why it had to happen the way it happened. I would never have left him otherwise. I am a creature of habit. Recent experience has taught me there is more out there than I knew, however, and I'm excited to see how far my world can extend. It might stretch all the way to Rome someday. Who knows?

Thank you for your very tactful inquiry about sheriff's-deputy-guy. No, he's not interested in me. No, I'm not interested in him.

Well, I might be the teeniest, tiniest bit interested, but I am keeping my distance and playing it cool. The last time I was into someone, if you recall, he threatened to remove some of my skin and bones for me. Forgive me if I'm a little cautious.

He comes over sometimes, at night, and the three of us play cards while the dogs chew bones in the corner. It's extremely wholesome, like an episode of The Waltons.

I will introduce you when you visit, but only if G promises not to do that thing where he kisses strangers on both cheeks. Come soon, because

Mina and I will need help hiring new staff for The Three Hounds.

Mina refuses to handle the hiring since the last two people she employed there are now doing KP in the Klamath County jail system, and I can't do it either, since I cannot tell the difference between a tsp and tbsp and…I might as well admit it…I don't even know what those STAND for, Wendy.

Off to walk the dogs. I love you. Talk soon.

Willa

P.S. Just figured it out. Teaspoon and tablespoon. You may go about your business.

Lucy's Apricot Bread

1 cup white sugar

2 TBSP softened butter

1 egg

3/4 cup orange juice

1/4 TSP baking soda

2 TSP baking powder

1 TSP salt

2 cups flour

1 1/4 cups chopped, dried apricots

1/4-1/2 cup real vanilla or vanilla extract

Preheat the oven to 350 F

1) Chop the dried apricots into small chunks and set them to soak for 30 minutes in the vanilla, plus 2 cups of very hot water.

2) Mix the flour, baking soda, baking powder, and salt together in a bowl. Set aside for later.

2) Cream the butter with the sugar until light and fluffy.

3) Add the egg, and mix well.

4) Stir in the orange juice and mix gently.

5) Add the dry ingredients, and mix until just combined.

6) Drain the apricots before folding them into the batter.

7) Pour batter into a greased and floured 9x5 inch loaf pan.

8) Bake for 55 minutes, or until just done.

9) Cool in pan for 10-15 minutes, and then turn out onto wire rack.

10) Enjoy!

Linda's Chocolate Chip Cookies

1 cup brown sugar

1 cup white sugar

2 sticks (1 cup) butter

2 eggs

2 TSP vanilla

1 TSP baking soda

1 TSP salt

3 1/4 cups flour

2 cups semisweet chocolate chips

Preheat the oven to 350 F

1) Mix the flour, baking soda, and salt together in a bowl. Set aside for later.

2) Cream the butter with the brown and white sugar until light and fluffy.

3) Add the eggs, and mix well.

4) Add the vanilla.

5) Add the dry ingredients, and mix until just combined.

6) Add the chocolate chips.

7) Use a spoon to scoop 12 golf-ball-sized blobs of dough onto a baking tray.

8) Bake for 9-11 minutes, until just done.

9) Repeat, with the second batch of dough.

10) Enjoy!

Lucy's Blueberry Muffins

1 cup lukewarm whole milk

1/3 cup sour cream

5 TBSP melted or softened unsalted butter

2 eggs

1/3 cup canola oil

2 TSP vanilla

1 cup white sugar

1/4 TSP baking soda

3 TSP baking powder

1/2 TSP salt

1/4-1/2 TSP cinnamon

3 cups flour

1-1 1/2 cups fresh or frozen blueberries

Coarse sugar for sprinkling

Preheat the oven to 400 F

1) Mix the flour, baking soda, baking powder, cinnamon, and salt together in a bowl. Set aside for later.
2) In a separate bowl, whisk the butter, oil, and sugar together until combined.
3) Add the eggs, and mix well.
4) Add the vanilla, sour cream, and milk, and whisk together well.
5) Fold in the dry ingredients, and mix until just combined.
6) Add the blueberries. Do not overmix.
7) Line a 12-count muffin pan with cupcake liners, or spray pan well with canola oil.
8) Divide batter into 12 parts, filling each muffin cup. Sprinkle with coarse sugar.
9) Bake at 400 F for 5-7 minutes, then reduce oven temperature to 350 and continue baking for another 20 minutes, or until a toothpick comes out clean.
10) Enjoy!

Also by Julie Titterington

The Doxies & Donuts Mystery Series

Death Pays A Call To The Three Hounds Bakery
Danger Lurks At The Three Hounds Bakery

The Desert Pines Mystery Series

Death By Association
Rapid Death
Death Benefit

About the author

Julie Titterington lives in the beautiful Willamette Valley with her husband and three children. When she's not writing or editing, Julie spends her time baking, eating, and reading mystery novels from the Golden Age, in that order.

Connect with Julie or sign up for her newsletter at authorjulietitterington.com

www.ingramcontent.com/pod-product-compliance
Lightning Source LLC
Chambersburg PA
CBHW061336310726
48974CB00001B/72